WIND AND DREAMS

WIND AND DREAMS

LINDA NORTH

SAPPHIRE BOOKS

SALINAS, CALIFORNIA

Cover Design by Linda North
Editor - Margaret Martin

Sapphire Books
Salinas, CA 93912
www.sapphirebooks.com

Printed in the United States of America
First Edition – June 2013

Dedication

This one is for you, Mom. Thanks for having all those wonderful books in the house when I was growing up.

Acknowledgements

A big thank you to Sue Hilliker, Carol Poynor, Angela Mula, and Q. Kelly. A special thanks to my wife, Danny Gail, for her belief in this story.

Thank you Chris and Sapphire books.

I am All That Has Been, That Is, and That Will Be.
No mortal has been able to lift the veil that covers Me.

Inscription on the temple of the Great Goddess Neit
in Sais as recorded by Plutarch.

Glossary

Ancient Egyptian Names and Terms

The ancient Egyptian language has five phases: Old Egyptian, Middle Egyptian, Late Egyptian, Demotic, and Coptic.

Ancient Egyptian hieroglyphics and hieratic (script) contained no vowels. Transliteration into English often contains variations in spelling, as rules are not standard. Since the details of ancient Egyptian phonetics are mostly unknown, transcriptions rely on Coptic for reconstruction.

The roles and attributes of the different gods and goddesses of Egypt evolved throughout history. Their importance also changed throughout history. Over time, many ancient Egyptian gods were absorbed into new deities or assumed the aspects of other deities. In my story, I used the more popular Greek names for the Egyptian deities.

ankh, wedja, seneb: life, prosperity, health.

Apis bull: A black bull with markings of a white diamond on its forehead, an eagle mark on its back, a scarab mark under its tongue and double the number of tail hairs. The bull represented the creator God Ptah, and later the incarnation of Osiris. The bull also represented the strength of Egyptian rulers.

ba: Ancient Egyptians believed the human soul consisted of many parts. The view held by many Egyptologists is that the ba is closest to the contemporary Western religious concept of a soul as it embodies the idea of personality.

Bast, Bastet: Bast was originally a sun goddess. The Greeks associated her with Artemis and she took on the aspects of a moon goddess. Her depictions are usually that of a cat or cat-headed goddess. Cats are sacred to her. She is the protector of the home, children, and pregnant women. Later, she incorporated many of the aspects of Hathor, especially as a patroness of dance, music, joy, and pleasure. The feasts held in her honor were ecstatic.

Bes: His depictions are as a fat, bearded dwarf. He is the god of childbirth, infants, and humor.

Black Land: The fertile area along the Nile River.

Copt: Native Egyptian Christians.

Coptic: Last stage of the ancient Egyptian script. It was used from circa 5th – 17th century A.D. and remains the liturgical language of the Coptic Church.

Demotic: An ancient Egyptian script in use from circa 8th century B.C–5th century A.D. The Demotic language is a development of Late Egyptian and shares much with the later Coptic phase.

Hathor: Ancient Egyptian goddess sometimes depicted with the ears of a cow or as a cow. Her name means "House of Horus." She is often shown wearing on her head a falcon, the symbol of Horus, or cow horns with the solar disc between them. She is associated with joy, fertility, love, sexual pleasure, the vulva, dance, music, and the feminine spirit. Festivals in her honor were often ecstatic and inebriated affairs.

henut: Mistress.

henutsen: Our mistress.

Horus: A solar deity. He is the son of Osiris and Isis and often depicted as a falcon-headed man. Egyptian kings are his earthly embodiment.

Isis: One of the most important and popular ancient Egyptian goddesses. She is associated with magic, healing, nature, children, and motherhood. Her name means throne and her headdress is often depicted as a throne. In later times, her headaddress is the solar disk between two cow horns. Isis came to represent the ideal wife and mother. Her husband is Osiris and her son is Horus.

Isisnofret: Beautiful Isis.

Kemet: Black Land. Name of ancient Egypt and refers to the fertile soil of the Nile flood plains.

Maat: The Ancient Egyptian concept of balance, justice, law, order, truth, and morality. Maat is depicted as a goddess who wears a white ostrich feather in her headband. The Maat feather is the weigher of the souls of the dead. The main role of the king was to uphold the concept of Maat.

Menes: Considered by tradition to be the first Egyptian ruler to unite Upper and Lower Egypt.

nebet: Lady. Neb is the masculine and means lord.

Neit (Nit, Net, Neith): One of the oldest deities in Egypt. Early war and hunting deity. One of her later aspects is as the virgin mother goddess who emerged from the primordial waters and created the Universe, gods, and mankind. This aspect included the belief that she was a combination of both male and female. Her son is Re. The most common depictions of Neit show her wearing the red crown (deshret) of lower Egypt and holding a bow and two arrows. Her cult center was in Zau (Sais) in the Nile delta. Feast of Lamps was held in her honor. The celebrants burned lamps in an outdoor feast that lasted all night.

Netjeru: Egyptian gods and goddesses.

nisut (nsw-bty, nisut-bity): King or ruler. Nsw-bty means lord of the sedge and bee and signified the king of both Lower and Upper Egypt.

Osiris: The god of the dead as well as fertility and resurrection. Osiris is often portrayed as a mummy. On his head is the tall, white crown of Upper Egypt with two ostrich feathers. He is the husband of Isis and the father of Horus. His brother, Set, killed him and cut his body to pieces. Isis and her sister, Nephthys, found the pieces and Isis resurrected him using magical spells.

Re (Ra): Sun god. He sailed his heavenly boat

across the sky and died at the end of the day, entering the underworld to be reborn each morning.

Red Land: The desert.

Set (Seth): the god of the desert, storms, and of foreigners. In later myths, he is also the god of chaos and darkness. He killed his brother Osiris and cut his body to pieces. He is the protector of Re's night barque as it travelled through the underworld. He killed the serpent Apep as it attempted to swallow the barque.

sistrum: A sacred rattle used chiefly in the worship of Hathor but is sometimes associated with other deities such as Bast. It was usually a simple metal or wooden loop attached to a handle. The loop held loose bars with metal discs that rattled when moved.

udjat: The Eye of Horus, an ancient Egyptian symbol of royal power, protection, and good health.

Two Lands: Refers to Upper and Lower Egypt. Since the Nile flows from south to north, Lower Egypt is the land in the north and includes the rich delta region. Upper Egypt is the land to the south.

uraeus: A rearing cobra and the symbol of the goddess Wadjet. It was worn on the crown, or as a circlet, to protect the ruler by spitting fire on their enemies.

was-scepter: A symbol of power and often seen in art as carried by gods, goddesses, and kings. It is shown as a stylized animal head at the top of a long, straight staff with a forked end. The head is thought by many to represent Set and symbolizes power and control over chaos.

Kemen Words

Fictional words based on ancient Egyptian.

Hemenisut: Queen. Wife of the king. Derived from the Egyptian phrase 'Hemet Nesw'. Hemet is the ancient Egyptian word for wife. Nesw is king.

Inet Suh Resutoo: Remenneit name for the Valley of Wind and Dreams derived from the Egyptian words for valley (inet), wind (swH) and dreams (resutw).

Keme: The Remenneit word for the Black Land or Kemet.

Kemen: Derived from the word Kemet and is the language spoken by the Remenneit.

Nesneit: Means 'Belonging to Neit.' The city and center of power in the Valley of Wind and Dreams built around the Temple of Neit, and founded in 391 A.D.

Parherry: House of flowers. Derived from the Demotic words for house (pr) and flowers (hrry).

Remenneit: The People of Neit. The people who reside in the Valley of Wind and Dreams and its vassal oases.

Setepenneit: Chosen of Neit.' Setepen is ancient Egyptian for elect or chosen.

The West: Remenneit belief based on the ancient Egyptian place where the soul of the deceased travels after death to await judgment in the Hall of Maat.

Other words and information

barque: Boat.

Deadwood Dick in Leadville; Or A Strange Stroke For Liberty. A dime novel by Edward L. Wheeler. First published in 1879. The description of the cover in my novel is from Beadle's Pocket Library No. 88, New York, copyright 1885.

electrum: A pale yellowish-white alloy of gold and silver, with trace amounts of copper and other metals. The ancient Egyptians sometimes used it to coat the tops of pyramids.

Hello! Ma Baby: Tin Pan Alley song written by Joseph E. Howard and Ida Emerson in 1899. The song is now in the public domain.

qirsh: The name for currency denominations in Egypt and the Ottoman Empire. The qirsh was minted in copper, silver, and gold in different denominations.

smashing, smashes, smash: Late nineteenth century words used to describe same-sex romantic friendships among American college women. Some women entered into a lifelong commitment and lived together, often called a Boston Marriage. Evidence does indicate that for some women there was a sexual element in these relationships. At the turn of the century, society began to look askance at these relationships, partly due to the work of Sigmund Freud and other sexologists, who were instrumental in recasting same-sex romantic relationships as aberrant.

wadi: Arabic word for valley. It can also refer to a dry riverbed.

Zerzura: Fabled city or oasis said to lie west of the Nile in Egypt or Libya. In writings that date back to the 13th century it is described as a white city and also called 'The Oasis of Little Birds.' The city is said to contain treasure and has a sleeping king and queen. The city was accessible by a road that led through a valley between two mountains. The gates to the city had a carving of a strange bird above them.

Prologue

Sais, Egypt
391 A.D.

The deep throbs of drums, clangs of sistrums, chants, and the heady scent of incense filled the air in the inner sanctum of the temple. The bronze braziers flickered with flames that made the ancient murals of the Gods and Goddesses come alive and dance.

Ancasta stood close behind Nofret, the Chosen of Neit. On her right stood Kiya and Delia, both Nofret's companions since her childhood, and priestesses of the Great Neit, as was she.

All three priestesses vowed to follow the Chosen of Neit to the Valley of Wind and Dreams that lay outside the realm of Caesar Theodosius, outside his decree ordering the temples of the Gods and Goddesses to close their doors forever.

The priests of the false Osiris from the east, the one nailed to the dead tree, now walked in the palace halls along the Nile. The people of the Two Lands lifted their voices in song to him by order of Caesar.

Ancasta and the other priestesses had prepared for this day as had the generations of priestesses before them. This moment was foretold at the birth of time, that Neit the Great, virgin creator of the Universe and all things, would leave her city in the Black Land and cross the Red Land to the hidden valley where her new temple would be built.

Nofret stood naked with the sheen of purifying oil on her body, her hair a loose black curtain down her back. She swayed slightly, arms by her sides, palms turned out toward the image of the Great One, carved from the trunk of a sycamore tree in ages past, and gilded with gold.

The life-sized image wore a red linen dress woven by the temple priestesses. On the statue's head sat the deshret, the flat-topped, round red crown of Lower Kemet. Her right hand held a gold bow and two arrows, and her left an oval shield.

The Venerated One approached, accompanied by two attendant priestesses. She carried the blessing of the Great Neit, passed from a long line of predecessors, stretching back through time before Nisut Menes made one the lands of Upper and Lower Kemet.

Stopping before Nofret, the Venerated One looked into her eyes. "Daughter of Kemet, you are the Setepenneit, the Chosen of Neit, who will carry her blessing to the new land. O blessed one, you are the spring from which the primordial waters shall flow and from which the Great Neit, eternal virgin, shall emerge in the time decreed to bring the Universe out of this chaos and back to Maat. Her son, Re, whom she created from herself, shall hide her new city, Nesneit, in the brilliant beams of the sun. You shall be as Horus, all seeing and all protecting. You are the nisut, the first ruler of Nesneit. Always strive to maintain Maat, rule wisely and in the name of the Great One. From this day forward your name shall be Merytneit, beloved of Neit."

The Venerated One peered past Nofret to her two friends. "Kiya and Delia, companions of Merytneit, serve her well. Lend her your loyalty and your counsel, and help her to build the new kingdom to come."

With a gentle smile, the Venerated One regarded Ancasta. "You, Ancasta, a stranger from the isle of the far north, are the chosen queen of Merytneit. Neit loves you and embraces you as a daughter. Your love for Merytneit will help keep her strong and true in the ways of Maat. It is your task to comfort Merytneit, to dry her tears, to share her joy, to love her and cradle her head on your breasts when she is weary, and to give her counsel. The protection and favor of Neit go with you."

Turning her attention back to Nofret, the Venerated One placed her gnarled right hand on Nofret's left breast, over her heart, and chanted the ancient invocations to call the Great One. Time seemed to unravel in a spiraling hoop. The Venerated One and Nofret jerked as if tugged by a rope. Ancasta caught Nofret against her and, with the aid of Kiya and Delia, lowered her to the floor.

As the two attendants caught the Venerated One, Ancasta heard a loud exhale of breath as the woman's *ba* passed to journey into the West.

She turned her attention to Nofret and watched her eyes open, the irises golden like those of the falcon of Horus.

Merytneit, the Chosen of Neit, and first nisut for Neit's people, took her first breath of life and fell into the blue eyes of her beloved, and into eternity.

Chapter One

Giza, Egypt
Giza Museum
March 04, 1901

O h, my, how horrid." Emma squeezed Rose's right hand. "I can't bear to look," she said while shielding her eyes with her hand and nudging Rose past the enclosed glass case that contained the mummy of a pharaoh.

Rose obliged her friend and hurried past though the mummified remains of pharaohs, queens, cats, and baboons. It did not bother her in the least. After all, her father, Arthur McLeod, was a dealer and supplier of Egyptian antiquities for private collectors, universities, and museums back home in America. As his secretary and consultant, with an eye for authentic pieces of ancient Egyptian jewelry and amulets, she was well acquainted with such relics.

Arthur McLeod expanded his business to include trips to the source itself, rather than to buy from a middleman who brought the antiquities to the American market. They arrived in Cairo five months ago, after closing up their home in Baltimore, and planned to stay for a year and a half.

Within a month of their arrival, Rose had met

Emma Walters at a social function hosted by one of her father's business contacts. The two women were close in age, Emma twenty-six and Rose twenty-five. Emma's father, Colonel James Walters, held an administrative position at the British Agency. His pastime as an amateur archeologist helped forge a friendship between him and Rose's father.

Emma grasped Rose by the arm and pushed her toward the room's exit and accidentally into another person. Rose stumbled back, stopped from falling by a firm grip on her arms. Her straw boater hat tumbled off her head onto the floor. Although startled, Rose found herself looking into the most beautiful and mesmeric eyes she had ever seen. The irises were golden yellow, the shape catlike, and the lashes black and long. These eyes captivated her. She *recognized* those eyes.

She mentally shook herself and searched the person's face. Only the eyes, arched black eyebrows, and the smooth brown skin surrounding them were observable. The end of a white and blue striped keffiye, the headscarf worn by Bedouin men, covered the lower portion of his face. A black cord, the agal, secured the keffiye to his head.

Rose assumed this was a young man, his height a tad above her own five feet five inches. A loose, open, blue robe covered his long, white tunic that was belted by a yellow sash with a silver dagger tucked into it. Around his neck hung a gold amulet called the udjat, the protective eye of Horus.

A swarthy, husky man in black robe and keffiye stepped to the young man's side. He gave Rose a menacing stare, his right hand wrapped around the hilt of the sheathed scimitar at his waist.

Dropping his grasp of her arms, the young man

stepped back, and spoke a few words in a low, alto voice to the man in black, who then backed away.

The young man focused his attention back to Rose, touched his right hand to his forehead, and imparted a slight bow. Rose couldn't help noticing the hand was rather delicate and small for a male.

"Please, excuse my clumsiness, lady." His English was accented but easy to understand. By the alto pitch of his voice and slight build, Rose now believed him a youth still in his teen years.

"I'm sorry. I'm the one—" Rose felt Emma tug her arm.

"Rose, let's go."

It was then Rose noticed the three women standing behind him. Each wore a galabeya, a long gown worn by Egyptians of both sexes, the women's often more colorful and ornate. Rich embroidery embellished their outfits, one a mulberry color, the other two blue. Their headscarves glistened with silver coins, and no veils hid their faces. One, the shortest of the trio, appeared close to Rose in age. Her smile was winsome and green eyes bright. The youngest woman looked to be no more than sixteen or seventeen. The oldest of the trio, a tall, handsome, dark brown-complexioned woman dressed in the mulberry galabeya, picked up Rose's hat and presented it to her with a friendly smile.

"Thank you, I—"

"Rose!" Emma pulled her away. Not even out of earshot she said, "Why I never. The uncouth desert savage had the audacity to put his hands on you."

Rose glanced back, startled to see those gold eyes fixed on her. She quickly focused ahead and followed Emma into the wide foyer.

"Who do you think he is?" Rose asked.

"How would I know? By the good quality robe he's wearing, I think he is the son of a sheikh. The dreadful man with him is his servant." Emma furtively glanced around then leaned close to Rose, her voice low. "The three women with him are probably his wives. Or his concubines."

"He looked to be a mere boy to me...not old enough to have a wife."

"Rose, you are naive. These natives are adults by the time they're twelve. Why, it's scandalous, the girls are married off before they're eleven, and often to old men. I've heard these desert nomads kidnap white women for concubines and lock them away in harems, never to see freedom again. I tell you, a young lady has to be vigilant." Emma gave Rose an assessing but appreciative look. "Your red hair and blue eyes would catch the attention of some old Bedouin sheikh who wants a young wife to dance for him."

"I can't dance. Well, not the kind of dance he would expect." Rose recalled the time three years ago when she and a couple of friends went to the Bijou Theater in Washington D.C. to see the entertainer, Little Egypt, and her exotic dance show. She had yet to see anything like it in Cairo, but did hear that in certain sections of town one could watch similar performances.

Emma clasped Rose's hand as they walked into another display room where a gaunt Egyptian man, in a white robe and red fez, pinned Rose with a cold and avaricious stare that sent a shudder of revulsion through her. She hurriedly averted her gaze as Emma led her to one of the display cases where her attention focused on a necklace in the center of the case. It was a gold udjat. Immediately her thoughts flashed to a pair of golden eyes.

ﯼﯼﯽﯾ

Al-Qahirah (Cairo)
March 04 1901

With her eyes shut tight, Meryt's peak neared as the nimble fingers rhythmically rubbed that pleasure place at the apex between her thighs, then entered her to stroke the inner walls. She brought her knees up higher and moved her hips in cadence with the caresses, now almost frantic for release. The woman's soft, red locks brushed along her cheek as Meryt turned her face into the graceful alabaster shoulder, her teeth grazing the flesh. The woman's arm embraced her tightly, drawing her closer against the side of her warm body. With a guttural cry, release tore from her.

"Rose!"

She collapsed and felt the careful removal of fingers from inside her. She hoped she hadn't spoken the name of the one she desired and imagined.

"So very ardent you are tonight." Tiye gently pushed the damp hair from Meryt's face and drew her head to her shoulder.

Tiye had given Meryt her first sensual experience and had been with her for fifteen years, ever since Meryt ascended the throne at age sixteen. Tiye was five years older than Meryt, and her maturity and level headedness were why the High Priestess had sent Tiye as first Companion. Meryt did not come to value these qualities until much later. It was the beautiful woman's dark skin, wavy black hair and intense black eyes inherited from her Sudanese grandmother that had enthralled the young nisut.

Companions were required to have never lain with a man and be lovers of women. Their duties were more than providing sensual favors. They included managing the nisut's palace staff, lending counsel, and acting as secretary. Meryt grew to love Tiye as she loved Hedjet, sent by the Temple of Neit as her second Companion seven years ago.

"I wonder what...or who...has stirred your passion so?" Tiye's voice held amusement.

Meryt involuntarily stiffened, waiting for Tiye to confront her with the truth.

"Rose." Tiye's whisper tickled Meryt's ear.

Meryt groaned in mortification.

Tiye laughed and kissed the top of Meryt's head. "We couldn't help but notice your fascination with the English nebet, or the desire in your eyes as you watched her walk away. Hedjet and I almost came to blows over who would come to your bed tonight, knowing how stirred your blood would be and that you would require attention. We agreed to both come to you tonight. However, Satiah cried because she has yet to share pleasure with you. We didn't think your bed big enough for four. Hedjet decided to stay and *console* the tearful Satiah. I think Satiah's first time with you should be alone."

Meryt let out another groan and sat up. "O Great One. No! I've no desire for the girl. She's too young... and has a sly air about her as if she's up to mischief."

"She's well past her first moon time and is soon to enter her eighteenth year. Hedjet tells me she's knowledgeable in the ways of pleasure." Tiye's voice became teasing. "And is very skilled at wielding the phallus."

Meryt curled her lip and threw up her hands. "I beg you, no details." The use of the leather instrument in pleasuring held no appeal for Meryt.

"If she displeases you so much, send her back to the temple."

"I might do that when we return to Nesneit." Five months ago the High Priestess persuaded Meryt to accept the daughter of a headman of one of the Valley's vassal oases as a Companion, believing it would strengthen his loyalty to Nesneit. Meryt now feared her agreement to accept Satiah might lead to the headmen and headwomen of other oases sending daughters to the Temple of Neit with expectations that they become Companions. The thought of the High Priestess assigning more 'Satiahs' to reside in her household was an unpleasant prospect.

"If Ahmose finds the English nebet, what do you intend to do?"

"I haven't decided." Since the museum visit that morning, she couldn't vanquish the young woman from her thoughts. She felt not only desire but also a strong wish to know this woman's heart and to share her own. Why she felt this way for someone she had never met was baffling. Yet, she sensed she did know her.

After returning to her residence in al-Qahirah, she had summoned her foster brother, Ahmose, who lived in the city and acted as her agent. She told him in detail all she could remember about the nebet. The only name she knew was Rose, the name the other English woman called her. She informed him he had ten days to find her, as the caravan would depart for home in two weeks.

Every two years Meryt, along with sixty-five of her caravan men, ten horse guards, eight foot guards, and six personal attendants, led a herd of two hundred white racing camels and forty quality horses across the desert to al-Qahirah to sell.

It was necessary when she left her kingdom to disguise herself as Zafar bin Abdullah, the eldest son of a sheikh of a distant oasis. The men currently lodged in the Black Land would never treat a woman as their equal, nor deign to do business with her.

Ahmose arranged for the customers to meet the caravan outside of al-Qahirah at Meryt's camp on the west side of the Nile where the haggling would begin. These rich customers came from all points of North Africa and the Middle East. Her white camels and quality horses brought in much gold, with which she purchased needed items of cloth, metal utensils, spices, coffee, tea, and other goods to take back to the Valley on her two hundred pack camels.

Meryt's thoughts flew to the beautiful English nebet. She had been able to tell that the nebet's figure under her gray skirt and white standup collar shirtwaist was nicely proportioned. Her hair was like flame and pinned up into a bun. She had a small nose with a slight up-tilt at the tip, and well-defined lips shaped like a bow. However, it was her large, brilliant blue eyes that had captivated Meryt. She knew those eyes. Did they spring from a prophetic dream sent by the Great One? They had spoken to her of a connection, perhaps from another time. If Neit so willed it, Rose would be hers.

"The English nebet may not be a lover of women," Tiye said.

"Any notion she may entertain of preferring

men can be cured if we have Satiah stand naked before her with a phallus strapped on. With Satiah's flat chest and that dark shadow of hair above her upper lip, she'd make a believable young man. That sight would send the nebet screaming into my bed and arms."

"Meryt, you have a wicked tongue." Tiye tried to convey disapproval, but Meryt heard the amusement in her tone.

"Let me show you how *wicked* my tongue can be."

The delight in Tiye's eyes was apparent and she smiled with eager anticipation as Meryt settled between her legs.

~ ~ ~ ~

The entrance to the narrow alleyway where Ahmose leaned against a shop wall gave him a clear view of the garden wall behind the Arthur McLeod residence across the road. Nothing about him stood out to draw notice from the passersby. His full-length, white robe with long sleeves was the common wear for most of the poorer men in al-Qahirah, as was his white skullcap.

It took seven days of having his men watch every hotel and club that catered to the English, to find Rose McLeod. Three days ago he sent a report to Nisut informing her of what he knew. One bit of important information was that the nebet was not English, but American. The only word from Nisut was to keep close watch until further instruction.

One of his trusted men, Rewer, had reported seeing a stranger slip over the garden wall last night. Rewer scaled a large crack in the wall to peer into the garden, observing as the jackal stood in the shadow of a tree and watched the lighted windows of the house until the lamps were extinguished for the night.

The jackal left, Rewer following him to the house of Hassid bin Hassid, a man known for his past as a slave trafficker. Since the abolishment of slavery in Egypt, at least officially, Hassid hired himself out as a guide for rich foreigners wishing to travel into the Sahara.

Over the past three years, several young white women from abroad had disappeared. Gossip was Hassid kidnapped these women and they ended up in harems in Morocco and Arabia. Not surprisingly, investigations led nowhere. Gold often had a way of ending the pursuit of truth.

All remained quiet at the McLeod residence. Ahmose's man watching the front of the house had earlier reported that the sole visitor was the nebet's friend, Emma Walters. Having arrived that morning, she had yet to depart, and it approached the noon hour.

As Ahmose watched, a man dressed in a white robe and red fez, climbed the garden wall and peered into the garden.

Rose McLeod, without doubt, was of interest to the jackal, Hassid.

ʬʬʬʬ

"I await your orders, Setepenneit." Ahmose sat on a low stool, avoiding Meryt's eyes. To look Nisut in the eyes would be an affront. Meryt had just received his report regarding the danger that threatened Rose McLeod. The meeting took place in the spacious, high-ceiled reception room of the residence built in the early 1600s by Merytneit the twenty-seventh, for times when a nisut visited al-Qahirah.

The chair Meryt occupied copied an ancient design, the feet carved in the shape of lion paws, the top of each front leg the head of a lion. The turquoise galabeya she wore glinted with embroidered gold and silver thread. Her thick, black hair hung loose, just touching the tops of her shoulders, and a net cap of gold strands covered her head, its edges strung with tube-shaped beads.

Tiye stood to the right of the chair and Hedjet to the left, to lend counsel if needed. Behind her chair stood Satiah, to observe and learn.

"Brother," Meryt's use of this word would let Ahmose know she was treating him as a family member and he need not be formal, "I want you to keep vigilance over the nebet for as long as she remains in the Black Land. Have her followed at all times. Tell your men I will have their heads if any harm comes to her."

"It shall be done, Sister."

She narrowed her lips for an instant. "We will deliver to this jackal, Hassid, a letter warning him that if he sends any of his pack to sniff around the nebet's house or trail her, their noses will be cut off. And if he attempts to carry through his plans, he will be hunted down and killed, and his body thrown to the dogs. Put the letter in a small box along with a live scorpion and send it to him tomorrow." Meryt saw Ahmose's faint smile, an obvious indication he liked the idea. "Find a big deathstalker scorpion."

"It shall be done, Sister." Ahmose now grinned.

"Henut," Tiye said, "you don't want to warn the

nebet's father so he can make arrangements to protect her?"

"No. The father would be no match for the cunning of a jackal such as Hassid. He might tell the authorities and they could interfere with Ahmose's surveillance and protection of her. I don't trust the authorities. Gold buys loyalties."

Meryt stood, and motioned Ahmose to stand. She drew him in for a quick hug. "May the protection of the Great One attend you, my brother. May the Gods hold you dear, as I hold you dear."

"Sister, it pleases me to serve you. I shall not fail you. May your reign be long. Ankh, wedja, seneb."

After he departed, Meryt addressed her Companions. "I am retiring to my suite and do not want to be disturbed." She entered her bedchamber, threw herself on the bed, and let out a deep sigh of bitter disappointment. In two days, the caravan would depart for home, leaving Rose far behind.

Last night she had made the decision not to approach Rose, not to intrude in her life. They existed in different worlds, and, in a way, they also existed in different times. Rose would never agree to go with her, to enter into a way of life unlike the one familiar to her.

It was the Great One's will that Meryt not have this woman. Yet, her Isisnofret, beautiful Isis, would visit in her dreams.

Chapter Two

My lovely Rose, were there any sweeter flower?" Emma murmured as she tenderly cupped Rose's face.

The two women sat on a blanket in the garden of the McLeod residence, hidden from view of the house by a row of oleanders that also shaded them from the fierce rays of the morning sun.

"Rose, I've fallen in love with you." Emma kissed Rose with gentleness at first and then with more fervor.

This declaration of love came as no surprise to Rose. Recently, she had sensed that Emma's sentiments for her had progressed beyond friendship. She hadn't encouraged Emma. Nor had she discouraged her, hoping her own sentiments would grow. Sadly, Rose felt only the fondness of friendship, and did not respond to the kiss. Emma broke the kiss and withdrew, creating an awkward silence.

Noticing the hurt in her friend's face, Rose said, "Emma, I'm sorry—"

"No. Don't say it. I know." Emma forced a smile without meeting Rose's eyes. "Well, I do need to return home. I promised Papa I'd do an inventory of the pantry and make a list of what we need." Emma quickly stood and straightened her skirt.

"Emma, we can still be friends?" Rose hastily got up and faced Emma.

"Of course we'll still be friends, you silly goose."
She took Rose's hands. "We'll have a jolly good time
when we visit the Sphinx and Pyramids next week. We
can even take a camel ride. It'll be great fun."

"I look forward to it." Rose felt disappointed
that her feelings for Emma hadn't bloomed. Would
she ever find that one woman who would inspire
love…and passion?

ᘐᘑᘓᘔ

"Ninety-five, ninety-six, ninety-seven." Rose
counted off the brush strokes through her hair, her
reflection looking back from the oval mirror above
the lowboy in her bedroom. She remembered when
a child how Momma would do this for her, and how
much she enjoyed it.

"A woman's hair is her crowning glory," Momma
would say. Rose never missed a night of brushing the
required one hundred strokes. Not even on the day
Momma died when Rose was twelve.

"Ninety-eight, ninety-nine, one hundred." She
placed the brush on the lowboy top and sighed as she
recalled Emma's declaration of love. What was wrong
with her? Emma was a handsome woman. Her fair
hair and hazel eyes drew looks of admiration from
men and jealous glances from women. She possessed
a good disposition, proper education, and made
a suitable companion. Rose thought if Emma had
attended Wellesley College, she would've been the
object of many smashes.

It was while attending Wellesley that Rose
discovered her romantic inclination toward the fairer
sex. She recalled the few smashes she had experienced

for fellow students. These never included anything beyond affectionate kisses and hugs. She longed to feel passion, to immerse herself in it, but she wanted...no, she needed that journey to be with a woman she loved, and one who loved her in return. Emma just wasn't the one. Not that Rose knew who 'the one' was. Maybe she was destined to be an old maid. She smiled dryly. By not marrying a man, society would indeed consider her an old maid. No one would consider housekeeping with a member of her own sex a marriage.

And if she never met 'the one'? Her life was far from empty. She had many good friends and an occupation she enjoyed. Her father planned to make her a business partner when they returned to Baltimore. Yet, sometimes she had a vague sense of restlessness as if a part of her searched for something more, but she had no direction or destination.

She pushed those melancholy thoughts aside and stood. She was just about to remove her lounging-robe and get into bed when someone knocked on the bedroom door. "Yes?"

The new servant, Layla, entered, carrying a teacup. Layla had appeared at their door that morning when Fatimah, their regular servant, failed to come back from a visit with relatives. The rotund Egyptian woman introduced herself as Fatimah's younger sister explaining Fatimah had taken ill, and she'd come to take her place.

"Miss Rose, I bring you tea. Good tea to make you have good dreams."

"Oh, I think it's a little late at night for tea. I'm about to retire."

"I fix this for you. You drink, sleep like baby." She held the cup out, Rose noticing the many rings on her plump fingers. "You make Layla happy and drink. I be sad if you do not."

Not wanting to disappoint Layla, Rose accepted the offered cup and sat back down on the stool. She took a sip and shuddered at the overly sweet taste. She gave Layla a smile. "It's really sweet tea." She steeled herself and took another sip. "Thank you." She handed the cup back to Layla. "I'm sure I'll sleep like a baby tonight."

"Yes, Miss Rose, you sleep like baby." Layla smiled as she watched Rose tumble from the stool and onto the floor.

Chapter Three

The reddening that heralded dawn crept up the eastern horizon and silhouetted camels with loaded packs on their backs. The cough of a camel drover as he cleared his throat, the occasional clangs of camel bells, and the bray of an ass carried through the stillness. The caravan was ready to start the long journey home. Meryt's red chestnut stallion, Bakhu, echoed the nicker of a neighboring horse. She held the reins close to the bit to keep his exuberance in check as she readied to mount. He pranced in place, eager to race the wind.

She swung the end of the keffiye across the lower part of her face, grabbed the pommel, and had her foot in the stirrup ready to hoist into the saddle when a distant shout caught her attention.

The dull thuds of galloping hooves striking the earth reached her ears, followed by the rattle and clack of wheels, as a bulky shape grew larger against the dawn sky.

"Yield the way, yield the way!" bellowed a voice she identified as her foster brother's. He brought the one-horse brougham carriage to a stop before her, causing Bakhu to skitter nervously and whinny. She called one of the caravan attendants to take charge of the fractious stallion.

The carriage horse's sides were dark with sweat, giving evidence of a fast and long drive.

"I have her—Nebet Rose." Ahmose could barely catch his breath. "I took her from Hassid's men."

Meryt hurried the few steps to the carriage and flung the door open, seeing Rose crumpled on the floor. She leaned in, brushed the long hair away from Rose's face and neck to place two fingers on the pulse point, relieved to feel a strong beat.

Ahmose came up beside her. "The jackals drugged the nebet." He quickly bowed his head. "Setepenneit."

Meryt pulled the end of the keffiye from off her nose, bent and sniffed Rose's mouth, detecting the sweet odor of a drug. She dismissed her stepbrother's formality. "Brother, were you followed?"

"I don't think so. I didn't take the Gezira Island route, as it would be easy for them to follow. Instead, I hired a small ferry to take me across the Nile. The darkness kept the ferrymen from seeing inside the carriage, so if anyone inquires about the nebet, they can offer no information."

"Thutmose," Meryt called to the closest of her personal guards, a big Nubian armed with a British Lee-Metford rifle. "Take men to the rear of the caravan. Let no one near that you don't know." She didn't want any surprises. "Take care of the carriage horse," she ordered a nearby man. "Bring me two blankets." Meryt's demand sent another of the caravan hands to carry out her request.

"I had arrived to take over surveying the garden," Ahmose said, "when Rewer, who was watching the main entrance, saw two men jump from a carriage and enter the house. Rewer ran to tell us. When we reached the front of the house, the jackals had just put the nebet in the carriage. While my men confronted them, I jumped in the carriage seat and hurried away."

"Henut," Tiye said from behind her, "send the men away, Hedjet and I will help you take care of her."

"Go, all of you, and await my orders."

The attendant arrived with the blankets and handed them to Tiye who spread one on the ground. "Take her out so we can see if she's injured, and if we should summon the healer."

Meryt took hold of Rose under the arms and started to pull her out. Hedjet and Tiye stood to each side of Rose and slid their arms under her back and hips. They eased her all the way out and carried her to the blanket.

Meryt knelt next to Rose and untied the sash of her blue robe, discovering a cream-colored nightgown that reached to the tops of her ankle-high blue slippers. The orderly and clean appearance of her attire indicated no violation had occurred. Besides, Hassid's customer would demand a virgin.

Hedjet covered Rose with a blanket and turned to Meryt. "Henut, what do we do? Return her to the father?"

Meryt gently ran her hand through the red hair, its texture silky, the color even more fiery in the rosy beams of Re's dawning light. She brushed a stray lock from the tranquil face and studied it for a moment before trailing her hand down a soft cheek. Rose looked like a sleeping goddess. *My Isisnofret.*

Once again, she stroked Rose's warm cheek. She closed her eyes and breathed deep as the thought of returning Rose to her father made her heart ache. Then the dawning of a smile appeared on Meryt's face and grew until its radiance chased the shadow of pain from her heart. Had not the Great One brought Rose to her? She could not refuse a gift from her Goddess. It was the will of Neit that she have Rose. This woman belonged to her now.

"She will come with me to the Valley of Wind and Dreams."

࿇ ࿇ ࿇ ࿇

Thirsty, so very thirsty. She hadn't enough spittle to wet her lips. If she could just dip her fingers into the Nile and bring the wetness to her tongue. No. The crocodiles were swimming near. She felt the reed barque jostle and shake as they hit it with their snouts.

Gazing up, she saw the Milky Way, a river across the night sky flowing from the past into the future. Although the sky was dark, she could see plainly about her. She dropped her gaze to the bow where a figure dressed in the white kilt of an ancient Egyptian stood, his back to her. He twisted his ashen head toward her. His red hair hung past his shoulders. His tall ears were erect and his eyes fiery embers. The lips of his long curved snout curled to bare his sharp, menacing teeth.

Set!

"Our father, who art in heaven, hallowed be thy name—" The words tasted like dust in her mouth. She didn't know if she believed anymore. Despite attending church for years, faith had slipped from her. For some time she suspected religion was but a construct of men. This secret she kept to herself for heretics still burned on the pyre of public censure.

Set laughed aloud, his breath a fierce wind upon her face, his voice thundering. "The upstart tribal god to the east holds no power here. In what shall be, he shall dissolve into the dust of time, as shall his son the pretend Osiris and with them the false prophet currently lodged in the Black Land. Their temples shall crumble when the Great One strikes the chaos from this age and restores Maat."

"Wake up. This is a dream," she spoke aloud.

"Dream, you say? As is sung in that silly nursery rhyme, 'life is but a dream.' Fitting, don't you think? We're in a boat and floating down a stream—a big stream. Metaphors," he chortled, "how I love them."

"This is a nightmare. You're not someone I would invite into my dreams."

He shrugged. "I have no choice but to be here. I am the protector of foreigners, and you have forgotten your way."

"Way? Where are we going?"

"That's up to you. Where is it you want to go?" Set spoke from behind her.

She twisted and saw that he now stood at the stern, oar in hand, dipping it into the water. "I want to go home."

"I await your directions."

She had no directions, or home. Home was more than a place on a map, or four walls. Home was what she searched for in her soul.

Another jarring jolt to the barque shook it, and she trembled. Was there no god to aid her? Maybe she should call to the gods of this land. "Divine Isis, Great Mother, you who have conquered destiny—*"A violent shake to the barque made her cry out. She'd tumble into the water, her soul swallowed into oblivion by the crocodiles.*

The night sky started to fade, and she took one last look at it as the sun rose over the horizon. Out of the sun's brilliant disc, flew the falcon of Horus. The falcon's eyes flashed gold and peered into her soul.

She heard the clang of a sistrum and the gentle voice of Isis. "Nebet Rose, wake up." The firm but soft hand of Isis clasped her arm to keep her from falling into the hungry jaws in the water.

Rose opened her eyes and tried to make sense of what she saw and where she was. It took a moment to recognize the long, white neck of a kneeling camel viewed from the back and the unsightly brown rump of a resting camel before this one.

She blinked, surprised at the view and alarmed to feel the warmth of a lap beneath her head. She hurriedly sat upright and gawked about, seeing she was in a roomy camel howdah. Beside her sat a woman dressed in a black abaya, the outer robe often worn by women over the galabeya. Beaded necklaces hung around her neck. One necklace stood out, a gold udjat, the protective eye of Horus. Gold and silver bracelets encircled her wrists, clinking when she moved her arms.

Rose studied the smiling, handsome woman with skin like chocolate, and dark, kind eyes. A black scarf covered her head, leaving bits of black, wavy hair visible. The woman looked familiar, but it was sometimes hard for Rose to tell the natives apart at first sight.

"Where am I? Who are you?" she croaked through a dry throat.

"I am Tiye. You are in the desert, in a caravan." The woman's accent sounded somewhat British to Rose. "Here, drink." Tiye handed her an hourglass-shaped water gourd.

Rose gulped down the tepid water, the overflow running down the sides of her mouth and chin.

"Not so fast." Tiye tipped the gourd down to prevent Rose from guzzling.

Her thirst quenched, Rose gave the gourd back to Tiye. She ran fingers through her tangled hair, noticing she still wore her lounging-robe and nightclothes, the slippers still on her feet. The last thing she remembered was Layla serving her tea.

"What happened? Where's my father?"

"You were drugged, and slavers stole you. Fortunately, the brother of Zafar, our headman, rescued you. Your father," she shrugged, "I don't know anything more."

"Drugged? Slavers?" *It was the tea.* The drug was in the tea Layla had given her. She became faint for a moment. Cold dread closed a fist around her heart. She needed to get home to see about Father. "My name is Rose McLeod. My father is Arthur McLeod. I have to return to Cairo. Get the man in charge—"

"Tiye." A young, petite woman with green eyes, caramel skin and pretty features, approached them. She was dressed similarly to Tiye. Her headscarf did not cover her black bangs and a raven-black braid fell in front of her left shoulder. She smiled when she saw Rose. "Ah, our guest is awake. I'm Hedjet. Come, let me help you out."

Rose took the proffered hand and stepped out of the howdah, almost falling save for the steady hold of Hedjet. "Thank you." Rose noticed that Hedjet's height came up to her nose.

Next, Hedjet assisted Tiye down from the howdah to stand beside Rose.

Rose shaded her eyes from the bright sunlight. Looking around, she took in the reddish desert speckled with dark pebbles and dusty stunted shrubs.

She directed her attention to Tiye, having to look up into her face. Tiye was tall for a native woman, in fact, taller than most of the Egyptian men.

"I need to talk to your headman, or the man in charge. Can you have someone get him for me?"

"In time. For now, we will eat and rest before the journey resumes. I'll find garments more suitable for you." Tiye strode away down a long line of standing and kneeling camels.

Groups of men squatting by cookfires stared at Rose with interest, making her conscious of her dishabille. She pulled her robe tight as she followed Hedjet to a tent, no more than a lean-to, but the shade was a welcome relief from the blazing sun. Several women dressed in abayas were gathered inside near a small fire. They stared at her with curiosity and friendly expressions, then continued to talk among themselves over tea.

Hedjet sat on a rug by a second small fire with a long-handled teapot in it. She patted the spot beside her for Rose.

A young girl, perhaps seventeen, sat across from them studying Rose with curiosity. Rose returned the scrutiny, thinking the girl would be attractive without the scowl. Dark hair peeked from her headscarf, and kohl lined her brown eyes.

"This is Satiah," Hedjet said. She spoke to the girl in a language unfamiliar to Rose. Satiah unfolded a tan cloth and removed a brown lump of sugar, placing it in a metal cup. She then removed the teapot from the fire and filled the cup, handing it to Rose. Hedjet gave Rose a piece of flatbread that she took from a basket.

Rose sniffed it in an attempt to determine if she

should chance eating it. She felt hungry, but wondered under what conditions the food was prepared.

"Eat, and drink your tea," Hedjet said as she slid a bowl of ripe olives in front of Rose. "It will be a while before we eat again."

Rose tentatively took a bite of the bread, finding the flavor palatable. Soon, Tiye joined them, laying a pile of clothes to one side before she partook of the tea and food.

"I need to speak to your headman," Rose said to Tiye.

"Later."

"How much later?" Rose's frustration made her voice strident.

"When next we stop...for the night."

Rose panicked. She would be further away from Cairo. "Take me to him! Now!"

Suddenly, she noticed all go quiet around her as the nearby group of women stopped their activities to gape at her. Tiye spoke, sending them back to what they were doing. She turned her attention to Rose. "You are in no position to demand." Tiye's voice was even. "Nor am I in the position to follow your request. Have patience."

Rose bit back a reply. Nibbling the bread in sullen silence, she listened, but couldn't understand the conversation between Tiye and the other two women. She thought it rude of them not to speak English.

The meal concluded and Tiye helped Rose slip into a black abaya over her nightclothes. Hedjet put a black scarf on her head that wrapped around her neck, which she could use to conceal her face from blowing sand or from those not meant to see her full features.

As a final touch, Tiye and Hedjet decked her out with several of their necklaces and bangles. Tiye said she would find a pair of sandals for Rose after they set up camp.

Soon the journey resumed, Rose sitting beside Tiye in the howdah, the slow gait of the camel rocking it back and forth like a barque on the Nile.

≈≈≈≈

With a sidelong glance, Tiye surveyed the profile of the sullen, young woman sitting next to her in the howdah. Tiye was but a simple priestess of the Great Neit, not one able to divine the future. However, even she could predict this woman would bring not only joy to Nisut's heart, but also strife. Strife Meryt was unaccustomed to as nisut and as a woman. Tiye feared this strife could rage through Meryt's heart, as a fierce sandstorm rages across the desert, stinging and smothering those without shelter.

Rose was a beautiful Isis and Tiye could understand Meryt's desire for this woman. It was hard to keep her heart from feeling a tiny nick from the claws of jealousy. It was not in the best interests of Nisut, or her household, for Tiye to entertain this dark emotion.

Those who entered into training as Companions must accept that the nisut could take other women to her bed. Jealousy had no place in a Companion's heart. She hadn't experienced jealousy when Hedjet entered the household. Satiah was another matter and not having anything to do with Meryt. That one might not ever find her way into Meryt's bed. It was Hedjet's bed Satiah found her way into, and that irritated Tiye.

Rose needed an ally, someone to help her adjust to a possibly bewildering and frightening new life. The wellbeing of Rose ultimately meant the contentment of Nisut. *That* Tiye wanted to see.

"Where is this caravan headed?" Rose asked, drawing Tiye from her thoughts.

"To the Valley of Wind and Dreams."

"Is that the name of your village or oasis?"

"It is the name of my home." Tiye was reluctant to reveal all. She thought it best to let Rose discover the truth a little at a time.

"Your English is very good. Where did you learn to speak it?"

A smile tugged at the corners of Tiye's mouth from the memory. "From Nebet Eliza Victoria Dartmoor. She was a distinguished elder from England. It was eight years ago that our caravan came upon Nebet Eliza on what she called a 'Grand Tour' into the desert, accompanied by friends. The jackal of a caravan leader made off with the camels and their goods, leaving them stranded. Our headman, Zafar, provided them safe escort to al-Bahariya Oasis. Along the way, Zafar became friends with the English nebet and invited her to go with us to our home."

Tiye recalled how Meryt and Nebet Eliza didn't know the other's language. One of Meryt's retinue had learned English from his time spent as a servant for an Englishman in al-Qahirah, and interpreted for them. That didn't prevent the two from forming a friendship, and soon they could understand each other without the interpreter.

"Nebet Eliza was the first English to see the Valley," Tiye said. "She became a part of our household and taught us English." Tiye let out a sad sigh. "Seven months ago her ba departed for the journey West. We mourn her leaving."

There was a sudden widening of Rose's eyes, as if she awakened to a truth. "Ba? That's an ancient Egyptian term for soul. Nebet...*lady*. Nebet is ancient Egyptian for *lady*. Your names—who are you?"

"The people of Inet Suh Resutoo, the Valley of Wind and Dreams. We are of Egypt as much as those who live along the Nile. Even more so."

"But you don't speak the Arabic like they do... unless you're Copts. I know the Copts still speak a version of the ancient Egyptian language. You're Copts."

"We are not Copts." Tiye weighed what to say next. "We call ourselves the Remenneit, the people of Neit. We worship the old Gods that sprang from Keme, what you call Kemet or Egypt, and from the hearts of her people. Our language we call Kemen."

"No one worships the Egyptian gods anymore. Well, there might be some in the Sudan who have incorporated tales of the Egyptian gods alongside the beliefs of Muhammad. But the old gods and goddesses of Egypt are myths, as are the Olympians of Greece and Rome."

Tiye's smile was shrewd. Rose was going on a journey. A journey of discovery that would take her into the realm of Keme as it might have existed if the old Gods and Goddesses still ruled supreme over the Two Lands of the Nile. And, perhaps a journey into her heart to discover something greater. The love of a nisut.

"You will see, Nebet Rose."

Chapter Four

The sun barque of Re slipped below the horizon and trailed fire, leaving the sky ablaze low in the west as the cloak of night drew over the desert from the east. Stars emerged to dance in the dusk. Meryt's heart sang with joy. The woman, Rose, was hers. She turned Bakhu toward her tent, toward the place where her beautiful Isis waited. She spurred Bakhu into a trot, two of the horse guards riding close behind.

All day she wrestled the urge to leave her duties and fly to Rose. However, her first priority was as a caravan leader. It had been hard to keep her thoughts on duty and not on what awaited her at the end of Re's journey across the sky.

Black tent after black tent she passed. There were men and a few women around their fires in conversation, or eating. Some of the caravan attendants had already retired, their tent flaps closed to keep out the desert wind that picked up since sunset. She wrapped the end of her keffiye over her mouth and nose to keep out the dust stirred by the breeze. Soon the wind would drive the others into their shelters to retire for the night.

In her black caravan tent, her private space was walled off from that of her Companions. She could choose to share her space with one or all of her Companions, if she wanted company or

pleasure. Taking pleasure with Rose was foremost
in her thoughts. Her desire and reason warred back
and forth. She felt certain Rose was a virgin, never
having lain with a man, or a woman. Meryt's ardor
might frighten her. Yet, her eyes hungered to gaze
upon Rose's beauty, her mouth thirsted to taste those
enticing lips, her hands yearned to explore the warm,
alabaster skin and trail through the burnished red hair
fine as silk.

Ahead, she saw two flaming braziers, one on
each side of her closed tent flap. They sat atop tall
poles, higher than a man's head. Underneath each
stood a guard to keep watch, each armed with a Lee-
Metford rifle. The guards stood at attention when she
halted Bakhu in front of the tent.

She dismounted and handed the reins to one of
the horse guards who had accompanied her. He would
take care of the stallion and have him ready for her
in the morning. She pulled off her leather gloves and
tucked them under her wide sash.

With her excitement high, she opened the tent
flap and entered. Her three Companions stood there
to greet her and act on any commands. Tiye removed
Meryt's black cloak, saying the meal was almost
prepared. Hedjet asked for her scimitar and ornate
silver baldric.

Straightway Meryt's sight alighted on Rose.
She sat on a cushion, dressed in a pale green galabeya
belonging to Meryt, her red hair a loose cloak about
her shoulders shimmering like fire from the reflected
light of a lamp. As Meryt's eyes drank in the goddess,
her Companions blurred into the background of her
awareness.

Rose hurriedly stood, her posture and manner

arrogant. "You will take me back to Cairo as soon as possible."

In a few rapid steps, Meryt stood before Rose, not bothering to remove the end of the keffiye from the lower portion of her face. Rose's haughty demeanor angered Meryt. No one had ever addressed her in such a way. She grabbed Rose by the left wrist and pulled her near. Her eyes skimmed over Rose's features and fixed on the expressive mouth, then lower to the slender, white neck.

"Let go of me!" Rose struggled to escape from the grasp. Balling her right hand into a fist, she hit Meryt on the left side of her head.

The blow stung Meryt's ear, but she managed to keep her grip tight and quickly catch Rose's wrist before the second blow landed. Rose cried out, frantic to break free, her strength no match for Meryt's that years of breaking horses and camels had hardened. The spirited fight in Rose ignited the fire of lust in Meryt. She pulled Rose closer, feeling the warm body against her. She wanted Rose naked beneath her, to douse her fire on the soft body she envisaged underneath the galabeya. Meryt was tempted to do something she'd never done: take an unwilling woman to her bed.

Then, a hand rested on Meryt's shoulder, and Tiye's calm voice sounded next to her ear. "Henut, please, let her go."

Tiye's words cooled Meryt's anger, and ardor. "Cease fighting me." Meryt's voice held a firm command as she gently pushed Rose a step back, hands still on her wrists.

Rose stopped struggling and looked Meryt in the eyes, her blue eyes widening in recognition.

"You," was all Rose managed to say.

Meryt let go of Rose's wrists as they stared into each other's eyes. With a slow lift of her hand to her face, Meryt removed the end of the keffiye revealing the truth to Rose.

≈≈≈≈

The sharp inhale of breath lodged in her lungs when the face was not of a male youth as expected.

"You're a woman!" Rose studied the attractive feminine face. Her cheekbones were high, complexion brown and smooth, her nose narrow and long, imparting an aristocratic air. Her lips were finely sculptured and full, now in a small smile. Her gold eyes were large, slightly tilting up at the outer corners, catlike, accentuated by arched, black eyebrows.

"I am more than a woman, though I am that, too. I am Merytneit, beloved of the Great Neit and her Chosen One. I am also nisut over her people."

The words left Rose speechless. The chosen of a goddess no longer worshipped? This was madness. The woman was insane. She was the daughter or wife of the headman, Zafar. Maybe all four of these women were his wives. It was unheard of for a woman to live and act as a man, especially here in this land where women were often hidden and veiled.

Rose couldn't ponder this madness. Her one thought was to get back to her father. "If you have any sway at all with your headman, Zafar, please tell him to take me to Cairo."

"I am Zafar bin Abdullah. It's the name and disguise I use when I take my caravan into the Black Land."

Rose could well understand this disguise, but

still found it a bit disturbing. "Then, take me back to Cairo. I must see about my father. Surely, you understand that."

"I have an agent in al-Qahirah, Cairo, the one who rescued you from the slavers. He had orders to check on your father as soon as he returned to al-Qahirah and is to immediately send word if things are amiss. A laden camel's gait is the same speed as that of a man's walk; a swift horse can make our current location in less than a day. No word has arrived. If no word is received by morning, take that as a sign your father is fine."

"Then we're not far from Cairo. Put me on a horse and send me back. I'm a fair rider."

"Know this, Rose. One does not refuse a gift from Neit. We will discuss this no more." Merytneit turned to leave.

"No, wait. I'll pay you if you take me back. My father will reward you."

Merytneit ignored her, rapidly striding away toward her section of the tent. Hedjet followed.

Tiye stepped close. "Ask no more to return to al-Qahirah, it will anger her. For now, speak to her only if she addresses you."

"Why won't she take me back to my father?"

"The answer is not mine to tell."

"I'll not give up." Rose glared at Tiye. "You can't keep me here against my will. I'll...I'll have the authorities arrest all of you for kidnapping."

Tiye stared at her for a moment in surprise, or disbelief, turned and spoke something to Satiah, the girl then leaving the tent.

Rose stamped her foot in frustration. Madness, this was madness.

᠁ ᠁ ᠁ ᠁

Rose's appetite was almost non-existent, but it would be rude not to try to eat the food offered, even though she wasn't sure what she was eating. Earlier, Satiah had returned accompanied by three women carrying pots and platters of food that they placed on the mat used to take meals.

They ate from copper bowls, using their fingers. One dish consisted of seasoned mashed peas or beans and was eaten by dipping bread pieces into it. She couldn't identify the seared chunks of meat on skewers. She hoped it wasn't camel. Surprisingly, the drink was a weak beer, evidence that whatever religion these women adhered to wasn't that of strict followers of Muhammad.

Rose surreptitiously looked across the mat at Merytneit. She was dressed in an ivory caftan that buttoned down the front, and wore a double strand of blue beads. Her black hair brushed the tops of her shoulders. Rose couldn't help but find her attractive. Attractive, or not, she needed to keep in mind that this woman, as Emma would say, was as 'mad as a hatter' and from all indications volatile and dangerous. She thought the wise thing to do was to heed Tiye's advice and keep silent until Merytneit spoke to her.

Merytneit fixed her stare on Rose. The look in those eyes disturbed her, but their intensity mesmerized. Unable to endure them for long she dropped her gaze. When supper ended, Rose watched as Merytneit spoke in Kemen to her three Companions who then left Merytneit and Rose alone.

Merytneit poured beer into her mug, took a

sip, then regarded Rose. "I am sure you have many questions as to who I am, and who my people are. Let me tell you our beginnings. In your year of 391 A.D., the temples of the Gods and Goddesses of Keme... what you call Egypt, closed their doors forever by decree of Caesar Theodosius. The only religion to be recognized was your Christian one. As prophesied in ages past, the Chosen of Neit led her worshippers out of Keme and to the Valley of Wind and Dreams. When her followers arrived in the Valley, the Great One's temple and city, Nesneit, were built. The first Merytneit was its nisut." Merytneit paused to take a sip of beer. "All nisuts are called Merytneit. I am Nisut Merytneit the thirty-fourth."

"Nisut? Isn't that an ancient Egyptian word for a pharaoh, or ruler?"

"Nisut is an ancient Keme name for a king."

"Are all of your pharaohs, or kings, female?"

"Yes, a nisut is also the Chosen of the Great Neit. She will manifest herself through one of us when the destined time of the Universe's emergence from chaos has arrived. She will then return the Universe to the rule of Maat. When the time nears for the old nisut to go into the West, a girl child is born with the gold eyes of the falcon of Horus, which destines her to be the next nisut. The old one passes the blessing of Neit to her when the time is decreed by the Great One."

All of this was balderdash, Rose not believing a word of it. "How is it there are no stories of this great city of yours or of female pharaohs? Egypt is full of stories of lost cities of gold and riches. Zerzura is one such place."

"Ah, Zerzura, the Oasis of Little Birds that lies in

the western desert in a valley between two mountains. Of course, like all fables, this one has jewels and riches and a queen and king. Not even in fable will you find the Valley of Wind and Dreams. Because to lend credence to a city and temple dedicated to a Goddess and the ruler a woman, is outside the wild imaginings of men. We know of the world but the world knows not of us. And we prefer it that way."

"How is it you haven't been discovered by explorers, or a caravan that's lost its way?"

"Neit charged her son, Re, to hide us in the bright rays of the sun. Only those having her permission find our city. Some are those who escaped slavers. The Great One led them to us. Tiye's grandmother was one who escaped those jackals. For some, Neit told them in a vision to journey into the desert, and they heeded her words and found us. They are welcomed and become citizens."

Rose shook her head. No. This was impossible. This was some tall tale. Maybe the oasis was so isolated the people developed their own language. But the names were Egyptian, as were the titles. They were just names and titles taken from myths of when Egypt was glorious, handed down through folk tales. That's all there was to it. This great city was just a small oasis with a population of a few hundred. Merytneit was likely the spoilt daughter of a tribal sheikh.

"You say you're a pharaoh, or nisut. Nisuts are supposed to be in their kingdoms ruling. But you're here." Rose couldn't suppress a smug smile.

"As you can see, here I am." Merytneit held her arms out from her sides, palms up. "Even a nisut has the wish to discover what lies outside her kingdom."

"Who presides over this great city while you're

away?"

"The High Priestess of Neit is my vizier. She has authority over the Valley's officials and manages other matters when I am away."

Rose felt disappointed. Merytneit had a ready answer for all her questions. She once again thought of her father. "My father, I'm sure he is worried about me. I have to get back to him, please."

The features of Merytneit became stern. "Ask me no more to return to al-Qahirah. I will have you write a letter to inform him that you are well."

Rose debated whether or not to say more, but Merytneit's hard features stayed her words. Tiredness descended and drained her. She needed to escape for a while, to be alone. "I'm tired and wish to retire for the night."

Merytneit scrutinized her for a second and nodded once as if she were dismissing a servant. "You have my permission. May your sleep be peaceful and your dreams sweet."

Rose stood and picked up a terra-cotta oil lamp from a low table and lit it from the flame of a bronze lamp. She walked to the curtained-off side of the tent where the three divided sleeping spaces were located. The center section was where the three 'servants' slept, the partitioned area toward the front was reserved for Merytneit, and a curtained space at the other end of the section was hers.

After placing the lamp on a table by the low, narrow bed, she pulled the blanket down from the mattress to check for insects and other creatures as Tiye instructed earlier. Finding no intruders, she slipped into bed, closed her eyes and reviewed the events of this day.

Why did Merytneit prevent her from returning to Cairo? Just what did she mean by *One does not refuse a gift from Neit?*

Chapter Five

March 19, 1901

My Dearest Father,

I hope you are well. I know you are worried about me, and I am sending this letter to help put to rest many of your concerns.

I am in excellent health.

The new servant, Layla, wasn't the person she purported to be. I strongly doubt she is the sister of Fatimah, and I worry harm may have come to that good woman.

It appears Layla was working for Hassid bin Hassid, a man of ill repute, who has a history as a slaver. Layla drugged me and Hassid kidnapped me. This evil man's plans were foiled, and I am currently in the care of a relative of my rescuer.

My host does not want his identity revealed, nor where we are located.

I do not know when I will see you, but know that I hold you in my thoughts, and love you dearly.

Your affectionate daughter,
Rose Grace McLeod

Rose placed the reed pen by the inkwell on the low table. She kept her seat on the carpet, reaching up to hand Merytneit the letter. Rose watched her read it. Its contents were terse, but Merytneit had given strict instructions regarding what she could write. This included not revealing Merytneit's gender.

This was day two of her captivity. The caravan travelled westward, taking her further from Cairo. Evening arrived and supper was done. All Rose wanted was to go to bed and sleep.

"I will send this to al-Qahirah tomorrow at sunrise. The messenger will go by horse." Merytneit turned, beckoned Hedjet over, and gave her the letter. "Take this to the messenger."

"Wait!" Rose's request stopped Hedjet from leaving. "Please. Have him wait for my father to send word to me."

Meryt motioned for Hedjet to leave the tent, then turned her attention back to Rose. "The messenger isn't coming back. He will stay with my man in al-Qahirah until I return."

This bit of news lent Rose hope of soon returning to Cairo. "When are you going back to Cairo?"

"Two years."

Rose quickly stood. "Impossible! I can't be away for two years. You must arrange for me to get back to Cairo."

"Ask me no more to return to al-Qahirah." Merytneit's voice was firm and her features stern.

"Why won't you let me go back to Cairo? Is it a ransom you want? I told you my father would pay you."

"Ransom? No ransom. It was the Great One's will that brought you to me. She gave you—"

"You can't keep me a prisoner! I demand that you return me to—Ahh!" A sudden grip on Rose's shoulders brought her almost against Merytneit. Merytneit slipped her right hand under Rose's chin, forcing her to stare into eyes that appeared of molten gold.

"You will not address me in that manner." Merytneit's breath was hot on Rose's face. "Do you understand?"

Rose held her tongue. The heat in Merytneit's eyes dared Rose to defy her. Rose tightened her lips, imparting her disdain with a flinty stare.

"Henut." Tiye approached. "I ask your forgiveness. I have been lax and haven't informed Nebet Rose the proper behavior toward one of your station."

"See that you do so." Merytneit let go of Rose. "She is now a member of this household, and you will instruct her on the appropriate conduct." She hurried off to her part of the tent. Satiah followed.

"Nebet Rose, I apologize to you. I have been lax in my duties and have failed to instruct you in the proper behavior when it comes to Nisut, and the rules of her household. Your lessons will begin tomorrow."

Rose debated on what to say. She wasn't a member of Merytneit's household, but a captive, nor was she a schoolgirl in need of lessons. These lessons, she was sure, wouldn't be ones she'd like or follow.

Chapter Six

Tiye was accustomed to the plodding gait of the camel and the jostle and sway of the howdah from their journey to al-Qahirah some weeks prior. She gazed beyond the open curtain at Hedjet riding alongside on her pregnant dark chestnut mare. Meryt had given Hedjet the mare when she first joined the household. Satiah trailed close behind on a bay gelding that was also a gift from Meryt. Both Hedjet and Satiah wore the outfits of Bedouin men. Since no followers of the False Prophet lurked nearby to see they were women, they left their faces uncovered.

Tiye had a fear of horses. She would walk all the way home rather than climb on the back of one. Her white camel, a gift from Meryt, suited her fine. Hedjet and Satiah both had a camel and howdah, but used them only occasionally. Tiye was sure the view from the comfort of the howdah was better than from the back of a horse.

This was the third day of Rose's rescue. Tiye regarded Rose while her focus was outside the howdah. "Nebet." This got Rose's attention. "I wish to see your interactions with Henutsen not so fraught with contention. What she commands, you obey. I don't think she will demand anything unreasonable. When she enters the tent, you stand in welcome. She has given you permission to call her Meryt when in private. When in public, always refer to her as Henut or Henutsen."

Tiye preferred to use the name 'Meryt' when it was just the two of them, or when the situation was personal. The young Meryt had been stricter in protocol when she first became Nisut. Tiye felt this had been due to her perceptions of power and self-importance. It wasn't until almost a year after Tiye entered the household that she had been granted the privilege of calling her 'Meryt.' However, the habit of calling her Henut remained.

"Henut. Isn't that a title like nebet?"

"It is an ancient Keme word meaning mistress or lady and is now a title of respect for the nisut, used only by a nisut's household, servants, and guards. Henutsen means 'our Mistress'. Those not of her household address her as Nisut Wer, which means Great King, or Setepenneit, which means Chosen of Neit."

Rose remained quiet. Tiye read her silence as cooperation. This would make her Henut happy. A happy nisut meant a happy household. As the silence stretched, Tiye watched Rose's brow knit and her lips tighten.

Rose stared at Tiye. "I am not a member of her household. I will give respect only if I am treated likewise. Tell your *nisut* that. And since she is not my mistress, I'll not call her henut."

Tiye sighed. *Stubborn and prideful.* However, Nisut was Nisut and her will would prevail.

Chapter Seven

Oil lamps cast a mellow glow over the tent's interior, and onto the two women engaged in a game of chess. Hedjet wore a triumphant grin as her black queen took Rose's white knight. She looked up at Rose with a coquettish smile. Rose dropped her gaze to the board and studied it, her concentration broken by admiration of the beautiful ivory and ebony playing pieces. Crusaders were skillfully carved from ivory, Saracens from ebony. The set looked old; the patina of age having mellowed the ivory to a rich gold color. Returning her concentration to the game, she made her move, hoping Hedjet would take the bait and open her king up to check. While Hedjet contemplated the board, Rose's thoughts turned to her present predicament. Seven days had passed since her 'abduction.' That's how she thought of it. The idea had occurred to her that rather than slavers, Meryt was the abductor all along. No, she really didn't believe that. Why wouldn't Meryt take her back to Cairo? She didn't want a ransom. What *did* she want from her? When she asked Tiye, her reply was to ask Meryt.

She would have to wait until Meryt returned to the caravan to ask questions. She left the morning after Rose wrote the letter to her father, having received reports of bandits. She and several guards were patrolling the road ahead and camping in the desert. Rose was relieved not to have Meryt watching her every move. She didn't like what she saw in her gold eyes. It unsettled her and was something that should not appear so boldly in the eyes of a proper young lady, or a gentleman. However, Meryt was hardly a proper young lady, was she? Her ways were queer, even for the natives of Egypt.

It was true that the people in this caravan treated her with respect and she did have command over them, but her claim to be a *pharaoh* was strange. Rose wasn't familiar with all the customs of Egypt, so it could be possible that some desert tribes had female chiefs. Tiye and the other two women obeyed her and attended to her every whim as if she were indeed royalty. Rose wasn't entirely convinced the three women weren't slaves, though Tiye said they had elected to be Meryt's Companions and were assigned to her by the Temple of Neit.

Rose supposed it was possible people still worshiped the ancient Egyptian deities and spoke a derivative Egyptian language. Tiye had explained that Kemen derived from both Demotic and Coptic. An element of Greek and Latin was introduced into the language as a few of the original settlers of Nesneit were of Greek and Roman descent.

Tiye and Hedjet didn't strike her as liars. She would concede to the probability of an isolated and distant oasis that held archaic beliefs and customs, but she thought they exaggerated when it came to a kingdom.

The drum of horses' hooves brought Hedjet's eyes up from the chessboard to look toward the tent flap. The riders stopped in front of the tent. Rose noticed Hedjet's enthusiastic smile as she stood and hurried toward the entrance, joined by Tiye and Satiah.

The *master* had returned. Rose remained seated and held her breath as a trickle of apprehension tensed her body.

Meryt entered and smiled upon her three Companions. She kissed Tiye on her cheek, then Hedjet and Satiah, receiving a kiss in return from each. She spoke words in Kemen to them. After Tiye took her cloak and Hedjet her scimitar and baldric, Meryt fixed her attention on Rose, a frown replacing her smile. Her angry glare caused Rose to drop her eyes to the chessboard. Before she realized it, a tight grip encircled her left wrist, and she was abruptly pulled up to stand before Meryt, almost pressing against her. She sucked in a sharp breath, frozen by the violent action.

"You will stand when I enter the tent and not ignore me." Meryt's tone was low and harsh, her eyes blazing.

Rose focused on the floor, wanting to end the confrontation. Meryt reminded Rose of a wild and dangerous animal. She'd heard to look a cougar, wolf, or even a growling dog in the eyes was to challenge them. The grip around her wrist tightened painfully. She lifted her eyes, stating firmly, "Let go, you're hurting me."

Meryt's hold lessened, Rose now seeing not anger in the expression, but an emotion even more disturbing. Rose turned her head away, only to have Meryt grab her chin, forcing Rose to stare into her gold eyes filled with desire. Her gaze dropped to Rose's mouth. Her hand moved up to softly stroke Rose's cheek.

Oh God, she's going to kiss me.

Meryt closed her eyes and moved closer. With

a cry, Rose twisted her head away from Meryt's kiss to have it fall on the corner of her mouth. Suddenly, Meryt let go of Rose's wrist, turned, snapped out something in Kemen and strode to her section of the tent, Hedjet accompanying her. Rose heard a loud, derisive sounding snort and glanced over at Satiah, seeing a nasty sneer on her face. Tiye spoke to Satiah who then exited the tent.

Tiye faced Rose, shook her head and frowned. "Why do you provoke her? She will now think I haven't been diligent in telling you how members of this household are to treat her."

"I apologize. Is there something I can tell her... can do?" Rose never intended to cause problems for Tiye who was kind and considerate toward her.

"Yes, remember to treat her with respect."

Satiah entered the tent, followed by two women carrying pots of food.

A little later, Meryt emerged from her part of the tent, dressed in a blue and green vertical striped caftan, her hair hanging loose to the shoulders. Around her neck hung a gold udjat. The eye's iris consisted of a gem that matched the color of Meryt's eyes. She took her seat by the mat, motioning the others to join her. Rose sat on the carpet by the mat, right in the line of Meryt's vision.

Supper consisted of boiled grain, a meat stew of goat or mutton, and flatbread. Meryt and her Companions conversed in Kemen during the meal. Rose avoided letting her gaze linger long on Meryt, not wanting to see what those gold eyes held if they should regard her. After supper, Satiah and Hedjet carried the bowls outside the tent. Rose moved near a lighted lamp stand where Hedjet had put a sewing basket and items of clothing that required mending. Earlier, Rose had offered to darn any clothes that needed it.

Tiye slid closer to Meryt's side, and they talked to each other in what appeared to be a private and warm conversation. Meryt tenderly smiled and stroked Tiye's face.

Rose blushed at this intimate exchange and diverted her attention to mending a tear in a robe.

Hedjet and Satiah entered the tent and joined Tiye and Meryt in conversation. When Rose glanced up to watch them, the three Companions focused on Meryt in what seemed to be adoration.

Hedjet stood and hurried to a chest against the back wall of the tent. She took a book from the chest, came back, handed it to Meryt and then sat next to her.

The title of the book was plain to see, and one Rose had read, *Alice's Adventures in Wonderland.*

"Shall I read in English," Meryt gave Rose a friendly smile, "so Rose will understand?"

That Meryt could read impressed Rose. She appeared to be educated, as did Tiye and Hedjet.

"Henut, Satiah won't understand a word you say," Hedjet said.

"Then Satiah can darn the garments."

Meryt spoke in Kemen to Satiah who looked crestfallen. She came to Rose, sat, and rudely snatched the robe and sewing needle from her hands.

"Here, Nebet Rose," Hedjet slid away from Meryt. "I have made a place for you."

"Come, Rose." Meryt offered Rose an inviting smile and patted the space beside her.

"I'm fine where I'm at."

All motion halted. Tiye and Hedjet glanced

nervously at Meryt and then to Rose. Even Satiah seemed to feel the crackle of tension as she stopped sewing to look around her with a puzzled expression. Rose detected the girl's posture tense when she focused on Meryt.

Rose noticed a flare to Meryt's nostrils, her mouth in a frown. The heat in Meryt's eyes caused a nervous flutter in Rose's stomach. Out of the corner of her eye, she caught Tiye's direct stare and the beckoning gesture with the fingers of her right hand.

Rose wasn't some servant to jump at anyone's beck and call. Meryt needed to understand that American customs were different, and Rose didn't intend to follow the 'when in Rome' rule. She was a freeborn American woman.

She noticed Meryt's eyes still fixed on her. Meryt stated something in Kemen while keeping her stare on Rose.

Satiah quickly shoved the robe into Rose's lap, then hurried over to sit by Meryt, her smile gloating.

Rose resumed sewing and listened as Meryt read the story in Kemen, the four women laughing at times.

When Meryt paused, Rose looked up to see those gold eyes fixed on her in what seemed like lust.

Another time she glanced up to see Meryt absently stroking Tiye's hair while she read. Were these Companions more than just Meryt's friends? They seemed to have more than just a friendly affection for Meryt, and she them.

She recalled the first time she saw them. She thought Meryt a young man. Emma even remarked the three women were 'his' concubines or wives. *Ridiculous.* Women didn't have concubines. Not even a sultana or Indian maharani would have them.

Rose finished her task and quietly waited for Meryt to stop reading. Meryt paused and looked at her. "I finished darning. Will you excuse me? I'm tired." It grated Rose to have to ask.

"You may go." Meryt's tone was casual and dismissive.

Rose lit a lamp from one already burning and walked past the four women.

"May your sleep be peaceful and your dreams sweet," Meryt said.

Not looking back, Rose nodded and went on to bed.

ﷺﷺﷺﷺ

"Argh," Satiah growled in anger and disappointment, sullenly rolling onto her side as the sounds of pleasure filled the tent. She snatched a pillow and pressed it over her head as an excited cry of passion assaulted her ears.

Once again, she received no invitation to share Nisut's bed and couldn't understand why. She was pretty and younger than those two heifers who were old enough to be her mother. Not Hedjet, but she was still old.

Nisut was old enough to be her mother, too. But Nisut was a beautiful Isis. She admitted Hedjet and Tiye were pretty for old heifers.

She was sure once in Nisut's bed she could satisfy her. She made Hedjet scream with delight when she rode her while wearing a phallus. True, Hedjet had told her Nisut forbade the use of a phallus when engaging in pleasure with her Companions. Too bad, because she held fantasies of riding Nisut until she screamed out in ecstasy, then have her beg for more. Nisut would soon make Satiah her favorite Companion.

But she was talented in other ways, too. She never had complaints from her conquests back home or from her teacher at the Temple of Hathor where Companions were required to receive instructions in how to pleasure a woman. Not that she ever needed lessons. She could have taught that old Hathor heifer a lesson or two.

She was the first from her village to have the honor of being a Companion. Almost two years ago her father, the village headman, had sent a request to the priestesses at the Temple of the Great Neit to take her as one of their order, and into training as a Companion. He had told them his daughter was a lover of women and modest in her behavior. The latter was a lie, but lover of women was the truth in more ways than he knew. Satiah's new and young stepmother could attest to that fact. Perhaps he did know, but his ambition was as great as her own. His hopes were that his daughter could influence Nisut to appoint him as chief administrator over several of the smaller oases.

She believed Nisut had started looking at her with interest, until the not English, but another word for one like the English. *Mercan? Yes, the Mercan nebet from far away who slithered like a poisonous serpent into Nisut's heart.* She saw how Nisut's eyes devoured the serpent woman. How she hungered for her.

The Mercan was beautiful, but cold. There was no passion in that one. Satiah had peeked one time through the edge of the curtain that divided the woman's private area from the other ones in the tent, and watched her wipe the sand and grime from her body with a wet cloth. Satiah had never seen a body the color of milk. The woman's skin was smooth, her body lithe, breasts rounded and tipped with pink nipples that made Satiah want to bite and mark them.

The Mercan lured Nisut with her beauty and had bitten her, the poison filling Nisut's heart with false love. If Serpent Woman were gone, Satiah was sure Nisut would look upon her with favor.

Why, just tonight Satiah had an honored place by Nisut's side when she read from the strange book. Nisut had even given her a smile and laughed when she did. Then Nisut would glance up to look at the Mercan and forget to read for a moment. Satiah knew Nisut wished it were the Mercan by her side and not Satiah.

Yes, the Mercan must be banished from Nisut's heart.

☙☙☙☙

The sounds of groans and moans drew Rose from slumber. She listened, wondering if she dreamed them. A long and fevered moan from a woman had her sitting up in concern, thinking someone suffered in pain.

She looked toward the curtain that separated her space from that of the three *friends* of Meryt. It was pitch black. She couldn't see a sliver of light through the gaps in the curtain. Then there was a series of short and breathy cries followed by one long strangled cry then laughter.

Silence fell, and Rose settled back down to sleep. She wondered what the cries and laughs were all about. Her eyes had barely closed when the frantic cries started again, this time sounding as if from a different woman.

She then heard the sound of two distinct female cries, loud rhythmic grunts and the other a series of throaty groans.

"O dear God in heaven." Realization slapped her hard. Those were the cries of women when experiencing passion, she was certain. Though she didn't have anything to base it on but instinct.

Shock and mortification flooded heat to her face. She had fallen in with libertines. But she couldn't help wondering who and how many were involved, and just what they were doing to cause such passionate sounds.

Chapter Eight

"Are you ill, Nebet?" Tiye asked the taciturn woman sitting next to her in the howdah. At daybreak, the caravan had resumed its journey west. In another day, they should come upon one of the small settlements on the outer edges of al-Bahariya Oasis. They would rest for a few days and go to a village souk to shop. Meryt would have her grand tent erected, and they might even have a feast.

Rose had seemed subdued since she first awakened. Soon after Meryt departed to perform her duties as caravan leader, Rose joined the three Companions for the morning meal. She seemed almost embarrassed, her cheeks reddening several times, and she avoided looking at Tiye's face when they talked.

Rose furtively glanced at Tiye then looked out the open front curtain of the howdah. She asked in a quiet voice, "Are you a...a..."

Tiye could see the crimson flush of her cheek that the headscarf didn't cover. She'd never seen a face turn so red. Perhaps it was due to Rose's pale skin.

Tiye waited for Rose to continue. When she wasn't forthcoming, she asked, "There is something you wish to know, yet you fear the question will offend me, or is it the answer that you dread?"

"It's really none of my business." Rose looked down at her hands.

"Let me decide that, Nebet, after I hear your

question."

Rose turned to her and drew in a deep breath. "Are you and the others Meryt's concubines?" Her words were rushed.

This surprised Tiye. Then she grinned, knowing why the question arose. Tent walls did little to keep in or out the sounds. She was sure the guards of Meryt's tent were aware of the nature of the cries they heard last night, too.

"As I told you before, we are Nisut's Companions. To be a Companion is a great honor. Our duties are to assist in the management of her palace staff and servants, arrange her schedule and provide counsel when she seeks it. We also offer friendship and company, and yes, Nebet Rose, give her physical pleasure when she desires it. That duty is one I enjoy rendering to my Henut."

"I...see." Rose's voice was strained. "It's just not something that's done in my country, and, well..." She dropped her gaze to her hands and laced her fingers together.

"Nebet Eliza compared Companions to the Ladies in Waiting who attended Queen Victoria. Except for the pleasurable duties." Tiye tried for her best Nebet Eliza accent. "A pity that. It would have done the Old Dear good."

Rose glanced at Tiye and giggled, though her face still kept its red hue.

Tiye felt sorry that pleasurable intimacies upset Rose. She understood from Nebet Eliza that *well-bred* young English nebets were taught to suppress their passions. They were not to have them. Part of it was religious beliefs. However, Nebet Eliza said much of it was male 'humbuggery' used to keep women suppressed. Rose came from America, but she spoke English and looked like the English women. From her reaction, she more than likely believed this 'humbuggery' to be true.

This did not bode well for Meryt enticing Rose into her arms. Then again, her Henut was a desirable woman and perhaps Rose would be drawn to her and discover passion. After all, women were naturally passionate.

She also suspected Rose was a lover of women. Hathor had gifted Tiye with the ability to look into a woman's eyes and see where her love interests lay.

"I know you aren't accustomed to our ways and don't understand them. I will help you. Don't hesitate to ask me questions or feel you will offend me."

Rose nodded and met Tiye's gaze. "What is it Meryt wants from me?"

Tiye knew Meryt's desire for Rose stood foremost. But she suspected there were reasons beneath the surface more intricate than even Meryt recognized, and when these reasons emerged, desire would play but a small part. Tiye's answer remained the same as the last time Rose asked the question. "That is something only she can tell you."

Chapter Nine

Rose relished having this grand tent all to herself if even for a little while. The caravan had arrived at al-Bahariya late yesterday. The pitching of this huge tent commenced almost immediately, by what seemed like the whole caravan crew.

After breakfast, Meryt took Tiye and Hedjet to shop in a nearby village, and they should return in the early afternoon. Rose didn't mind not accompanying them, but Satiah did. She was left to see to Rose's 'needs', as Meryt had worded it. Rose thought this odd as the girl couldn't speak English.

Satiah was unhappy as evidenced by the baleful stares she'd directed at Rose. She disappeared after bringing Rose a meal of rice, bread, cheese, and dried dates.

The maroon cushion Rose leaned against was comfortable and enticed her to stretch like a cat as she read the adventures of young Master Hawkins and Long John Silver. She finished the chapter and placed the book on the carpet.

The chest containing twelve books written in English was hers to explore since asking Meryt's permission last night after supper. Meryt had agreed with a pleasant smile, naming all the books written in English that the chest contained. By Meryt's friendly manner, Rose thought it safe enough to press her for answers as to why she was being held captive, but before she could ask, Meryt was called away to handle caravan business.

She gazed up at the voluminous tent ceiling of almost white, which filtered the bright sunlight to a muted glow shining into the spacious common area.

This tent was the biggest and finest one Rose had ever seen, and consisted of three separate tents, one attached on either side to a huge one that was the common area. The common area held a storage room in the back, which contained trunks, spare cushions and other items. This had a back entrance for servants.

Meryt's room was in the left tent, and Rose and the three Companions' on the right. In the right section was an entrance leading into a passageway with two curtained off private spaces on each side. Rose's area was located at the end on the left side, and Tiye's across on the right. Satiah and Hedjet's rooms were in the front by the passageway entrance.

Rose hoped that any nocturnal soirées between the women occurred in Meryt's section. She thought it far enough away not to have her ears assaulted by the sounds. Her cheeks burned just remembering. Her thoughts strayed to places that made her uncomfortable with the images they provoked. Images that weren't all repugnant.

She quickly directed her attention to surveying the common area, admiring the colorful and luxurious carpets in different patterns. Scattered about were cushions, low stools, floor lamps, and two tables. Fastened to the tent walls were tapestries woven in floral patterns.

She smiled ruefully, comparing this to a harem. Not that she'd ever been inside one. From what she learned about Meryt's Companions, she thought her imagination not far from the truth.

A commotion outside the tent caught her attention. She straightened, ready to spring to her feet in a show of respect if Meryt entered. It grated her to do this. The main reason to comply was for Tiye, not wanting to cause her any trouble. She was relieved that Meryt never kissed her cheek when she entered the tent.

The sound of female voices and laughter let her know Meryt's household had returned. The tent flaps parted and an excited Tiye and Hedjet entered followed by four guards toting two wicker chests. The guards placed the chests on the floor and then departed.

"Nebet Rose!" Hedjet's expression was one of happy excitement as she took Rose's hand and pulled her up. "Come and see what garments we have for you."

"Yes, come and see." Tiye's eyes were bright and her grin wide. She opened a chest for Rose to peer inside it. There were clothes in many different colors, along with other items. Tiye removed a wooden box out of the chest and handed it to Rose.

"Open it, Nebet." Tiye almost bounced on her toes.

Rose opened the box, seeing a beautifully carved ivory comb, a brush, a hand mirror, and hairpins.

"Oh, my, what a lovely set. Thank you." Rose was happy to receive the gift. She'd appreciate her own brush and hairpins and not having to borrow them. Now she could resume her routine of brushing her hair every night for one hundred strokes.

"See what else we have for you." Hedjet took the box from Rose and placed it on the floor. "Henutsen had us choose only the best garments and things for you."

"I picked this one for you." Tiye held up a square of blue material and unfolded it to reveal a galabeya decorated with silver embroidery. She put it up against Rose to see if it would fit.

"It's very pretty, thank you." Rose felt uneasy accepting the clothes, knowing Meryt's money bought them. But she needed her own clothes, especially since her current outfits belonged to Meryt.

"I have a mirror in my room you can use to see how the garments look on you," Hedjet said.

"I may do that later." Rose had seen the large, oval floor mirror and had wondered how it was packed on a camel to prevent breakage during the journey.

The two women's enthusiasm became contagious and she soon enjoyed examining the clothes and lightweight under shifts. There was a pair of long, white pants, called sirwal, worn by men under their robes or with a tunic. Women sometimes wore them as under drawers. She also received two pairs of sandals, a pair of slippers and a pair of tan leather boots.

Now it was Rose's turn to admire the contents of the other chest containing articles of clothes for Tiye and Hedjet. They had even purchased outfits for Satiah.

"Where is Satiah?" Tiye looked around.

"I don't know. I've not seen her in a while."

"She better show up soon. Henutsen will be back after she checks on things, and she will want a bath. Satiah needs to make arrangements for the water."

"Bath?" Rose's voice held hopeful anticipation.

"Yes, yes." Hedjet's tone and smile were ones

of delight. "Not one like we would take at home, but close enough. The water is plentiful here. It's just too bad we can't take the oasis with us."

"Nebet Rose, I have some bath oil with a nice fragrance you can borrow," Tiye said.

"That would be nice." Rose offered a pleased smile.

"It's one of Henutsen's favorites, she's partial to the fragrance," Tiye added.

Rose's smile froze. Was that when the oil was on Meryt, or on her Companions? *Harem. This is a harem.* Rose prayed Meryt didn't think of her as the latest acquisition.

Chapter Ten

Cool water sluiced in refreshing rivulets over and between Meryt's firm breasts, down her flat belly and slim thighs before it splashed into the shallow, copper washbasin in which she stood. Tiye poured another bowl full of water down her back, took a towel from Satiah and held it open as Meryt stepped into it.

Tiye patted her dry, then got a flask of cinnamon scented oil from a nearby table, poured a few drops into her palm and rubbed her hands together. She massaged the oil onto Meryt's skin.

The agile touch of warm hands caused the tingle of desire, but this did not spark in Meryt the wish to share pleasure with Tiye. Her thoughts were on her blue-eyed beautiful Isis, wishing it were her elegant hands massaging her. She couldn't stop a smile when imagining it and what other sweet touches would follow. She looked up to see Tiye's shrewd expression and lifted her eyebrows in question.

Tiye smoothed the warm oil over Meryt's shoulders and down her breasts, causing the nipples to stiffen. "Perhaps Nebet Rose will sweeten her regard for you if you attend to her feelings tonight, and every night," Tiye said. "After all, one does have to cultivate and care for a grape vine to have it yield sweet grapes."

Perhaps Tiye offered good advice, Meryt thought, but it irritated all the same. She knew Rose held contempt for her and wouldn't favor her with 'sweet' regard. Her contempt made Meryt furious. She'd pray to the Divine Hathor to help soften Rose's heart.

"That is true, O Wise Priestess. I don't want sour grapes."

A chuckle from Tiye, and Satiah's laugh was derisive.

Meryt glowered at Satiah. "Take from the smaller chest a gown...the sky-blue one. Then get the blue faience necklace and the sandals that match the gown's belt. Take them to Hedjet and tell her to give them to Rose. Tell Hedjet to inform Rose they are gifts from me and she is to wear them when we dine tonight." She wanted to see Rose in one of her finer gowns worn on intimate dinner occasions with her Companions, usually ending in a night of pleasure. Its cut was along the same line as one of the traditional patterns of her kingdom. She always traveled with a chest full of the traditional outfits, finding an opportunity to wear them.

Meryt had arranged the menu with the cook after she returned from taking her Companions to the souk. The idea hadn't occurred earlier, and she was relieved when the cook said she bought chickens and fresh produce at the souk that morning. They also had dried apricots, figs, and honey to make pastries.

Tiye took a robe from the top of a chest and held it for Meryt to slip on. "What do you want to wear tonight?"

"Select something that will fit the occasion."

"As Nisut or as the attentive suitor?"

"Something that will make me into a Hathor, O Wise Priestess." *For I will need divine intervention.*

Rose knelt on the floor, her head bent over the copper washbasin, eyes closed in ecstasy, as Hedjet washed her hair. A soft groan of pleasure escaped her as the woman's fingers massaged her scalp. Earlier Rose had stood in the basin and washed the grime and sand from her body. While it hadn't been a full bath, it far surpassed wiping with a damp cloth as she'd done for the past ten days. Water was plentiful at the oasis. It felt delicious to be clean, the floral perfumed soap and oil leaving a pleasant scent on her skin.

Hedjet poured water from a copper bowl over Rose's hair to rinse out the soap. She squeezed out the excess moisture and removed the white towel draped across Rose's shoulders that protected her clean shift from dampness, and wrapped it around Rose's head.

"Sit on the stool so I can dry your hair and comb out the tangles," Hedjet said.

Rose did as instructed, Hedjet kneeling behind her to dry her hair with the towel. Hedjet took a comb from the top of a table and started at the bottom of a damp lock of hair, working up the strand to remove snarls.

Satiah called Hedjet's name from the other side of the curtain. Hedjet bade her enter. Rose saw that Satiah carried a bundle of folded clothes on which rested a pair of finely crafted sandals along with a belt and what looked like items of jewelry. Satiah spoke to Hedjet in Kemen and then shot Rose a hateful scowl.

"Nebet Rose," Hedjet said, "Henutsen wishes you to accept these gifts and wear them when you dine tonight." She spoke again to the girl. Satiah went to the bed and put the items upon it.

Rose didn't like the idea of accepting gifts from Meryt, but she had already taken the clothes bought for her, so what was one more gift? She would thank Meryt for the clothes and other items.

"When it's time to dress, I will assist you," Hedjet said.

"I think I can manage to dress myself, thank you, Hedjet. Is this dinner in celebration of a special or holy day?" Hedjet had informed Rose earlier that Meryt had a special dinner planned, and she would help Rose bathe and prepare for it. Rose had refused the offer of assistance with her bath, but accepted Hedjet's offer to wash her hair. Rose hoped the words 'special dinner' meant there would be more on the menu other than the usual fare of flatbread, rice, beans, unidentified meat stew, and dried fruit. She wondered if Meryt had invited any guests. If she did, they would probably be the caravan leaders.

"No, Nebet Rose, it's not a holy day."

"Is it just us dining tonight, or has Meryt invited others?"

"You are the only one to have the honor of dining with Henutsen."

Rose stilled, thinking she had misconstrued what Hedjet said. "Surely you, Tiye and Satiah will attend?"

"Only you, Nebet." Hedjet's tone was bright and her smile wide. "It's a great honor to dine alone with Henutsen. Many would envy you."

Rose sucked in a sharp breath, wondering what this dinner portended. She experienced trepidation that she'd be alone with Meryt, recalling how those gold eyes stared at her as if she were—She didn't want to fathom what those eyes held.

For a moment, she considered not attending the dinner, but she knew that would anger Meryt. She sensed that anger was far more dangerous than what she had so far observed, and was not something she wanted to provoke.

Hedjet finished combing Rose's hair. "I'll return at sundown to take you to Henutsen." Hedjet and Satiah departed.

Rose reached for the bundled apparel on the bed and examined the sandals. Nickel-size discs of lapis and gold adorned the white leather straps. The jewelry consisted of a beaded faience collar and looked similar to those seen worn by the ancient Egyptian women and goddesses rendered on tomb walls. Next, she examined the belt, noticing the white leather set with lapis and gold and how it matched the sandals. Before she touched the folded sky-blue apparel, she could tell it was delicate, almost sheer.

With apprehension, she picked up the attire and unfurled it, her breathing stilled. To her it was indecent. The blue sheath was translucent and would reveal whatever she wore beneath it. The design looked similar to sleeveless Roman or Greek tunics and she realized underclothes were not worn under it.

Did Meryt think of her as a Companion who would provide entertainment...or heaven forbid, engage in intimate pursuits with her? Closing her eyes, she drew in several long breaths to steady her nerves. She had never suffered the vapors, and she certainly wouldn't have them now.

She went to the clothes chest and removed three galabeyas, placing them on top of the bed. She decided on the substantial ivory galabeya with blue and gold embroidery of blossoms around its neck and down the front. The sandals would be the only thing she'd wear from the presented items. She'd pin up her hair and present an elegant and modest appearance, her manners those of a proper lady, above reproach...and, approach.

Chapter Eleven

Hedjet held open the curtain for Rose as she entered the common space. Rose surveyed the luxurious room cast in a golden glow from the bronze stands that held lamps filled with fragrant oil smelling of jasmine. Numerous candles decorated the dining mat amidst platters of fruit and food. To Rose, all of this looked like a romantic setting, or the scene for a seduction.

A sudden movement snared her attention. She watched as Meryt abruptly shot to her feet from the other side of the mat and strode rapidly up to her, stopping at arm's length.

With a scowl, Meryt looked Rose over from head to foot. She focused on Rose's face. "Why do you not wear the gown and necklace I sent to you?" She looked from Rose to Hedjet who slowly shook her head and dropped her gaze to the floor.

Meryt returned her scrutiny to Rose.

Rose noticed the fury in Meryt's eyes and decided it prudent to answer. "I wished to wear this instead."

Meryt crossed her arms over her chest. "*You* wished? Did you now? What *you* wish is of no consequence. Where are the things I wanted you to wear?"

"They're in my room."

Meryt turned her attention to Hedjet. "Go get

them and bring them to me."

A sharp clap of Meryt's hands and loud words in Kemen summoned a woman from the curtained off area behind the dining mat. She stood before Meryt with head and eyes downcast. Meryt spoke to her in a few commanding words.

The woman rushed to the mat, picked up a bronze carafe, grabbed a cup and poured into it a red liquid Rose guessed was wine. She hurried back to Meryt and gave her the cup. Meryt dismissed her with curt words. A self-satisfied smile played on Meryt's mouth as she sipped the wine and studied Rose over the cup's rim.

Rose frowned and looked contemptuously into Meryt's eyes, noticing how the kohl outlined them and the green paint on the lids made them appear more gold. Red ochre tinted her lips. Around her head, she wore a gold band edged with tiny, dangling green beads. Rose thought her beautiful. But that beauty harbored the cruelty of a cobra. She lowered her sight to the collar of gold with green trapezoid tiles hanging around the edge. Her eyes fell lower to take in the pleated sheath of white linen, a green sash circling her waist with its two ends falling below her knees. A hot blush flooded Rose when she noticed the near translucence of the gown's material that revealed the hint of brown skin and shapely breasts with dark nipples.

A hushed sound behind Rose drew her attention to Hedjet bowing her head in deference as she held out the folded dress with the necklace and belt on top to Meryt.

Meryt brought the cup to her lips and drained the contents, then tossed the cup aside. "Put them on the floor and leave us."

Hedjet placed the items on the floor. Out of the corner of her eye Rose saw Hedjet give her a concerned glance before she departed.

Meryt's eyes were dangerously bright and intense as they swept over her. With a curt nod, she motioned to the galabeya Rose wore. "Take it off."

Rose was shocked, her breath caught in a sharp inhale.

Meryt's stare hardened into one of hawkish intensity. "I order you to take it off."

Rose swallowed and stood straight, ire making her teeth clench. "I will not."

Meryt stepped forward, close enough that Rose detected the subtle fragrance of cinnamon. "You think to disobey me?" Meryt's smile seemed to be one of amusement.

Rose bit back a sharp retort, deciding to show contempt through silence.

"You will learn, Rose, that you are to obey me. I am nisut here. My will is supreme."

"I'm not one of your subjects to jump at your commands." Rose gave Meryt a sharp and scornful look.

Meryt smirked as she looked Rose over leisurely. "My beautiful Rose, how defiant you are. How very refreshing, and should I say, stimulating. Your very voice and manner tell me you have spirit. No one has broken you. But I can break you, Rose, if I so choose. Break you and have you beg to please me in all ways."

"You disgust me!"

"Disgust you? Do I now?" She paused, her smile smug. "You *will* do what I ordered, or I'll have Hedjet summon two of my men to remove your garments for you. The choice is yours."

With effort, Rose fought down the urge to beg Meryt not to do this. What choice did she have? Meryt would do what she threatened, of that she was certain. "Did you not hear me?" Meryt's eyes narrowed.

Rose pulled the galabeya up and over her head and dropped it to the floor. She stood straight, now wearing only the under shift. She lifted her head high, focused on the far tent wall, and held her posture in a defiant pose. She wouldn't let Meryt shame or break her.

"Take off the rest."

Coldness and a mild breathless sensation hit her. Rose closed her eyes, swallowed hard, and with determination, overcame reluctance. She stared at Meryt with disdain as she removed the shift and let it drop. *She will not shame me. Do not give her the satisfaction.* Meryt moved closer, her smile fading as her eyes searched Rose's face then dropped to her breasts. Meryt circled Rose, plucking the pins from the back of her hair. As her hand ran through a strand of hair Rose heard a slow indrawn breath. She felt the warm stroke of Meryt's hand down her spine to the small of her back, causing an involuntary shiver to skitter across the base of her neck. A soft caress swept across her right shoulder as Meryt continued around her.

Once in front of her Meryt stepped back, eyes caressing Rose's breasts, lingering before continuing their journey lower.

Rose flushed, fighting the urge to grab the discarded shift to cover herself and hang her head in shame. *No, be strong. Don't let her win. Never let her win.*

With contempt, Rose glared at Meryt, seeing

her eyes bright and her mouth slightly parted. Rose recognized the look of lust when it presented itself. It took all her willpower not to panic. She choked down a sob of anxiety.

"Isisnofret." Meryt's voice was a whisper. "You are a teardrop shed by the divine Isis when her beloved Osiris died. The tears became sparkling jewels. Neit does love me to give you to me."

One does not refuse a gift from Neit. Rose recalled Meryt's words from the first night of her captivity. She became lightheaded for a moment from the realization of what that meant…and why Meryt held her captive. She kept silent, her nakedness making her feel too vulnerable to protest.

Meryt stared for a few seconds longer, and then abruptly bent to take the necklace from the top of the clothes. "Dress in the garment I gave you." She returned to the mat, sat and leaned against a cushion, keeping her eyes on Rose.

Despite the trembling of her hands and her awareness of Meryt's eyes on her, Rose managed to slide on the dress and fasten the belt around her waist.

"Come, Rose. Take your place by my side."

The shine of a hairpin from the red carpet on which Rose stood caught her eye. She picked it up, along with two others, and twisted her hair to pin it up.

"Leave it down," Meryt said.

Rose dropped the pins and looked at Meryt. "What are your intentions?"

Meryt appeared confused for a second before she smiled. "To have you join me in dining. Is that such a distasteful thing for you to do?" Meryt patted the place by her side. "Come sit."

Rose hesitated, reluctant to move forward as her thoughts ran in one direction.

"I don't bite my dinner guests." Meryt's tone was amused. Then her voice held a command. "Come here, Rose."

"And after dinner?" Rose held her breath. Her question wasn't only for now, but also for what lay beyond this night.

Meryt lifted her eyebrows in surprise. "Ah, I see. You wish to know if I will request carnal favors from you, do you not?"

"Yes." Rose's heartbeat pounded in her ears.

"You surprise me, my little virgin, to let your fancy stray in that direction. Do you wish to join me in my bed after we dine? I promise the pleasure we share will be delightful."

"Certainly not! You think me a...a libertine?"

Meryt laughed. "Oh my exquisite jewel, I think you many things, but not a libertine." She paused, her voice now serious. "I have never forced a woman to lie with me, and I never will. I am Nisut, and that alone makes women eager to come to my bed. In time, you will come to Nisut's bed. You will do this willingly. For now, I wish only to dine with you."

And pigs might fly. Rose wasn't a possession, and she'd never go willingly to *that* woman's bed.

※ ※ ※ ※

Even though Rose kept her posture and walk stiff as she came toward the dining mat, she had an enticing sway to the hips that Meryt found sensual. Rose sat by Meryt, keeping her posture rigid.

Meryt took the necklace from where she had laid

it on the mat. "Turn so I can put the necklace on you."

Rose turned, gathered her hair and lifted it. Moving close Meryt circled the necklace about her neck, pausing to savor the tantalizing brush of hair against her face. Its flowery scent launched a hot flood through her veins. She fought the desire to take Rose into her arms and kiss her senseless, to tear away the dress and feast upon those enticing pink nipples. She roused herself and fastened the hook, letting her fingers briefly fondle the velvety skin of her neck, feeling Rose tense.

"Turn toward me," Meryt ordered. Rose did so, and Meryt adjusted the necklace. She smiled as she drank in the sight of her. This woman's beauty and spirit delighted Meryt. She focused on Rose's tempting lips and let her gaze slide down to her bosom to enjoy the hint of pink nipples through the semi-transparent material. An involuntary clench of desire between her thighs caused her to shift position. She wanted Rose and entertained the brief thought of taking her to bed tonight, though she knew Rose would be reluctant.

It was true she had never forced her attentions on a woman, but Rose stirred the desire to take her and to wake in Rose the desire for Meryt. She wanted to tame her spirit, but not break it. Already, she regretted her earlier actions. She must make an effort not to let the disdain Rose felt toward her drive her to behave as a beast.

Meryt reached for the platter of roasted chicken while knowing the food would have the flavor of dust in her mouth, for she hungered to feast on the soft lips and skin of the beautiful Isis beside her. But for now, that hunger must not be fed.

Chapter Twelve

The slight jostle of the bed, the feel of a body scooting close against her back, and a warm hand placed on her lower abdomen roused Tiye from sleep. She pressed the hand firmly on her stomach, the heat bringing some relief from the cramps that often accompanied the onset of her moon time. She had retired early after taking an herbal draught to lessen the symptoms.

"Hmmm, what brings you to my bed? Surely you don't tire of Satiah already."

"Be nice. Jealousy isn't a garment that fits you well. Especially for one who's a Companion. It goes against our teachings."

"That only pertains to Nisut. And I'm not jealous." However, Hedjet was no nisut, and Tiye did experience jealousy when it came to Hedjet sharing pleasure with anyone other than Meryt and herself.

She recalled the time a little over seven years ago when she informed Meryt that running the household and arranging state functions had become too much of a burden and she needed help. Meryt had agreed to accept another Companion.

When Tiye first went to the Temple of Neit to request a Companion, she surreptitiously observed the new candidates. Hedjet was sixteen at the time, Tiye thinking her much too young for the responsibilities of a Companion. Yet the petite, pretty woman's sweet

smile and green eyes had attracted Tiye. She knew
Meryt also would find her alluring.

Soon after the young Companion came to live in
the palace, Tiye had fallen in love with her. To her joy,
Hedjet expressed the same sentiment for her.

Hedjet's sigh was deep. "Henutsen...she...she
was cruel and hard tonight. Rose...she..."

Tiye stilled and then rolled onto her back, voice
sharp. "What are you saying? Did she take Rose to her
bed?" Tiye held her breath, certain if that occurred it
had to be because Rose was pressured.

"Henutsen sleeps alone." Hedjet related all she'd
heard, admitting she also peeped through a gap in the
curtain.

"This is not good." Tiye shook her head. "Rose
defies Henutsen and she reacts like a..."

"Nisut?"

"Perhaps as some nisuts have acted in the past.
Henutsen is a nisut, true, but she has never acted in
this manner before."

"Rose is a fool to defy her. It only makes
Henutsen more determined to assert her will and
show Rose she is to be obeyed. Rose should accede to
the simple requests of Henutsen."

"I have told Rose this but she heeds not my
advice."

"What can we do?"

Tiye pondered this question. Perhaps she should
talk to Meryt about her behavior. Or should she wait
and see if things escalated and then intervene? She let
out a slow hiss of breath through her nose. "We will
watch and only intercede if things become dire."

"Dire? In what way?"

"Henutsen wants Rose in her bed. If she presses

and Rose refuses, she might try to force her—"

"No, Tiye, Henutsen would never force a woman to lie with her. I heard her tell Rose that tonight."

"That was tonight. Who's to know what the birth of a new sun will bring." Tiye did not want to think Meryt capable of such an act. However, the strife Tiye feared had entered Meryt's heart, and she reacted as the worst sort of nisut, with arrogance and belief of entitlement.

They remained quiet. Tiye would say a prayer tomorrow at sunrise to the Great One to guide Meryt back onto the path of Maat and to smile favorably upon Rose.

Her thoughts then turned to how besotted Meryt was over Rose and her beauty. "What does Rose look like unclothed?"

"She would not allow me to help her bathe, just wash her hair, so I only saw her from the back as she stood naked before Henutsen. What I saw was delightful, so very delightful. Rounded firm buttocks and shapely legs. Ah, that glorious sunset hair falling down her white back stopped my breath. I can imagine the view of the front is just as wonderful. I would be inclined not to want to share such an Isis, so we may never get permission to share pleasure with her."

"O Divine Mother Isis. Can you think of nothing else but sharing pleasure with the new women Henutsen brings into the household?" Tiye felt a stab of jealousy, not about Rose but about Hedjet sharing pleasure with Satiah. Meryt granted Tiye and Hedjet her permission to engage in physical pleasure with each other when Hedjet first became part of the household. Permission was also granted for Satiah. However, unlike Hedjet, the girl did not charm Tiye. She hoped

Meryt would send the girl back to the temple when they reached home.

"If you weren't thinking about it too, then why did you want to know what she looked like naked?"

Tiye had to admit she did think about it one…or two times. Tiye snickered. "Rose would run frightened into the desert if we were to invite her to our beds. Such a chaste little virgin, that one."

"These foreign white-skinned women are passionless and unnatural."

"It is how they are raised. Their religion is an affront to Maat, similar to the False Prophet's religion that infests the Black Land. They don't have goddesses or celebrate womanhood. Physical pleasures are viewed as sinful. However, a woman is a woman, after all. I am sure if the fire is hot enough, that little pot will boil over."

"The passion is an inferno in Henutsen. That little pot may already be starting to steam."

Both women tried to smother their laughter to keep from waking the whole tent.

"Do you think Henutsen will make Rose a Companion?" Hedjet asked.

"That I don't foresee happening. She's not a priestess."

"A concubine?"

"That is a tradition long out of fashion. The last nisut to have concubines was Merytneit the twenty-eighth. Or was it the twenty-ninth?"

"Twenty-eighth. She had twenty, and four Companions. The story told is she required a priestess of Hathor to live in the palace and prepare potions to increase her ardor."

"Those potions don't work."

"How do you know?" There was silence before Hedjet's voice exploded out of the dark. "You didn't give Henutsen—"

"Shuss. Keep your voice down. Henutsen doesn't need a potion."

"You didn't put it in my drinks, did you?"

Tiye smothered a laugh into her pillow. "You? Who's always like a she-cat in heat? The potion would probably kill your ardor."

"Then I conclude that you have tried it for yourself." Before Tiye could deny it, Hedjet continued. "If not a concubine, then what?"

A pregnant silence grew with another possibility.

"Surely not queen," Hedjet said.

Tiye thought about this. The last nisut to take a queen was Merytneit the thirty-second.

Since Hedjet and Tiye were priestesses, this precluded either of them from being Nisut's wife, or queen. This was a rule going back to the first Merytneit. A priestess was sworn to serve her Goddess first. A queen's duty was to serve the nisut.

They remained silent, each pondering that possibility.

"If the Great One so wills it," they said in unison.

Chapter Thirteen

Meryt pulled the cloak tightly around her against the chill of a desert morning. Diamonds dusted the indigo sky. Their brilliance glittered and dazzled. Re had yet to be reborn. All was deep silence, no wind stirring the sands of the nearby dunes. Peace walked in the desert this morning, awaiting the birth of a new day. She knelt onto the cool sand and placed the small, wooden chest before her, opened it and removed the gold figure of Neit, reverently positioning it on the top of the chest to face the east.

Meryt bowed before the image and sang.

O Divine One, mysterious and great, who by a thought created herself.

You are the breath given, the breath taken, and the breath yet to come.

She who by a word created the Universe from void.

She who by a word separated the land from the waters.

She who is the mother of mothers to gods and humankind.

She who is the circle of light with no beginning and no end.

I am humbled before you.

Your presence awes me.

I heed to your will.

I sing paeans to your glory.
O Great One, The All, The Eternal.

She petitioned the Goddess for her protection over her people. Then she beseeched forgiveness, for she had failed to follow Maat.

She felt ashamed. She had humiliated Rose. That Tiye knew of what happened was not in doubt. Before leaving, she had seen the look of disappointment and condemnation in Tiye's eyes. Meryt knew by Hedjet's guilty look and avoidance of her gaze that she had spied and reported to Tiye. Meryt could not apologize, to ask for Rose's forgiveness, as Nisut's actions were always right, even when wrong.

Not only did she feel shame, but also guilt. These emotions seldom visited her. Rose's contempt infuriated and made her lash out. No one had ever defied her. She had acted on it as a despotic nisut, when instead, it was the woman within herself she wanted Rose to know, to come to love.

She understood it was Nisut who attracted women. It seemed just about every vassal oasis she visited had a daughter, or daughters of the headman, offering to lie with her. Even the daughters and sisters of some of the Valley's administrators and officials sought her bed. A few times, she'd taken up the offers, aware it wasn't the woman they wanted, but the prestige of having bedded the nisut. At first, it hadn't mattered. Now, she refused the offers, not wanting to be a conquest.

Even with Tiye and Hedjet, her power and position had enticed them to enter the service of Neit in hopes of becoming Companions. It was true they had grown to care for her, to love her. However, she often wondered if their affections would hold true if she went back to being Benret, the daughter of a baker.

Benret. That name she hadn't heard since becoming Nisut. She was born late to her mother, a woman in her forty-fifth year. Her older sister and brother already had families of their own. She was told by the priestesses that her mother had lived long enough to gaze into her eyes and see not the indeterminate color of a newborn, but the gold eyes of the falcon of Horus. *"Neit has honored me,"* were her last words.

The Great One's design once again manifested. The one destined as the new nisut and Setepenneit was born. The midwives had summoned a priestess of Neit who took her from her mother's husband. He was happy to accept the stipend from the temple and rid himself of a girl child believed sired by Neit, as were all the nisuts before her. A respectable family had been selected to foster her, and the priestesses of Neit educated her in the art of ruling a kingdom.

As was tradition, the introduction to her predecessor occurred on her ninth birthday. She often wondered what emotions the old nisut struggled with when looking into the gold eyes, like her own, knowing the time for her departure to the West approached? What would her own thoughts be when that time came?

Closing her eyes she recalled the day she became Nisut. In the sanctum of the Great Temple, she stood naked before the statue of Neit. The draught of dreams she drank, the aroma of incense and the swish-clangs of sistrums, chants, and beats of drums opened the eyes of her ba to the land of the old Gods awaiting the age they would return to the Two Lands. The Great One had appeared and touched her heart, filling it with light and fire. Then blackness fell. When she opened her eyes, she was Nisut Merytneit the Setepenneit.

Her sight drank in the majesty of heaven, the creation of Neit, and she wondered why the Great One had given Rose to her. Was part of the mystery she saw in those blue eyes in Giza that day the one destined to love not Nisut, but love the woman, Benret?

She felt drawn to Rose, not merely by desire but also by the awakening of another emotion. It confused her. She dare not name it, for to name it might make it so, and its power scared her. But could she refute it? Was it a part of her destiny? Fixed and immutable?

"As you decree it, Great Neit, so it shall be."

Chapter Fourteen

Random sparks from the bonfire shot streamers into the night sky. Rose sat on a low stool next to Meryt under the tent's canopy watching the dozen or so women illuminated by the fire and moonlight perform an ancient dance. Hedjet said Meryt had dedicated the feast to Hathor, Goddess of love, passion, and the feminine spirit. Rose wryly thought it appropriate given the libidinous nature of the relationship between Meryt and her Companions.

Voices of men and women blended in harmony, accompanied by drums, flutes, stringed instruments, and rattles. This wasn't the music of Islam, but it had an oriental sound. Nor was this dance like any of the ones performed by Little Egypt. But, it was joyful with swaying steps, twirls and swirls, and she could imagine this dance performed before the pharaohs of ancient Egypt.

She furtively glanced at one of the two guards standing nearby, then to Meryt beside her seated in an ornate chair. It was reminiscent of a chair taken from a pharaoh's tomb and on display in the Giza Museum. Meryt wore not the robes of a desert chieftain, but a galabeya type gown of gold cloth. Her headband of gold, no more than a finger's width, was shaped like the body of a cobra, the snake's head the size of a man's thumb, its hood extended. This headband was the uraeus and a symbol of the Goddess Wadjet, protector of Egyptian rulers and the land. Hanging around her neck was the gold udjat.

She imagined Meryt as Cleopatra, Queen of Egypt. Though, Meryt probably carried more Egyptian blood than Cleopatra who was of Macedonian descent. Who was to say Meryt didn't carry the blood of pharaohs? She did look every bit a queen, and the people of this caravan considered her one. Meryt turned to her and smiled, and Rose quickly averted her attention back to the dance. She searched for Hedjet and Tiye among the women dancing around the fire. They had tried to entice her to join in the dance, but she declined.

The two women had drawn her out of her room yesterday morning, following her humiliation the night before. They gave her comforting hugs, with concerned expressions, the only indication that they were aware of what had occurred, for which Rose was thankful. She did not want to discuss it. Then they engaged her in playing the ancient Egyptian game of Senet and games of Old Maid, Snap, and Seven-Up taught to them by Nebet Eliza. During the game of Old Maid, Rose insisted the two not call her Nebet or Nebet Rose, but Rose. She liked these two women. They had giggled, each one saying her name without the title in front of it. She knew this pleased them.

Meryt wasn't around yesterday, or earlier today. Tiye said she attended to duties in preparation for the feast. Rose had been relieved, not wanting to interact with Meryt. She had retired to bed early last night before Meryt had finished her duties. Another one not around much was Satiah. She disappeared during the day. Rose was glad not to be subject to her baleful glances.

Earlier today, Tiye and Hedjet had excitedly

discussed the feast and what they planned to wear, giving Rose advice on which of her galabeyas would fit the occasion. She decided to wear her blue one with a double strand of blue beads and amulets Hedjet had given her to keep away the evil eye. She hadn't been in the mood for a feast but understood it would be an affront to her 'host' if she didn't attend. A weary sigh escaped her. Last night's sleep was restless, and this left her drained of energy. It was late; the feast had been going on since sundown.

She caught Meryt's attention. "I'm tired. Would you mind if I retire?" It galled to ask, but she didn't want to provoke Meryt's anger.

"May your sleep be peaceful and your dreams sweet."

With a nod and false smile, Rose entered the tent, took a lamp from a low table and lit it from the flame of a lamp hanging from a stand. She opened the curtain and stepped into the passageway of the private section. She let out a startled cry to see a man at the end of the passageway in front of the curtain to her room, carrying a straw basket and a lamp. Then she released a sigh of relief when she saw that it was Satiah dressed as a Bedouin man. Satiah seemed surprised to see her. She rapidly strode past Rose, giving her a sneer as she exited into the common area.

Rose entered her room and placed the lamp on a table by the bed. She removed the necklace and galabeya, leaving on the shift. She knelt by the bed to turn down the blanket. It required some effort to free the edges from the mattress. A quick inspection of the surface showed no insects or other uninvited guests. She was about to extinguish the lamp and slip onto the mattress when a slight movement, under the blanket, at the very foot of the bed caught her notice. A strong tug drew the blanket to the end of the bed.

The breath caught in her chest, and her heart jumped into her throat at the horrific sight. A shrill scream, loud and long, tore from her as she fell back onto the floor in an attempt to flee. She screamed again and scrambled back along the floor until she came up against the tent wall.

The palm-sized, yellow-green creatures skittered about on the bed with their tails held high, showing the stingers, two engaged in a battle to the death. The curtains abruptly parted, and Meryt and two guards stood frozen for an instant when they saw the terrible tableau on the bed. Meryt barked out words in Kemen. One of the guards ripped the cover from the mattress, folding it over the scorpions. He spun and left with the lethal bundle. The other guard keenly glanced around, searching for more creatures.

This was all too much for Rose. She started to tremble. Hugging her knees close to her chest, she began to cry.

A comforting arm encircled her shoulders, and a calm voice murmured close to her ear, "I won't let anything harm you. Come with me so my man can search the room."

With Meryt's aid, Rose stood on shaky legs. She clung to Meryt as they left the room and went into the common section of the tent just as Tiye and Hedjet entered. Meryt spoke to the two women in Kemen. Hedjet nodded and went into Meryt's part of the tent, carrying a lit lamp.

Tiye came to Rose and put an arm around her shoulders. "Come, we'll go rest now." She led Rose to Meryt's room and over to a mattress, big enough for two, or three. "Henutsen said you were to take her bed tonight, Hedjet and I will stay with you."

"You won't leave me, will you?" The trauma still fresh in her mind, Rose relived the horror over again.

Tiye softly touched Rose's cheek, her smile gentle. "No, Rose, Hedjet and I will protect you as a lioness protects her cub."

⟣⟣⟣⟣

Stealthily, Satiah darted behind a patrolling caravan guard to the rear line of tents. She then sprinted to the lean-to shelter by the tie line of horses, snatched up a blanket, saddle, and bridle, then hurried to her gelding.

The sounds of celebration stopped, letting her know the camp had been alerted that something was amiss in Nisut's tent. She had to get away. Even if the deathstalkers filled Serpent Woman's body with poison, she might still live long enough to tell of what she saw. Nisut would take the word of the Mercan, and it would be hard for Satiah to defend herself against the truth. If fortune and the Gods were with her, it would take some time to sort out the events and discover her absence.

The horse readily accepted the bit. She threw on the blanket, then hefted the saddle onto his back, pulled the cinch and tucked it into the cinch rings. With skill honed from many years of training her own mounts, she was securely in the saddle and off to al-Qahirah. The few Egyptian coins she had would not last long, and she would have to find a way to obtain more. She'd disguise herself as a man and would try to get work as a groom.

Her gelding was seasoned and accustomed to desert travel and could easily make it to al-Qahirah in five or six days. There were wells along the way, and a few settlements where she could find forage for her horse and purchase food for herself. The moonlight elongated the shadows of the date palms she passed, and the distant fires of another caravan resting for the night let her know she followed the right path.

The caravan she came upon was huge. She raced past the seemingly endless row of camels and tents. Finally, leaving the caravan behind, she headed toward al-Qahirah. Perhaps staying in al-Qahirah was a bad idea. Ahmose lived there and he would receive word of her treachery and look for her. Once she reached al-Qahirah, plans should be made to go to Alexandria or somewhere else.

It angered her to know she was now an outcast from her home. Word would spread to her father and he'd disown her for disgracing him. No oasis or village in the shadow of Nesneit would accept her.

She snickered when recalling the Mercan's screams of horror. "May Ammut devour the living heart from your body, Mercan." Then her thoughts focused on the one that spurned her. "May Nisut swallow bitter tears when she watches the woman die." She hoped if the Mercan didn't die that her body would burn in agony from the poison.

A low shadow darted out of the night in front of the horse. He abruptly halted and reared, throwing Satiah hard upon the pebbled ground. Her breath whooshed out in a loud grunt. The horse sped away, leaving Satiah lying limp in the desert dust.

ﷺ ﷺ ﷺ ﷺ ﷺ

Tiye carefully lifted her hand from Rose's waist to slip quietly out of bed. The lamp from the floor stand sputtered, about to go out. She took a lamp from a table by the bed and lit it from the dying flame. The lamp cast its light over Rose nestled along Hedjet's side with an arm thrown across the Companion's waist.

Rose was now her friend, and Hedjet's friend. To invite a person to call you by your name and not include a title, such as neb for men and nebet for women, meant you wanted to be friends. Friendship required responsibilities of loyalty and support. It gladdened her heart that Rose was now a friend, for she liked her.

Earlier, Hedjet had prepared Rose a sedative draught, one that would calm her nerves. She and Hedjet got into bed, Rose between them.

Before Rose fell asleep, Tiye inquired if she noticed anyone not of Meryt's household enter the tent today. Rose said only Satiah was in the tent when she entered to retire. Tiye asked what Satiah was up to when Rose saw her. Rose told her, and then proceeded to relay what had happened. Rose became upset and asked if she thought Satiah had put the scorpions in the bed. Tiye said she didn't know, but Henutsen would find out.

On her way through the common area, Tiye spied a lidded straw basket on the floor. She picked it up and shook it to see if she could hear anything rattle or scurry about inside it. She heard nothing and placed it back on the floor. One of Meryt's guards could open and examine it more thoroughly in the morning.

She entered into the passageway to the private section and opened the curtain to Satiah's room, not surprised to see the empty bed. She stepped across the passageway to Hedjet's room where Meryt slept. She knelt by the bed and shook Meryt awake. "Meryt."

"Huh." Meryt sprang into a sitting position and rubbed a hand over her face. "Five deathstalkers. If they had stung her…" She stared at Tiye. "How is she?"

"She sleeps soundly." She frowned. "One deathstalker crawling into her bed is possible. Five?" She shook her head. "Rose said she almost didn't see them as they were concealed at the bottom of the bed by the blanket that was tucked tight." A shiver ran down her spine. "I think the scorpions were deliberately concealed by the blanket in such a way as not to be able to move. Rose would have slipped into bed, and the movement of her legs would have loosened the blanket to free them. Satiah is nowhere about. I think she may have had a hand in this."

"Satiah," Meryt spat out vehemently. Her expression became puzzled. "But why?"

Tiye shrugged. "Jealousy. That you find Rose desirable is plain to see. That you have no desire for Satiah is also plain to see. I've seen the disdainful way she looks at Rose. For the last two or three days she has been absent from sight for long periods. I thought she was visiting a friend from her village who's a goat herder in the caravan."

"She might be innocent—though I doubt it. That one has a sly way about her. Did she think to get away with this?"

"Satiah probably assumed Rose wouldn't check the bottom of the bed before she slipped in. One deathstalker sting Rose could survive. The sting from two or three?" Tiye shook her head. "Satiah ran because Rose saw her in front of her room holding a basket. I found a basket on the floor in the common area. Satiah knew Rose would connect her to the scorpions and tell us."

Meryt got to her feet and picked up her discarded galabeya, pulling it on.

"Get one of my guards. I will arrange a search party for the she-jackal." Meryt's features hardened. "She will die for this."

Chapter Fifteen

The sun inched down to the western horizon as evening crept into the eastern sky. Rose surveyed the hushed throng of camel drovers and other caravan attendants, some standing under date palms, at a discreet distance from the open front of Meryt's tent.

In the tent's front, under a canopy, Meryt sat in her ornate chair, dressed in the gold galabeya and cobra headband she'd worn the night of the feast. In her right hand, she held a polished wooden was-scepter, its forked tip resting on the ground. The carved, stylized head represented Set with his big ears and elongated snout. The staff was a symbol of power representing Set's dominion over the forces of chaos and storms.

Behind the chair at Meryt's right shoulder, stood Hedjet dressed in a dark blue galabeya, her expression stony. Rose knew she was there to lend advice should Meryt ask. Two guards, dressed in black robes and black keffiyes, stood to either side of the chair, sheathed scimitars belted around their waists.

Rose stood some twelve feet away on Meryt's left, Tiye by her side as interpreter. The accused stood between two guards and in front of Meryt some ten feet away. Her demeanor was far from humble, almost defiant. She talked in an impassioned voice and several times pointed at Rose, spitting contemptuously on the ground.

Tiye whispered close to Rose's ear, "She said you are an evil spirit and have Nisut under your spell. You will sway Nisut to do your bidding."

The search party had captured Satiah on the Cairo road two mornings ago only a few hours after she had absconded. When they found her, she was stunned and bruised. The horse was found a short distance away, safe and sound.

Meryt's face was impassive as she listened to Satiah's defense.

Tiye continued. "She states you put the scorpions in the bed and blamed her because you hate her and you're jealous of her. She says she knew you would fill Nisut's heart with your poisonous lies and Nisut would believe them, so she fled."

Rose muttered out of the side of her mouth, "I would rather drink a gallon of castor oil than come anywhere near a scorpion."

Meryt addressed Satiah in a firm and loud voice.

"Nisut states your whereabouts can be accounted for at all times," Tiye said. "However, Satiah's cannot. As an American nebet, you would have no knowledge of how to trap scorpions and would not know where to find them. Whereas, Satiah has grown up in an oasis surrounded by desert and would have such knowledge."

Satiah started to protest vehemently until Meryt raised her hand and spoke in a firm voice.

"Nisut has made her decision," Tiye told Rose.

When Rose learned of Satiah's capture, she had inquired what the punishment might be. Tiye had said that it was up to Nisut, that Nisut followed Maat and the decision would be just. It was a serious offense to try to kill someone. The penalty could be death, flogging, imprisonment, banishment, or compensation to the victim. Rose guessed, given Satiah's young age, that Meryt would sentence her to a mild flogging or imprisonment for a short time.

All was silent save for the clang of a camel bell. Rose felt as if the world held its breath waiting for Nisut's decision. Meryt's eyes, even from where Rose stood, seemed like those of a falcon fixed on Satiah, the all-seeing eyes of Horus, or Re. Meryt stood and addressed Satiah solemnly, her voice carrying across to the quiet throng.

Satiah was stunned, her mouth open and eyes wide in disbelief. The two guards seized her. Satiah screamed and fought to get away as the guards dragged her through the crowd. Rose heard what sounded like curses shouted at Satiah who now wailed, the sound chilling Rose to the marrow.

"She will be taken from the camp tomorrow and beheaded." Tiye's expression and words were stark.

No! This couldn't happen. To Rose, Meryt seemed carved from stone. Hedjet's face appeared a frozen mask, no emotion evident.

"You can't do this!" Rose moved toward Meryt.

"Rose! No!" Tiye grabbed Rose's arm.

Rose shook off the grip and rapidly strode to stand before Meryt, aware of the confused eyes of the spectators upon her, and hearing low murmurs.

"Leave. Go into the tent," Meryt ordered gruffly as her face flushed dark red under the brown cheeks. Her lips tightened. Her eyes blazed.

"Meryt, you can't do this. I'm alive and she doesn't deserve to die." Before she could draw in a breath and continue, Meryt sprung to her feet, delivering a hard slap across Rose's left cheek that snapped her head to the right.

Shocked, Rose brought her hand to her stinging cheek, staring at Meryt in bewilderment. No one had ever raised a hand to her. Even as a child, her parents had spared the rod.

Meryt's two guards stepped forward with their scimitars drawn. Meryt addressed them in a commanding voice. They put the scimitars back in the sheaths and backed away, but the two remained alert.

Tiye stepped beside Rose, grasped her arm and growled into her ear, "Silence, you fool. Don't force her to have you stripped and flogged before the people. Come with me."

Rose stared at Meryt, seeing the coldness in her face and eyes. Ice seeped into her veins knowing that this was Nisut and Nisut would not hesitate to punish her. She let Tiye take her to Meryt's room. Meryt had insisted Rose and the two Companions take it, for which she was grateful. Rose was not ready to sleep in her own bed, so recently the scene of horror, nor was she ready to sleep alone. She turned to Tiye, seeing an expression of disappointment.

"Stay here." Tiye spun away and hurried out of the room.

Rose felt sick and helpless. She couldn't allow this to happen. This was unjust. Yes, Satiah deserved punishment. Possibly locked up for a time, but the girl didn't deserve death. There must be some way to appeal to Meryt.

She remembered the coldness in Meryt's eyes. No. Nisut's eyes…and shivered.

Rose swallowed down the sudden bile flooding her mouth. How far was she willing to go to save a life?

The dance of shadow and light cast on the wall that divided Hedjet's room from the common area alerted Meryt that one of the Companions was approaching. She wondered which one it would be. She wanted no company tonight and would send her away.

Immediately after court, she had retired to contemplate her decision. Was an order of death truly in keeping with Maat? Only twice before had she meted out death. One was for the murder of a child and the other for the murder of an elderly couple by a thief. Those sentences were just. However, this one? Satiah only attempted murder.

She watched the light move into the passageway. The curtain to the room parted, the identity revealed in the golden glow of the lamp.

Rose. Meryt quickly sat up, remaining silent. Rose's eyes were dark reflecting pools in the subdued light, her body still as the statue of a beautiful goddess. Only the slight lift and fall of her bosom beneath the white shift lent evidence that this woman was flesh and blood.

"You have come to plead for me to spare her life."

"Yes."

The low light of the lamp colored Rose's hair deep bronze. Meryt wanted to bury her hands in it, to have it cover her bosom and face as Rose lay atop her. She knew what price Rose would pay for Satiah's life. She smiled wryly, feeling sad. Had she not told Rose she would come to Nisut? Rose would give herself to

Nisut. Benret would once again remain untouched, the eternal virgin. Perhaps Neit required it of her.

With a quick push off the bed, she stood before Rose. Taking the lamp from her hand, she used it to light the one on the bedside table, then placed the lamp on the floor and stepped away and in front of the large, oval mirror. She watched Rose's eyes widen at the sight of her nakedness.

Meryt studied Rose's left cheek, grieved to see a small bruise from her slap. Yet, to let Rose get away with challenging her decision openly, before the people, would have weakened Meryt in their eyes. She rotated Rose toward the mirror and stepped behind her, placing her hands on Rose's arms.

She peered over Rose's left shoulder into the mirror. They studied each other in the reflection, their eyes meeting. Meryt pulled Rose against her, feeling the slight quivers, aware they did not spring from passion.

She leaned her head on the silky hair, inhaled the sweet scent, feeling the heat of desire infuse her. "Is this the ransom you will pay for her life?" She stroked her hands down the length of the smooth arms, the warmth from Rose's body flooding her senses.

"Yes." The word was almost inaudible.

"I accept the ransom price. But know this, Rose, you are mine now, in all ways. You will no longer thwart my commands—or my desire. I will have you in my bed when it so pleases me. Is this not so?"

Rose released a long, shaky sigh. "Yes."

The word was a turning point. Rose could not refuse her, refuse her passion. Meryt would not deny herself this woman. She would be gentle and try to awaken in Rose the desire she herself felt, but knowing that if Rose never felt it, Meryt would still take her again and again to satiate her hunger.

Slipping her right arm around Rose's waist she drew her tight against her body, then placed a hand under her chin tilting Rose's head back against her shoulder. Her soft hair brushed Meryt's cheek, and she nuzzled her face into it to breathe in deep the heady scent of this woman. With a slight twist of Rose's head Meryt brought her lips to her cheek to place a tender kiss on the bruise in an unspoken apology, then gently slid her mouth over Rose's lips, just enough to feel their heat. She deepened the kiss, the sensation almost dizzying.

Parting from the kiss, she returned her sight to the mirror and lifted Rose's shift to uncover the beauty upon which she gazed a few nights ago. Her eyes still hungered for the sight. Light from the lamps gilded Rose's pale skin gold, revealing the crisp, red hair between her legs, and the alabaster breasts made to fill a woman's hands, to cushion a lover's head after she was spent from passion, and to give comfort when it was required. Rose lifted her arms, Meryt removing the shift and dropping it to the floor. Once again, Meryt slipped an arm around Rose's naked waist, feeling the silken skin of Rose's back on her breasts and the firm buttocks against her groin.

"Isisnofret," Meryt whispered as her eyes drank in the beauty of Rose's reflection. Almost with reverence, she cupped Rose's breasts, holding them as if they were offerings to the reflection in the mirror. She ran her palms over the coral nipples, feeling them stiffen, not in passion she was sure, but a mere reaction from the touch. Her mouth watered to suckle the nipples, and a strong twinge in her core released dampness between her legs. She watched as Rose followed the path of her hands as they moved over her curved waist and to her hips to massage the soft skin over her hipbones. She glided her hands over Rose's flat stomach, slipping her right hand down to the edge of crisp hair.

Meryt sucked in a breath, closing her eyes against the rush of desire. With abandon, she turned Rose to face her, crushed her supple body against hers, breasts pressing breasts, abdomens and thighs touching. She slipped her hand through Rose's hair, bringing her head close to crush their mouths together. She pushed her tongue forcefully at that line between Rose's lips.

Meryt pulled back. "Open your mouth for me," she demanded in a groan.

Rose parted her lips, allowing Meryt entry. Meryt gently slid her tongue over Rose's that lay placid to the touch. She knew she was the first to kiss her in this way, that Rose had never felt the full passion of another.

Tightening her grip in the red hair, she pulled Rose's head back to break the kiss and brought her mouth to the visible throb of pulse on Rose's ivory throat, sucking and grazing her teeth along it.

The ache between her thighs brought forth a groan, and she led Rose to the bed. Slipping back onto the mattress, she pulled Rose on top of her. Wrapping Rose tightly in her arms she exalted in the feeling of soft breasts on her own and silky hair against her face. Warm breath wafted along the side of her neck as Rose's head rested on her shoulder. Rose no longer shivered, but she was far from relaxed. Meryt could feel her tenseness. She smoothed her hands down Rose's back, lightly squeezing her firm buttocks.

"Sit up." Meryt placed her hands on Rose's shoulders and pushed her gently up.

Rose now straddled her waist, Meryt feeling the rough hair at the apex of Rose's thighs against her stomach. She pushed a lock of hair from Rose's cheek, seeing the closed eyes, the mouth slightly parted, and a tremor to the bottom lip. She squeezed Rose's firm breasts, running her thumbs over her nipples. Watching them harden and the areolas pebble, she hungered to take them into her mouth, to taste, and savor them.

Meryt groaned as her core tightened and pulsed. She wanted Rose beneath her, wanted to immerse herself in the heat, feel the solidness against her as she quenched her need along a warm thigh.

A cry escaped Rose. Not one of passion, Meryt was certain, but of anxiety.

"Look at me, Rose."

Rose opened her eyes, Meryt seeing what seemed like fear in them. She carefully pushed Rose from her to lie on her side. She studied her. She ached for Rose, wanted her with a hunger she'd never felt for another. This woman belonged to her, a gift from the Great One. Why shouldn't she have her in the way she wished? Yet taking Rose would break her and destroy her spirit, and that she did not want.

"I am Nisut," she said sadly. "My people obey me without question. If so desired, I could have any woman I want. None would say a word, or even dare look displeased about it. That's not what I want. I want to know that it is not Nisut, but Benret the woman, who is desired, and sparks passion." *And inspires love.* That fervent wish would remain unspoken. To speak of it would open up her heart and leave her vulnerable.

Rose remained silent, her eyes now reflecting confusion.

"I'll not force you, this I swear to you. I will woo you. I think woo is the word the English use when they want to win a woman's favor, is it not?"

Rose nodded, wetting her lips. "It is."

"Then I'll woo you. I have never wooed a woman, so be patient with me."

An uneasy silence returned. Meryt couldn't prevent her eyes from drinking in Rose's naked body. She quickly realized what she was doing and tore her gaze away. She pushed off the bed and grabbed Rose's shift from the floor and tossed it to her, then donned her own. Once Rose was dressed, she reached out her hand. "Come. I will return you to your bed. Morning will soon arrive, and we need rest."

Tentatively, Rose took the offered hand, and Meryt pulled her up to stand.

Rose slipped her hand out of Meryt's grip. "And Satiah?"

"I will spare her and keep her under guard. Her father is headman of one of the oases located close to Nesneit. We stop there to rest and I'll return Satiah to him. She will be banished from ever entering the Valley of Wind and Dreams."

"Thank you."

"Don't thank me. Never challenge me in front of my people again. I'll have no choice but to punish you for your insolence. I am Nisut and I am always right. If you want to petition Nisut, go through Tiye and Hedjet. They will hear you and if they think your petition has warrant they will present it to me."

Rose nodded and dropped her gaze.

Meryt cupped Rose's chin, forcing her to meet

her eyes. "You are a member of my household, and you *will* defer to me. As I am head of household, you may come to me with any concerns that pertain to my household, and I will take into consideration what you have to say. However, my decisions are final."

"Yes."

That one word was said dispassionately, yet Meryt saw the spirited woman in Rose's eyes. She knew Rose would challenge her. Not challenge Nisut, but Benret the woman, and this pleased Meryt.

ঌ৶৶৶

Tiye hadn't expected to see Rose until morning. And was surprised to see that Meryt accompanied her. When Rose had slipped quietly from bed, Tiye stealthily followed her. She stood beside the curtain of Hedjet's room long enough to hear the reason why Rose went to Meryt. It had saddened her to know that what Rose offered Meryt was not to share pleasure they both would enjoy, but offered herself as a trade for Satiah's life.

Tiye slipped from the bed, allowing Rose to slide in next to the sleeping Hedjet. Hedjet was a sound sleeper. Tiye often teased that she could sleep through cattle stampeding across the room.

"Come with me," Meryt whispered in Tiye's ear and took her hand.

They went to Hedjet's room, both sitting on the bed.

"Rose offered to lie with me in exchange for Satiah's life." Meryt sounded a little sad.

Tiye remained silent, not wanting to volunteer that she knew.

Meryt continued. "But that's not why I'm going to rescind my order to execute Satiah."

"Some will think Rose has swayed you to change your judgment. They might not have understood her words, but her actions spoke disagreement with that decision." Tiye knew Meryt wasn't comfortable with her verdict, and that Rose probably had no influence to rescind the decision, but this needed saying.

"Truthfully, I needed no swaying. My judgment was done out of anger. That's why I want your and Hedjet's help."

"What will you have us do?"

"Scatter the seeds of talk among your friends that Rose petitioned Nisut to have Satiah compensate her for the attack and Nisut agreed. Nisut, in her benevolence, spared Satiah's life but will forbid her from ever entering the Valley of Wind and Dreams, and demand Satiah's father pay compensation. He has some fine Arabian brood mares, and I wouldn't mind acquiring a select few to mate with Bakhu. Of course, the mares will belong to Rose, and I'll make arrangements with her."

"I think that should work. Hedjet and I will spread the word tomorrow."

"Good."

"Word will travel fast. When we reach home, what has occurred will be repeated. Having the mares in the caravan will prove that compensation was rendered."

"That is so." Meryt closed her eyes as she rubbed a hand through her hair. "She left my bed still a virgin. I wanted her, burned and ached for her, but I couldn't take her. It would have destroyed her spirit. I promised her I wouldn't force her. I'll wait until she comes to my bed because she desires me. If she ever does. I think she finds me unattractive and distasteful. I admit I treated her with disrespect, and I am perhaps not deserving of her favors."

Tonight was full of surprises. Tiye never knew Meryt to admit her actions were wrong, or to doubt her appeal to women. "You are a beautiful woman with a passionate and kind nature. The women who are worthy will see beyond Nisut and want the woman. Be the woman for her and not the nisut." Tiye had wanted the nisut in the beginning. However, over time, she had watched as the conceited and arrogant girl matured into a lovely and generous woman... when not being Nisut. It was the woman Tiye grew to love.

Meryt grinned and gently touched Tiye's face. She didn't have to say the words 'I love you,' for Tiye to know she did. Those words were never spoken between them. Tiye knew Meryt's heart would always hold her, as well as Hedjet. She also knew there existed in Meryt's heart a special place that only a special woman could fill. For Tiye, Hedjet filled that special place in her heart. Perhaps Rose would dwell in that place for Meryt.

Meryt's grin disappeared, a serious look replacing it as she squirmed uneasily. "Ah, tell me what you know about, ah, wooing a woman."

Tiye chuckled. "I think I may have some suggestions."

Chapter Sixteen

Rose let out a tired sigh, and rolled onto her side in an effort to get comfortable. She adjusted the pillow beneath her head and then yanked up the blanket. The subdued sounds of conversation reached her ears from the common area of the small caravan tent. She had retired to bed as soon as supper ended.

It had been a long day starting at dawn and had continued until the sun touched the western horizon. Her calves ached, and her feet were tired, as she had spent part of the day walking beside Tiye instead of riding in the howdah. Rose had no idea the al-Bahariya Oasis covered the area it did. She always thought of an oasis as a place surrounded by sand and containing a well or spring fed pool, and maybe a few date palms. The caravan route through the oasis took them past hot springs, ponds, thick groves of date palms, olive groves, fruit orchards, and numerous settlements.

The oasis lay in a depression surrounded by dark hills and cliffs. The ancient caravan route wasn't all flat, and parts were difficult to trudge. Swarms of flies, a number of them biting, buzzed about both humans and animals, and the dust blew in thick swirls at times.

Weariness, accompanied by low spirits, kept Rose quiet throughout supper. Meryt also seemed subdued, as did Tiye and Hedjet. She avoided eye contact with Meryt, not wanting to look into those gold eyes after what occurred the night before last.

As much as she tried not to think about that night, the images would run over and over in her mind. The emotions she felt left confusion. She was angry and mortified. But what disturbed her most of all was she had become physically heightened from Meryt's kiss and touches.

Rose held no fondness for Meryt. The woman was autocratic and possessed a host of unsavory characteristics. Meryt's humiliation of her still angered. Yet, she didn't find her repulsive. Meryt was an attractive woman, and the sight of her naked in the lamp's muted glow had certainly been enticing. She had reminded Rose of a panther, all sleek muscles and svelte. Her brown skin was warm, breasts high and round, the nipples a darker brown, her hips slim and legs long and shapely.

A bolt of arousal raced through her when she recalled the full press of Meryt's heated flesh against her own. Then there was Meryt's kiss and the hunger it had ignited. It had frightened and confused her, leaving her stunned and unable to respond. If Meryt hadn't stopped when she did, Rose would have given in to desire, and she'd have regretted it the next morning.

Why was it someone who had no regard for her, who treated her disrespectfully, that she had this response to? Why couldn't it be Emma?

"Rose?"

"Yes?" She recognized Hedjet's voice.

"Henutsen requests your company." Hedjet stepped into the room, carrying a lamp.

"Tell her…" She was about to say she had retired for the night. She sighed, recalling she'd agreed to heed Meryt's commands as part of the deal for Satiah's life. "Tell her I'll be right there."

"I'll wait and take you to her."

Rose got up from bed, hurried over to the clothes chest, removed the blue galabeya, and put it on over her shift. She removed the hairbrush from its box and tidied her hair. Hedjet led her to Meryt's room and opened the curtain for Rose.

For a moment, Rose's steps faltered. She straightened, determined not to let Meryt cow her down as she walked into the room. She heard the slight rustle of the curtain as it closed, aware that she was alone with Meryt.

Several lamps lit the room, casting a warm radiance over Meryt on the bed with her legs crossed and feet bare. The pale orange caftan she wore gave her skin a warm glow.

She looked Rose over and smiled invitingly. "Come. Sit across from me."

Rose sat facing Meryt, legs crossed and back rigid.

"Hold out your left hand to me," Meryt said.

Cautiously, Rose extended her hand. Meryt grasped her arm, holding it close to the elbow as she slipped a bracelet over Rose's hand and onto her wrist.

Rose studied the gold bracelet, noticing its delicate floral filigree design, the width that of her forefinger. No matter how pretty, Rose couldn't help but wonder if it signified a mark of ownership. The Companions wore a multitude of bracelets so maybe it was just a gift.

"It's very pretty." Rose looked up to see Meryt's pleased smile. "Thank you."

"It is a gift...from Benret."

I want to know that it is not Nisut, but Benret the woman, who is desired, and sparks passion. Rose recalled Meryt's words.

"Who's Benret?"

"She's the daughter of a baker who was raised to be nisut."

"You?"

"Me."

This surprised Rose. That seemed so common. She thought a ruler would come from a noble family.

"All nisuts are virgins, never lying with a man, so we don't have children to inherit the position." Meryt grinned. "It is said that the Great One brings into being only nisuts who are lovers of women."

This declaration did not surprise Rose. After all, Meryt did have two 'concubines.'

"Your parents, where are they?" Rose asked.

"My mother journeyed into the West soon after my birth. Many believe Neit is the sire of all nisuts. My mother's husband...I was never in his care and met him only a few times. He departed to the West seven years ago. On occasion, I see my sister and brother. It is my foster family that I hold close to my heart. Ahmose, the one who saved you from the slavers, is my foster brother. My foster parents reside in the Oasis of Montu. My foster father is head of the caravans that journey up to Siwa and Alexandria, and some of the coastal cities of Libya."

"I thought your caravan was the only one to go from your kingdom, and every two years."

"There are a limited number of caravans under my control that are permitted to trade the olive oil and other goods from our oases with the outside world a few times a year. The leaders are ones I trust not to reveal our whereabouts, and the attendants are men known for their loyalty."

Rose's first thought was that this was a way to get to Cairo sooner than two years' time, if she could persuade Meryt to send her back.

"I know about your father," Meryt said. "Yet you have never spoken of your mother."

"My mother died when I was twelve. I'm an only child."

"I am sorry about your mother."

They fell silent. Rose knew Meryt was sincere in her condolences.

"Tell me of your America and your life there," Meryt said. "Do you know Calamity Jane?"

"Calamity Jane?"

Meryt twisted to reach behind her, picked up a paper book from beside the pillow, and handed it to Rose.

Rose examined the cover of the slightly tattered Beadle's Pocket Library dime novel with its illustration of Calamity Jane, her two pistols drawn and pointed at a ruffian. She read the title aloud, "*Deadwood Dick in Leadville; Or A Strange Stroke For Liberty.*"

"Calamity Jane is queen of the cowboys. She rescued Deadwood Dick from outlaws." Meryt's expression and voice reflected conviction.

Rose couldn't keep the amusement out of her voice. "Where did you get this?"

"In al-Qahirah at a shop that sells books. I have other ones like this back home that tell of Kit Carson and Buffalo Bill that I bought on my last trip to al-Qahirah."

"I haven't met Calamity Jane, or Kit Carson. But I did see "Buffalo Bill's Wild West" when they held a performance in Baltimore in 1898."

Meryt's eyes widened, her face beaming. To Rose, she looked almost like a child on Christmas morning. Meryt scooted closer to Rose until their knees touched. "You must tell me. Tell me all!"

Meryt wanted to know everything about the show, even the colors of the horses and their names. Rose relayed everything she could remember about the skits and costumes.

Later, as Rose lay in bed, her thoughts were on her visit with Meryt. She had enjoyed their conversation. Meryt was an attentive listener, asking questions about America. She seemed to have a particular interest in cowboys, Indians, and outlaws, and was disappointed Rose didn't know any of the characters she'd read about in her dime novels. Rose didn't have the heart to tell her most of the stories were tall tales.

Then there was the gift from Benret. Was that Meryt's way of declaring the wooing had begun and it wouldn't be by Nisut, but by the 'ordinary' woman? Not that Rose knew what an ordinary woman was in Meryt's culture. Maybe they were like Hedjet and Tiye. Or, heaven forbid, Satiah. She hadn't gotten to know any of the other women in the caravan due to the language barrier.

But, as pleasant as Meryt acted tonight, it didn't change the fact that she was still arrogant and autocratic.

Rose was almost asleep when she remembered: *Calamity Jane is queen of the cowboys.* Rose laughed.

Chapter Seventeen

Meryt watched alertly from Bakhu's back as the dapple-gray Arabian mare Rose sat astride shied away from the cream-white pillar of chalk standing sentinel in the yellow sand of the Sahara al-Beyda, the White Desert. The mare's name was Izza, Arabic for honor, and Meryt had presented her to Rose yesterday. She had bought the mare in al-Bahariya a day before the caravan left the oasis. It had pleased Meryt to see the delight in Rose's eyes when she led her outside the tent and presented the mare. Rose at first tried to refuse the gift. Meryt had informed her one did not refuse a gift from Nisut. Rose had patted the mare's neck, thanked Meryt, her smile shy.

Rose was by no means an expert rider, but Meryt saw she was experienced enough to handle the gentle but spirited mare. The strangeness of the rock chalk formations in the shapes of minarets, pillars, mushrooms and fantastical beasts were something the mare was unaccustomed to seeing, and they confused her.

She and Rose were a couple of miles ahead of the caravan on the southern road toward al-Farafra Oasis. The caravan had left al-Bahariya four days ago, their destination some three weeks away, barring problems. They were already delayed by three days due in part to the extra time spent in al-Bahariya Oasis meting out justice to Satiah.

Since the night in Meryt's room four days ago, when she presented Rose the bracelet, there seemed to be a waning in the tension between them. Rose acted more at ease with her, and the wariness in her eyes lessened. Meryt had started giving Rose a kiss on the cheek when she returned to the tent at the end of the day and was pleased that Rose didn't flinch from this.

Meryt endeavored to control her open desire for Rose by not staring at her, though that was difficult to do. She wanted Rose, and it proved hard not to let her eyes drink in the woman's beauty. Tiye told her the hunger in Meryt's eyes for Rose was evident for everyone to see, and this made Rose uneasy. Meryt had replied her eyes were made to look at beautiful things, and they acted on their own accord, but she'd try to control them.

Meryt urged Bakhu into a canter, the mare following. This area of the desert had always fascinated her with its chalk shapes, the yellow sand covered by wind-blown drifts of white chalk. She halted Bakhu next to a squat knob of chalk and dismounted, Rose bringing Izza to a stop a dozen steps away.

"Why are we stopping?" Rose asked as Meryt strolled up to the mare.

"Dismount, I want to show you something."

Rose dismounted and stood by Izza. Even though Rose wore the desert outfit of a man, consisting of white robes, tan boots, and a white keffiye held in place by a black agal, she still looked very much a woman. Meryt couldn't prevent her appreciative gaze from lingering, and saw Rose's cheeks pink as she uneasily looked down.

Meryt removed her gloves and took Rose's left hand to lead her to a patch of cream-colored soil. She slid the scimitar from its sheath and started to move the sand with the weapon's tip as she studied the ground. After placing the scimitar back into its sheath she picked up a small, white object from the ground. Taking Rose's left hand, she placed what she'd found in her open palm.

Rose plucked the object from her hand and held it up to study. "It's a fossilized seashell."

"Yes, far from the ocean. It comes from the time when Neit emerged from the waters of Nun and separated the land from the waters."

"Some would believe it comes from the time when Jehovah covered the Earth with a great flood to destroy mankind for their wickedness."

"You speak of Noah and his great barque that carried a mated pair of every type of beast in creation."

Rose smiled, her voice amused. "Why does it not surprise me that you know that?"

Meryt returned the smile. "Is it because I am Nisut and Nisut is all knowing?"

Rose laughed, the sound delightful to Meryt, making her feel tingly.

"I suspect it's because Nisut is educated. Is education required to be a nisut?"

"I don't really know. The priestesses of Neit educated me. I learned to speak and write English from Nebet Eliza. I have a library at home containing many books written in English that I collected on my past journeys to al-Qahirah. I have more that I am taking back home that are safely packed."

"More Wild West adventures about cowboys and Indians?"

"It is my misfortune that the only one I found was the one you saw the other night. I did manage to find the complete works of William Shakespeare this time. Nebet Eliza said it's required for every library."

"Oh, indeed, Nebet Eliza is right." Rose again studied the seashell. "May I keep this?"

"It is yours."

Rose slipped the shell into a pocket inside her robe. She smiled shyly, their eyes meeting. Rose didn't drop her gaze, and Meryt noticed warmth in her blue eyes that made her breath catch. She fought hard to keep from taking Rose in her arms and kissing her. Rose's smile faded and she averted her gaze. Meryt knew Rose saw her desire and felt uneasy.

Rose turned and faced the west. "You said last night it would take about three weeks to reach your valley."

"Yes, in two or three days the journey will become difficult. We may need to travel at night when it is cooler, as the hot season is close upon us. If we stray from the route, we could perish from thirst. There are not many oases so the main source of water will be from wells that are a distance apart. When we reach Ipu Oasis, we will need to rest a few days there, and also rest at Iunyt Oasis."

Meryt heard Rose sigh, the sound one of unhappiness. Still looking to the west, her profile to Meryt, Rose asked, "What is it you want from me? Why are you doing this? Taking me away from my father?"

Meryt turned Rose toward her. Hands on Rose's shoulders, she gazed into her blue eyes. "I do believe our meeting was decreed in an age past by the Great One. She brought you to me, gave you to me." She shook her head, "Why? I don't know. I only know I will not, cannot let you go. Perhaps in time we will know." What she wanted from Rose, for now, would remain unanswered, as Meryt was unsure what that answer might be.

"It's wrong, Meryt. What you're doing to me is wrong. No one can give a person to another. It's slavery. My country had a war not long ago to free slaves."

"You are not a slave. My kingdom does not have slavery." Meryt's words were vehement. "You are a member of my household." Rose was hers, a gift from Neit, a gift to respect. Once again, she experienced shame and guilt, and not only due to her disrespectful treatment of Rose, but also due to Rose's unhappiness. Feeling these emotions made her angry. "You will not refer to yourself as a slave again. Do you understand?"

Rose remained silent, but Meryt could see that Rose, too, was angry. Tears started to pool in Rose's eyes. "Please. Let me write to my father again so he'll know I'm safe and well."

"There is no one I can send at this time that would be able to make the trip to al-Qahirah and back to the caravan before we enter the desert of sand. It would be too dangerous for them to cross the desert in an attempt to find us."

"Will you forever prevent me from seeing my father, or writing him?"

Meryt drew in a deep breath. "When I return to al-Qahirah, you will come with me and arrangements will be made for you to see him."

"Two years, Meryt? He'll have returned to America, not knowing what has become of me."

"When we reach Nesneit, I can make arrangements for one of my caravans to take letters to Alexandria and have them sent to him. I think they have a postal service there."

Meryt could see that her offer didn't seem to lessen Rose's unhappy look.

"I feel as if I'm a prisoner."

Meryt pressed a finger on Rose's lips. "We will speak no more of this." Meryt swallowed hard against anger. "Come. Let us ride back to the caravan." Meryt strode back to Bakhu, not wanting to see the unhappiness in Rose's eyes, and feel the emotions it provoked.

They rode back in silence, Re in his sky barque the only witness to what words had passed between them.

࿐ ࿐ ࿐ ࿐

With a glance, Rose viewed the red orb of the sun as it ascended between the eastern horizon and heaven to start on its timeless journey across the sky toward the west. Drovers checked packs and tightened girths on camels in preparation for the trek home.

Tiye held Rose's left hand and Hedjet her right, as they made their way to the line of horses drinking their water ration from goatskin buckets held by grooms and riders. The mounts had their morning feed before the stars started to dim with the first gray of dawn.

"There they are!" Hedjet dropped Rose's hand to hurry up to her chestnut mare, Cleopatra, and the lanky-legged chestnut colt the mare had foaled last night. They were in a roped-off corral separate from the other mounts. Hedjet patted Cleopatra's head, the mare pushing her nose against Hedjet's chest. The colt stood by his mother while warily eyeing the trio.

Cleopatra had foaled after sunset, Hedjet and a groom attending the birth.

Hedjet went to the colt and hugged it about the neck. "Come pet him. He needs petting every day to get accustomed to handling."

"I think I'll just look at him." Tiye dropped Rose's hand and stood back from the mare.

"He won't bite you." Hedjet petted the colt and kissed it on the white star between his eyes.

"His mother might." Tiye eyed the mare nervously.

"She won't hurt you if you don't get between her and the colt."

Tiye made no move toward the foal. "I can see that he is a...ah...handsome boy." She sounded not at all convincing.

"Such a timid gazelle you are. Why don't you run along and visit the donkeys. I heard one had a foal, and they named it Nebet Tiye, after you."

"Better the donkey than that stinking flea bitten mangy goat herding bitch the caravan drovers named Nebet Hedjet, after you."

"You dried teat old heifer." Hedjet snatched up a piece of dry horse manure. "Here, go and gather dung for the cook fires." She threw the manure at Tiye's retreating back, missing her.

Rose snickered. The fact that the two quarreled in English let her know they weren't serious but entertaining her.

"Pet him, Rose."

Taking slow steps, so as not to startle the colt, Rose walked up to stand by Hedjet and rubbed the colt's head. "What are you going to name him?"

"Hmmm." Hedjet shrugged. "I don't know.

Bakhu is his father and he is named for the mountain where the sun rises. I was thinking because he is red like Bakhu, I could name him Manu, which is the mountain where the sun sets." Her smile was bright. "Why don't you name him?"

"Yes, Rose, why don't you name him?" Meryt said from behind Rose, causing her to start and take a step back from the colt. Meryt came up to Rose and stood close beside her, Rose stiffening. Since their desert ride yesterday, there was an awkward uneasiness between them, again. This uneasiness had carried through supper last evening. Rose had excused herself early last night, feigning tiredness.

Rose noticed Meryt wore a white, knee-length tunic and a blue sash around her waist with a pair of cuffed riding gloves stuck into them. Her white sirwal bottoms were stuffed into a pair of brown boots. The keffiye was white as well, making the brownness of her skin stand out in a becoming way.

Today, Rose and Tiye wore galabeyas, Hedjet dressed similarly to Meryt with a dagger tucked in her sash along with a riding whip. Since they had left the main caravan route, a few of the women had opted to don desert garb like that of the men.

"Henut, how do you like him?" Hedjet stepped back from the foal.

Meryt was silent for a moment as she studied the colt. "He has sturdy legs and a nice breadth of chest. His nostrils are large to draw in air. I see a lot of Bakhu in him. He'll make a fine mount."

"I think so, too. He's a fine boy and will make a good start to my herd."

Meryt turned her attention to Rose. "Hedjet's eyes are shrewd when it comes to horses and their strengths and weaknesses. She assisted me in finding Izza for you."

Rose gave Hedjet a smile. "I'm very pleased with her."

"Honor him, Rose," Hedjet said as she fondled the colt's ears. "Give him a name."

Meryt circled her arm around Rose's shoulders and squeezed them in encouragement.

"What is the Kemen word for star?"

"Seba," Hedjet said.

"I will name him Seba, for the one on his forehead."

"An auspicious name. It fits him well." Meryt tightened her embrace about Rose's shoulders, bringing her close against her side. Meryt's scent was slightly spicy from the body oil she favored, Rose finding it pleasant.

"Yes, an auspicious name." Hedjet stepped up to Rose, stood on her toes, and planted a peck on Rose's cheek. "Soon, you'll have horses of your own to name."

Meryt had informed Rose that she would receive some Arabian mares from Satiah and her father as compensation for the attempt on her life. Rose had wanted to refuse, but Meryt said she must take them so her people would see that Maat was served. Meryt also informed her she would like to mate Bakhu with some of the mares.

Meryt removed her arm from around Rose's shoulders. "I'll take Rose to Tiye's camel." She gave Rose a questioning look. "Unless you want to ride Izza. I can have a lean-to erected so you can change into riding garb."

"Maybe I'll ride after we stop to eat. I'm still a little tender from riding yesterday."

"You should have told me. I would have rubbed liniment on your tender parts."

Hedjet snickered. Rose blushed. "I wasn't that tender." Rose was surprised Meryt looked a bit sheepish.

"I need to go and saddle Sah," Hedjet said, referring to the bay gelding that had belonged to Satiah and was now hers. "Rose, we can ride together later, if you wish. I will ride alongside Cleopatra and Seba so I can take them aside and let Seba nurse."

"I think I would like that."

Hedjet nodded, then strode toward the tack tent.

Meryt took Rose's hand and they walked toward Tiye's camel. One of Meryt's guards followed a discreet distance behind, leading Bakhu. They passed by the line of camels and drovers. A few drovers noticed Meryt and bowed their heads in respect, Meryt giving a slight nod in acknowledgement. Meryt still held her hand and Rose noticed the smooth, warm feel of the fingers and palm. The softness, no doubt, was due to the oil she'd seen applied on them by Tiye, and the use of riding gloves.

"Rose, I want you to write a letter to your father tonight. One of my men will leave tomorrow to take it to al-Qahirah."

This was good news. Then again, maybe not. "Your man won't be able to get back to the caravan, will he?"

"No, he'll stay with Ahmose in al-Qahirah. Ahmose will put him to good use."

Rose was quiet as she thought about this. The man might have family in Nesneit and would miss seeing them for at least two years. Meryt could have ordered him to do it even though he didn't want to.

"He's looking forward to it and is impatient to go." It was as if Meryt read her mind. "Write the letter tonight."

"I will." This gesture by Meryt by no means made up for the fact that Rose wouldn't see her father for at least two years. But, she would be gracious about the offer. As the old saying went, you can catch more flies with honey than with vinegar. Maybe Meryt would change her mind and take her back to Cairo sooner.

They came to the kneeling camel. Tiye stood next to it, in conversation with the drover. Tiye smiled when she saw them. The man bowed his head and stepped away.

"Here," Meryt said, "I'll help you two into the howdah. We leave in a short while."

"Henut, take care." Tiye kissed Meryt on the cheek, receiving one in return. Meryt assisted her into the howdah.

Next, Meryt turned to Rose, giving her a quick kiss on the cheek. Rose hesitated for a moment before returning the kiss. "Thank you, Meryt. Henut." Rose furtively glanced around to see if any of the drovers heard her slipup. Meryt grinned as she helped Rose into the howdah, then pivoted and walked to Bakhu.

Rose watched as Meryt mounted Bakhu and rode to the head of the caravan. She thought she might like to ride Izza later, alongside Meryt. She thought back to Meryt's mention of rubbing liniment on her backside, and how it would feel to have those graceful hands on her again, remembering how they caressed down her back and squeezed her buttocks on *that* night. She felt her face heat, both from a stab of arousal and annoyance at herself for allowing desire to surface.

"Rose, are you ill? Your face is very red." Tiye looked Rose over with concern.

"I'm fine. Just fine."

❧ ❧ ❧ ❧

April 9, 1901

My Dearest Father,

I hope this letter finds you well. I am in excellent health and treated well. At this moment, I am many miles from Cairo. I cannot give you my location, as my host does not want it revealed.

What I have to tell you might be difficult for you to understand. There is a good possibility I may not see you again for at least two years. I do not wish for you to wait for me but to return home when your business in Egypt has concluded.

When I return to Cairo, I will contact James Walters, or someone in the American Consul General's office to aid me in contacting you.

I will try to write to you as often as possible. That may be difficult due to my location.

I love you. My thoughts and prayers are with you.

Your affectionate daughter,
Rose Grace McLeod

Rose handed the letter to Meryt, watching as she scanned it and then passed it to Tiye.

Meryt turned to Rose. "Stand up and give me your hands."

With slow deliberation, Rose stood, feeling

soreness in her back and thigh muscles. Her buttocks felt raw. Rose knew it was due to staying in the saddle too long. A part of Rose's day had been spent riding Izza alongside Meryt. A couple of times, she had ridden beside Hedjet as she rode at the end of the caravan to keep an eye on Cleopatra and Seba.

She stuck out her hands, palms down. Meryt took both of them with care to turn them up and scrutinize the palms. Not lifting her sight from Rose's hands, Meryt called out, "Hedjet, go get the healing ointment." She led Rose over to one of the carpets near the burning lamps, grabbed a nearby cushion and knelt by it.

"Come, Rose, sit." Meryt patted the cushion.

With somewhat stiff and ginger movements, Rose eased onto the cushion.

"I noticed when you sat for supper and to write the letter, you seemed to favor your backside." Meryt carefully took her right hand and again looked at the palm. "Your hands are red. You don't want them to blister. Blisters are dangerous and can become infected. I have a pair of gloves that will fit you. As for your backside, I can cover the saddle seat with a thin cushion made from sheepskin."

Hedjet returned with a small, earthenware jar, Tiye right behind her. Both women knelt on the carpet close to Rose, Hedjet handing the jar to Meryt.

Meryt scooped out a gob of the yellow ointment and rubbed it on Rose's right palm. Her touch was careful and soothing. Rose noticed her clean and manicured nails. Meryt administered the same treatment to Rose's left hand.

"Before you go to sleep, Tiye will see if you need any treatment for your backside."

"I can do it, Henut." The eagerness in Hedjet's voice had Rose glancing up at her to see an enthusiastic smile.

A sarcastic snort came from Tiye. Rose turned to see her frown and give a slight shake of her head. "Henutsen requested me to do it."

"Tiye will do it," Meryt said.

Although Rose didn't relish having her backside examined, she was glad Tiye would do it. Hedjet was a little too ready to administer *help*. As for Meryt, Rose was both disappointed and relieved that she didn't offer to do it. But she knew presenting her posterior to Meryt might be a temptation, not only to Meryt but also to herself. The thought of those graceful and warm hands doctoring her rear caused a shiver of excitement to race down her spine.

"That will be fine," Rose said quickly.

Tiye handed Meryt a cloth to wipe the ointment from her hands.

After she cleaned her hands, Meryt settled next to Rose and touched the tip of her right forefinger to Rose's nose. "The sun has made your nose red."

The keffiye Rose wore provided inadequate shade from the sun. She tried to keep the end draped around the lower portion of her face, but often found it uncomfortable so left her face uncovered.

"I have skin lotion that will help," Hedjet said.

"Thank you," Rose said.

"Too bad we don't have a straw hat like the ones I saw the English nebets in al-Qahirah wear when they were out exploring the city," Tiye said.

"I'll try and keep my face covered when out in the sun." She was thankful she didn't freckle like most redheads.

"When next you ride," Meryt said, "I'll show you how to arrange the front of your keffiye over your brow to give more shade to your face." Meryt smiled and added, "I would like to read aloud tonight. I think Rose should pick the book."

"Yes, Henut, read to us." Hedjet plopped down on the other side of Meryt and cuddled close to her.

Rose bit her bottom lip while deciding which of the twelve books in English would be a good choice. "I would like you to read *Black Beauty* in honor of Seba's birth."

Hedjet clapped her hands. "I like that one."

Meryt moved nearer to Rose until their shoulders touched. She shared a smile. Rose didn't move away, enjoying the warmth that radiated through her veins from the contact.

"I'll get it." Tiye walked over to the chest of books.

"If I had a black colt, I'd name him Black Beauty. Seba, he's a beauty, too." The pride was evident in Hedjet's voice.

"That he is, and a good start to the herd you intend to build," Meryt said.

Tiye returned with the book and handed it to Meryt then sat next to Hedjet, wrapping an arm around her waist.

"If I read something we don't understand, we can have Rose explain it to us," Meryt said.

"I would be happy to oblige."

Meryt started to read, Rose enjoying the sound of her voice. She found the scent of Meryt, and the warm arm pressed against hers, very pleasant.

Chapter Eighteen

Tiye watched as Rose dealt out the cards for their game of Go Fish. She placed the remainder of the stack on the low table. Six days had passed since they veered off the al-Farafra road and headed west into the desert.

Rose and Meryt's relationship had improved over the past few days. Tiye thought it due in part to Meryt allowing Rose to send her father a letter. Rose treating Meryt respectfully also fostered this improvement in the relationship. When Meryt returned to the tent at the end of the day, Rose now greeted her with a kiss on the cheek.

For the past four days, Meryt's days had been long, starting at sunrise and sometimes ending long past sunset. This was a perilous route of the desert, with shifting sand dunes. Seasoned desert scouts rode ahead of the caravan to find the right route that led to the wells and oases. Often tempers became frayed between several of the drovers, prompting Meryt to assert her role as nisut to settle disputes.

There were a couple of nights when the household played cards together, or Meryt would read to them while Rose sat by her side. Tiye could see the desire in Meryt's eyes, along with tenderness when she looked at Rose. Rose ignored it, no longer becoming flustered. For the past week, Meryt retired to bed alone, not summoning any of her Companions for company. Except for tonight.

A woman's ardent cry came from Meryt's section of the tent, Tiye identifying it as Hedjet's.

Tiye peered up, watching Rose's face flush bright crimson.

"Does it make you jealous?" Rose asked, as she arranged the cards in her hand.

"No, it pleases me that my Henut is happy. To be a Companion is to forsake jealousy for we understand Nisut may seek pleasure with others." She imparted to Rose a meaningful look. "And love others."

"I don't understand it. I admit I can understand being physically attracted to more than one person. But love, love that combines both the spiritual and physical, how can you love more than one person in that way?"

"Spiritual love is often separate from the physical. The love of the Divine seldom enters into the realm of the physical, though it has happened. We mortals can love many people in different ways. Does one blessed with many children love only one and forsake the rest?"

"No. But that's a different love one has for children, not like that between a husband and wife."

"Yes, but it's still love. Not the love you mean, I know, however that love springs from the spirit, and one can love many with the spirit. When spiritual fuses with the physical, it can embrace others."

Rose studied her for a moment, Tiye recognizing her attempt to understand. "Is this a part of your religious beliefs?"

"It's a part of the philosophical beliefs of the priestesses of Hathor. One of Hathor's titles is that of the Goddess of Love, especially physical love. True,

Companions are priestesses of Neit, but we do receive training by a priestess of Hathor in," Tiye paused as she considered her next words, "how to please a woman. The different philosophical aspects of the nature of love are also taught to us, and not only how it relates to the physical aspects." Tiye fixed her attention back on her cards. "Do you have any nines?"

"Go fish."

Tiye drew the top card from the deck.

"Do you have any fives?" Rose asked.

"Go fish. Do you have any queens?"

Rose plucked a queen from her cards and handed it to Tiye.

"What beliefs do the Remenneit hold about love?" Rose asked.

Lately, Rose had been asking her and Hedjet questions about the Valley and her people. Rose had been curious to know if they truly believed Re sailed his sun barque across the sky and their belief in many gods and goddesses. Tiye had explained that the more educated among them knew the Earth was a planet that revolved around the sun. The Netjeru, or gods and goddesses represented certain aspects of the Divine. That mummification of the dead, and building structures for the afterlife, were no longer practiced. The dead were interred in one of the many natural caverns in the western walls of the Valley.

Many now believed in only one aspect of the soul, the ba, which encompassed the personality and passed on to the afterlife. The philosophical and spiritual beliefs of the priestesses of Neit were that some individuals would be reborn into the earthly realm to fulfill a destined role.

With a triumphant smile, Tiye laid down four

queens, and then looked at Rose. "Most hold similar beliefs as you...that love is meant to be shared between two people only. For a person to have more than one love interest at one time is looked upon askance by many."

"However, Nisut is outside the boundary of rules for the common person," Rose said dryly, her expression sardonic.

"Yes, in that regard. Nisut is allowed many lovers without censure. In the past, nisuts had concubines, though that tradition is no longer followed. Even when a nisut takes a wife, or queen, to have a Companion or Companions is still expected. This is how it has always been and no one questions it."

"Wife?" Rose's eyebrows lifted. "How can a woman marry another woman?"

"What you term a marriage is a bond between two people to join with each other as mates, be they a man and a woman, two men, or two women, though the last two are not common. These arrangements are not religious affairs and we don't view them as wrong as does your religion. Love isn't a sin, nor is sharing physical pleasure."

"Can an agreement of marriage be entered upon by more than two?"

"That has occurred, but is rare. Mostly, a man builds a house and asks a woman to move in with him. If she wants him as a mate, he seeks permission from her parents if she still lives under their roof. Do you have a four?"

"Go fish."

Tiye drew from the deck. "That is the usual way. However, my mother built a house and asked my father to move in with her."

Rose's look was one of skepticism.

"I speak the truth. A woman can ask a man to be a mate. Many women own property and have trades. My mother was wealthy because she owned a herd of cattle. She built a fine house and asked my father to move in. His parents considered it a good match. They hosted a big feast and a Chantress from the Temple of Hathor was hired to sing songs that would insure the union be blessed with physical pleasure and fertility. I was born nine months later."

Another heated groan came from Meryt's section of the tent, Tye seeing Rose blush. That groan belonged to Meryt.

"Do you have any sevens?" Rose asked.

"Go fish."

Rose took a card from the top of the deck. "Will Meryt be assigned a wife by the Temple of Neit?"

"Nisuts pick their own wives. They're not required to take one."

"Does Meryt have a prospective wife in mind?"

Tiye thought she did. Rose. But, Meryt might not realize it. Yet. "Perhaps. Perhaps not. Do you have any jacks?"

"Go fish."

Chapter Nineteen

Ipu Oasis

The conversations and laughter flowed around Rose. She could understand a few words, but not enough to follow the discussions. The large dining mat held a variety of dishes from fruits, pastries, vegetables, breads, baked doves, and slices of roasted goat haunches. The drink was a fruity wine, Rose's goblet already having been filled twice. Nisut and her household sat on padded, low stools, each with a small table before them. The other guests sat on thin cushions and partook of the food laid on the mat. A group of male and female musicians sat not far away, playing gay tunes on harps and percussion instruments.

Their host was Ptahmose, commander of Nisut's garrison at the farthest oasis, named Ipu and under Nesneit's control. The garrison's main function was to prevent intrusions into the territory of Nesneit by unknown caravans, slavers, and the rare Imohag raiding parties that sometimes crossed over from Libya.

One of Meryt's horse guards had ridden ahead to alert them of their arrival. The caravan had arrived at midday. The Commander had prepared in advance to receive his nisut with as much pomp as the small settlement of eighty-five soldiers, and their families, could muster.

Meryt had ridden Bakhu into the oasis. The
stallion's bridle had dripped with tassels as did the
saddle blanket, and his tail and mane were braided
with colorful ribbons. Meryt had worn white Bedouin
robes, a red cloak, and red keffiye held by a gold agal.
Tiye had informed Rose that red was the color of the
dress the Great Neit wore, as was her crown. The
oasis' women sang festive songs and performed the
high, trilling ululations. The soldiers marched ahead
of Meryt, beating drums. When Meryt pulled even
with the crowd, many fell to their knees and lowered
their heads.

Rose had noticed that the women were dressed
in festive galabeyas and headscarves decorated with
silver coins and beads. The required dress for this
formal dinner was surprisingly different. Meryt and
her household and twenty dinner participants were
dressed in clothes that were customary for occasions
such as this. She had the strange feeling of having
stepped into a theater production of *Antony and
Cleopatra*. What the women wore looked similar to
the dresses she and Meryt had worn on the night they
dined together, but not as transparent, thank goodness.
If Meryt had ordered her to wear a dress like the one
she wore on that night, she would have disobeyed and
accepted the punishment, short of torture involving
scorpions.

Ptahmose, his officers, and his two sons were
dressed in blue short-sleeved tunics that looked
Roman. She found it a bit disconcerting to see the
kohl around their eyes and paint on the eyelids. They
also wore jewelry and beaded collars.

Meryt wore a pleated ivory dress, and a pleated

short cape that lent the appearance of wide sleeves reaching the elbows. A gold sash, heavily embroidered with red thread, girdled her waist and hung almost to the ankles. Around her head was a gold ribbon embroidered in red that matched the sash. Her concentric beaded collar, consisting of red and gold beads, reached the upper portion of her bosom.

She made an attractive picture, and Rose found her gaze often taking in the sight. Meryt caught her looking a few times and smiled, which caused Rose to blush, but she shared smiles in return.

Tiye and Hedjet each wore a linen dress with a Roman look. Tiye's was the color of butter and Hedjet's blue. The collars they wore were made of blue and green beads, and they donned other items of jewelry, including headbands.

As for Rose, she wore a dress given to her by Meryt. It was accordion pleated and in a pale lilac. Her concentric collar consisted of tiny flower-shaped beads in white and pink. Hedjet had applied kohl around her eyes and blue paint on the eyelids. Meryt had told her how beautiful she looked, Rose seeing the admiration in her expression.

Next to Meryt's right sat Ptahmose and his wife, on Meryt's left was Rose, then Tiye and Hedjet. To Hedjet's left were seated an officer and his wife. The other diners sat across the mat.

The conversation flowed freely between all, except for Rose. She sipped her wine and glanced across the mat, her sight stopping on Ptahmose's youngest son, his eyes intent on her. His expression seemed one of libidinous interest. He couldn't have been more than fourteen. He lowered his gaze, seeming embarrassed. He wasn't the only one that stared at her. Throughout the meal, she caught Ptahmose's older son scrutinizing her, and an officer giving her a lascivious leer. What she saw in their eyes was far from curiosity. It was lust. She glanced up to see them once again staring at her. She ignored them and took the last sip of her wine, the cup refilled immediately by a male attendant.

Tiye leaned over and whispered, "If those sons of Set keep looking at you as if you were a honey cake they wish to eat and Henutsen sees them, she will have their eyes plucked out."

"So you noticed, too?"

"They are not subtle. Neither are Ptahmose's two nieces and two daughters who are staring at Henutsen as if she too were a honey cake."

Rose looked up to see the group of four young women, their eyes focused in the direction of Meryt with speculative interest. Rose doubted all four were romantically inclined toward the fairer sex. It was Nisut's title and power that attracted them.

Rose leaned close to Tiye. "Will Henutsen also pluck their eyes out?" While out in public, Rose referred to Meryt as Henutsen or Henut.

Tiye sniggered. "No, she has become accustomed to it. There is always some headman's or headwoman's daughter hoping to get Henutsen's notice and be invited to her bed."

"Do they succeed?" Rose hadn't meant to ask, but it slipped out before she could think.

"In the past they sometimes did. The offers hold no appeal for her now."

It bothered Rose to know that about Meryt, even if it had occurred in her past. She could understand, well, almost understand Meryt having Companions.

She knew Meryt had an emotional attachment to Tiye and Hedjet that carried over into the physical. Not that she condoned it. But, casual trysts were altogether another thing. It reminded her of the old custom of droit du seigneur, where the medieval lord had the right to take the virginity of his serfs' maiden daughters.

"Are you discussing me?" Meryt leaned close to the two women, her conversation having concluded with Ptahmose and his wife.

"We were discussing your admirers," Rose said.

"I have many, which ones?"

"The ones desiring to be in your bed tonight," Tiye said.

"Do you speak for yourself, Tiye?"

Rose covered her mouth to try to suppress a laugh.

"I speak of the herd of four love-struck young heifers across from you."

Hedjet leaned part way over Tiye to say, "The last time we were here, Henutsen didn't cull the herd. Henutsen should choose all four to atone."

"All four? Do you take me for an Apis bull?" Meryt lifted one corner of her mouth in a wry grin and spoke low, even though the host and none of the guests could speak English. "As always, Ptahmose has informed me members of his household are at my *service*. I think he means his two daughters and two nieces, though he probably wouldn't be averse to his wife. I prefer the wife. Though after one night with me, she would no longer want Ptahmose, or any man ever again. Ptahmose has served me ably and I wouldn't do that to him."

Both Companions snorted derisively.

Rose surprised herself by finding this remark humorous instead of scandalous. The wine must have gone to her head.

"I thought you the Chosen of the Great Neit and not of Hathor," Tiye said in jest.

Meryt's grin was lopsided. She placed her left hand on Rose's back, rubbing lightly. "I see Rose has garnered the admiration of a few bulls."

"Will you pluck their eyes out for me?" Rose enjoyed the feel of Meryt's hand on her back.

"I think changing them into oxen would be more suitable. However, I have a more efficient way to discourage both our problems, if you will follow my plan."

This intrigued Rose, wondering what Meryt's plan entailed.

"It will save your admirers from having their eyes plucked out. Or other parts."

"I might be inclined. Do tell me your plan."

Meryt leaned in and kissed Rose tenderly on the lips, lingering for a long moment.

Rose felt her cheeks heat and lips tingle. Meryt leaned in again and kissed her. Rose pushed from her awareness the soft and pleased sounding chuckles from Tiye and Hedjet. Meryt's kiss deepened. Rose responded this time by relaxing her lips, only Meryt existing.

☙ ☙ ❧ ❧

The sound of a high-pitched, female shriek followed by laughter brought a smile to Meryt as she walked the shady path through the grove of palms, her two guards following. The path led to a wooden gate in a high, whitewashed mud-brick wall and to the sentry standing in front of it. The man stood at attention, the two escorts halting, not following her through the gate. She walked on a few yards through a garden and to a high trellised area of grapevines. She sniffed, catching the scent of moisture. The sound of splashing water and female chatter reached her ears.

Meryt had left the tent at daybreak to perform caravan business, finishing a short while ago. She had returned to the tent to change into a fresh galabeya before seeking out her household and joining them.

This was a private garden, a part of the grounds of the ancient house Ptahmose lived in and was hers and her household's for the day. Its various plants were able to flourish due to the natural spring located on the grounds. The trellised grapevines partly hid an arbor with the vines arched overhead. She walked through the portal and under the bower that provided shade from the afternoon sun. The sound of splashing water and talk grew louder.

She stopped in the dappled shadows at the end of the short tunnel of vines to gaze at her Companions in the pool. Centuries ago a gray stone border was built around the spring and formed a rectangular pool some fourteen feet long and ten feet wide. At one end of the pool was a trough for the spring's water to trickle out and irrigate the garden. A stately date palm grew at each corner of the pool, shading the water from Re's bright beams. Stone benches were situated on the east and west sides of the pool.

She smiled when seeing the delightful sight of her two Companions. Tiye stood in the water that reached to her upper thighs. Her skin was the color of dark honey, her form tall and stately, her breasts ripe and firm. The water came up to Hedjet's hip tops, the young woman as slender as a gazelle, the large nipples of her small breasts puckered from the cold water. She chuckled when Hedjet splashed water onto Tiye, only to receive a splash in return, both women playfully screeching.

Although this view was beautiful, her eyes sought the sight of what she longed to see. At the far end of the pool, Rose leaned against the pool wall, the water covering her shoulders, red hair fanned out and floating around her. Rose laughed as she observed the two women and slapped a spray of water toward them. She stood, causing Meryt to catch her breath as the white shift, almost transparent from wetness, hugged her figure. Meryt feasted her eyes on the rounded breasts and the coral nipples taut from the cool water. Then she languidly ran her sight down to the trim waist and flared hips.

"Isisnofret," she whispered.

Rose glanced up and immediately stilled as she watched Meryt walk toward the pool. Tiye and Hedjet spied Meryt and stopped their play.

"Henut, come join us." Tiye's smile invited.

"Yes, Henut, the water is cool." Hedjet's smile equally inviting.

"What say you Rose? Is the water cool?" Meryt eyes boldly caressed Rose's body.

Rose blushed and crossed her arms over her breasts, not meeting Meryt's gaze. That Rose wore the shift was no surprise. Meryt knew her culture had taboos against baring one's body. From Nebet Eliza, she learned English nebets were taught to be modest, overly so, when compared to Remenneits, and to suppress their passions. She assumed that American nebets behaved similarly. Still, the nakedness of her two Companions did not appear to embarrass Rose.

"It is." Rose met Meryt's eyes for a moment before she uneasily focused on the water.

A mild hurt beset Meryt. Last night at the feast, Rose's actions had indicated her regard for Meryt was deepening. They had exchanged gentle kisses, Meryt's main intent to let others know Rose belonged to her, and that she desired none of the others who would offer themselves as a bedmate.

The smiles Rose had bestowed on her had been amiable, and many seemed flirtatious, as did some of the exchanges of words. Meryt had realized that some of the relaxation in Rose's demeanor was likely due to the wine, but she was inclined to believe not all of it was. They had left the feast late, escorted back to the tent by Meryt's guards. They had straightway retired, Meryt sleeping alone.

She moved to a nearby bench and removed her garments, stacking them on the bench's surface. Stopping at the pool's edge for only a moment, she stepped in, "Ahh, cold."

"I can warm you up, Henut," Hedjet said as she waded over and wrapped both arms around Meryt's torso. She stood on her toes and kissed Meryt on the mouth.

Meryt returned the kiss, pulling Hedjet's wet body tight against her and running her hands down the slickness of it to squeeze the firm buttocks. Arm around Hedjet's waist she drew her down into the water to sit beside her against the pool wall.

Meryt held the other arm open for Tiye who slid into the water next to her and pressed close. Tiye ran her right hand up and down Meryt's inner thigh as the two kissed.

Meryt watched out of the corner of her eye as Rose pushed out of the pool and stretched out on a bench in the sun facing away from them.

"I think we've embarrassed Rose." Tiye sounded concerned.

"Embarrassed?" Hedjet asked. "Why? She quickly got over any embarrassment when we disrobed." Hedjet giggled. "Did you see her face redden to the color of her hair when she first saw us?" She stroked Meryt's thigh and teased, "It is Henutsen's beauty that has sent her from the water. She's embarrassed because my Henut has her starting to boil like a little pot over a hot fire."

"Ugh. Hedjet," Meryt warned.

"We favor Henutsen with affection and she us, and this is what embarrasses her," Tiye said.

Meryt remained quiet, knowing Tiye was correct. Anything that hinted of physical pleasure made Rose uncomfortable and the three of them sharing affection had sent her running.

"Why should this embarrass her?" Hedjet leaned over and gave Meryt a kiss, taking her bottom lip between her teeth and lightly nipping it. She snuggled back against Meryt's side. "She has ears and hears when we pleasure one another. You yell like a mating cat when you peak. Everyone in the caravan is aware of what goes on in Henutsen's tent."

"Mating cat?" Tiye reached across Meryt and splashed water onto Hedjet. "You scream like a woman birthing her first baby. A 'big' baby."

Hedjet dashed water at Tiye, the spray hitting Meryt in the face. Tiye splashed water back toward Hedjet. A battle ensued as both women smacked water toward each other, the shower splattering Meryt.

"Ahh." Meryt frowned, wiping the water from her face. "Cease or I'll apply a flail across your backsides."

"Henut, I deserve to be punished." Hedjet rubbed catlike against Meryt's side, her smile flirtatious.

Tiye delivered an exaggerated sigh and shook her head. "How unfortunate, we left the flail at home."

This information did not discourage Hedjet. "There is a patch of cane growing by one of the marshy pools where we are camped. I can find a nice cane."

This was a pleasurable pastime Meryt and Hedjet shared, Nisut administering punishment to her offender. Tiye wasn't partial to it, and Meryt knew Rose would not understand. Yet who knew what hidden fantasies she entertained. Meryt yearned to know them all and to grant them all.

Meryt watched Rose and sighed. Would she ever let Meryt into her heart? Would she ever come to her bed? She thought once Rose tasted passion, she'd become an enthusiastic participant. After all, Rose was a woman and, despite her upbringing, women were naturally passionate.

Meryt gave Hedjet a wry smile, knowing she was about to disappoint her Companion. She would make it up to her when they reached home.

"Nisut in her benevolence absolves you of your crime...this time."

≋≋≋≋

The heat from the bench surface warmed Rose's skin through the wet shift. Rose lay on her stomach, the heat of the sun on her back. She wouldn't be able to stay in the direct sun for long, due to her complexion.

The women's playfulness carried to her ears. She could easily pick out each woman's voice.

Yet, one particular voice caressed her senses as if a hand smoothed down a cat's back, the cat arching sensually into the touch. She closed her eyes tighter in an effort to dispel this feeling that both excited and frightened.

She moved uneasily from a pang of arousal when recalling Meryt stepping into the pool, her body displayed proudly and without shame, her attractive curves and warm brown skin. A groan escaped when remembering the heat of that body and the soft breasts pressed against her.

She was in danger of losing all sense of propriety over this attraction to Meryt. She felt a stranger to herself, not recognizing the woman she was becoming, had become, with an awareness of emotions she'd always romanticized. Yet, hadn't she always longed to feel passion? How naive to think passion a welcoming fire confined to the relative safety of a hearth made of love. No, passion was a spark from a lightning bolt that struck a tree in a forest. That spark could cause a wild fire, consuming all.

Her lips slightly opened and relaxed remembering the affectionate and tender kisses Meryt had given her last evening at the feast. She had returned the kisses, and it wasn't just the wine that had lowered her defenses and caused her response. The kisses were not like the fervent one from the night she'd offered herself to Meryt. The tenderness in them awakened an ache to go back to that time and to the kiss of fire, allowing it to sweep her into desire and its ultimate fulfillment.

Ice and Fire. Meryt was both. As nisut, cold and autocratic, dedicated to duty, possessing a sense of entitlement. Maybe that's how it was with all who were in power. Meryt's belief that Rose was hers, a gift from Neit, property, appalled her. In all fairness, some men in her acquaintance held the same view of their wives and daughters. Women were chattel, passed from the care of one man to the care of another. Except the difference here was, Meryt was a woman. However, her power as nisut would put her on an equal footing alongside any imperious male in Rose's acquaintance. No. Rose knew no man in her acquaintance who wielded the power Meryt seemed to possess.

Then there was Meryt the woman who held a childlike joy for learning. Rose recalled her interest in stories of the American West with its cowboys and Indians and Meryt's fondness of reading aloud to them, and sharing laughter. When not acting as nisut, she displayed warmth and love to the two women in her life. When Meryt allowed her feminine nature to emerge, she was considerate and kind, and a woman of fire in her passions.

The passionate encounters the three women shared intrigued her. The sounds they made when engaged in 'pleasuring,' as Tiye called it, made her wonder what the three, or two, were doing to cause such ardent cries. The sounds and her visualizations were stimulating. These three women shared a bond, a love Rose couldn't fully understand, but one she was beginning to respect and maybe even envy.

Images and sensations of *that* night standing in front of the mirror, once again flooded her thoughts. Meryt naked, pressed against her body, the feel of warm breasts and hardened nipples touching her back, and the brush of the crisp hair of Meryt's private place against her rear.

And if Rose allowed passion to sway her into Meryt's arms, what then? She could become one of three in Meryt's life. *That*, she couldn't accept. The fear of this physical attraction to Meryt paled beside a greater one. The fear that she could easily lose her heart to Meryt.

Chapter Twenty

With a hard tug, Rose tightened the girth and tucked the strap ends into the cinch rings. She placed her hand on the pommel and shook the saddle to make sure it sat securely on Izza's back. Placing her left foot in the bronze stirrup, she pushed up and into the saddle, the rein slipping out of her gloved hand. She leaned forward in an attempt to reach it. Hedjet stepped over and handed it to her before mounting Sah, and the two women trotted their horses to the end of the caravan. They were on the trail west again, having left Ipu Oasis two days before.

The morning sun had yet to clear the eastern horizon and heat the cool air that lingered from night. Rose drew in a deep breath, smelling the dung fires and the aroma of food, tea, and coffee, along with the musty wool smell of camels. Over the past few weeks, she'd grown accustomed to the odors.

They passed laden camels, some standing while others still rested on the sand, not inclined to move despite the prodding by their drovers. A strident, harsh female voice startled Rose. She scanned the line of camels in an effort to find the source. The strident shouts continued and drew Rose's sight to a woman on a camel. It was Satiah with her features twisted in a grotesque mask of hate. Satiah hurled words sounding like curses, even as the drover slapped her leg with a livestock prod.

Hedjet stopped to scream invectives back at Satiah, accompanied by a shake of her riding whip. She then tapped Sah lightly with the whip encouraging him into a canter, Rose following, until they reached the end of the caravan among the goats and donkeys.

Hedjet slowed Sah to a walk and turned to Rose beside her. "Too bad Henutsen didn't order the she-jackal stripped and flogged before everyone in the caravan." Hedjet's expression was severe. "I would have offered to flog her and loved doing it." She brightened as she gazed past Rose and pointed her whip. "Look, there's Nebet Tiye."

Rose twisted her head, noticing a gray jenny nursing a tiny charcoal foal.

"Oh, how precious she is." Rose remembered Hedjet telling Tiye a baby donkey carried her name. She watched as the foal vigorously nursed, its tail wildly wagging.

There was a laugh from Hedjet. "Little Nebet Tiye takes after Big Nebet Tiye when it comes to the enjoyment of teats." She made a loud suckling sound.

It took only a heartbeat for Hedjet's words to register. The statement surprised Rose but didn't shock. She felt a chuckle escape. Who better to know than Hedjet…and Meryt?

Lately, her thoughts had a way of straying down *that* enticing path, especially after the serenade of fervent cries two nights ago coming from Meryt's section of the tent. Hearing them made her wonder if she'd ever experience passion as fervent as that. Not that she would engage in the sort of relationship the three women shared. She wanted to find that one special woman with whom she could share passion. Uninvited, a vision of Meryt invaded her thoughts.

She tried to shake free from the memories of ardent lips kissing her and the feel of supple hands on her naked body.

She urged Izza into a trot toward the front of the caravan. All at once, Sah raced past and away from the caravan. Hedjet glanced back at Rose with a challenging grin, the ends of her blue and white striped keffiye flapping like wings. Izza snuffled and tossed her head, eager to follow. Rose encouraged the mare with a shout and gave Izza free rein as she leaned forward, feeling the whip of mane against her face.

The two horses ran neck and neck, racing alongside a broad, dry streambed. Izza passed Sah and they continued to follow the streambed as it led into a bend. All at once Rose registered a dozen or so blue-robed men on camels, some sixty yards away, emerging from the streambed. With a hard pull on the reins, she brought Izza to an abrupt stop, almost catapulting over the mare's head. Before she could get her balance, Izza reared. Rose tumbled to the ground, and the mare galloped away.

"Rose!" Hedjet halted Sah beside her prone figure, quickly offering Rose her hand. "Imohags! Hurry!"

Rose pushed to her feet. Feeling pain in her right hip, she gingerly hurried the few steps to Sah and grabbed Hedjet's hand with her right hand and the pommel with her left to pull onto the horse. Unexpectedly, a camel was beside them, the rider pointing the long barrel of his antique musket down at them. Rose froze when she looked into his blue-veiled face, hard eyes staring down at her.

Hedjet threw her whip at the camel's head, causing it to shy, the abrupt motion making the man's musket fire into the air. By a quick action of her hand, Hedjet removed her dagger from its sheath and flung it up toward the veiled rider.

The sharp reports of gunfire came from the direction of the caravan, giving Rose hope that help was on the way. All at once, another camel was to the front of them. Rose tried to pull onto the horse, but slipped, almost pulling Hedjet from the saddle as she landed hard on her rear, her keffiye falling off. She scrambled to her knees, feeling hands grab her around her waist from behind, then half pick her up, and drag. She struggled to get free from the assailant, trying to pry his hands loose from her waist.

Hedjet maneuvered Sah between Rose's captor and his kneeling camel. A loud and long warbling ululation from Hedjet sounded, and suddenly, Rose was roughly thrust to the side and crashed to the ground. She struggled to her feet, the pain in her hip making her stumble back. Looking up, she witnessed the blue-robed rider rush toward Hedjet with his sword held above his head, ready to strike. Sah reared up, his front hooves pawing the air in front of the man backing him up. The man charged again with raised sword. Hedjet urged Sah into another rear to halt the aggressor.

Rose hurriedly scanned the ground at her feet for a rock to throw at the attacker when the pound of horses' hooves and shouts of men surrounded her. She looked up to see Bakhu charge out of a swirl of dust and knock the attacker to the ground, Meryt on the stallion's back swinging her scimitar down at the prone man's head. The arrival of one of the horse guards blocked Rose from seeing the fight's conclusion.

All was chaos, gunfire, shouts of men, squeals

of horses, and bellows of camels. Amidst it all Hedjet rode up alongside her, holding out her hand to Rose. Rose grabbed it and the pommel. Hedjet snatched the back of her robe and tugged her across the front of the saddle, the air in her lungs expelled in a huff.

"Hold on." Hedjet pressed a hand on Rose's back.

The only thing Rose was able to do was hang draped over the saddle's front like a sack of grain. There was a shrill whinny from Sah. A jarring movement forced air out of Rose's lungs a second time.

Sah went into a full gallop. Rose closed her eyes against the stomach pain from jostling against the pommel. Soon Sah stopped, and voices surrounded her. Hedjet issued orders. A drover helped Rose off the horse and onto the ground.

Hedjet sat beside her. "Are you injured?" She brushed a lock of hair back from Rose's face, her expression concerned.

"No," Rose said, breathlessly.

A woman knelt by Rose handing her a cup of water. The water was tepid but relieved Rose's dry throat.

"Thank you." Rose gave the cup back and the woman refilled it from the goatskin water bag that hung from her left shoulder, passing it to Hedjet.

After Hedjet drank the water, she motioned over one of Meryt's black-robed guards. They conversed for a few seconds before the guard turned and spoke to two drovers who then hurried down the line of camels.

"Meryt! What about Meryt?" Rose felt her blood freeze, not knowing the outcome of Meryt's fight with the attacker.

"I'm certain Henutsen is fine. She's skilled with the scimitar." Hedjet grinned. "Neit will protect her."

Rose threw her arms around Hedjet's neck and hugged tight. "You saved my life."

Hedjet patted and rubbed Rose's back in a comforting way for a moment. "The Imohags saw that we were women. They would rather take us as slaves than kill us."

Rose wasn't sure of that, the image flashing through her mind of the ruffian charging Hedjet with his sword. But death might be preferable to what she imagined slavery to those captors would entail.

"Hedjet!"

Hedjet sprang to her feet and into the arms of Tiye who kissed each cheek and enveloped her in a tight hug. The two spoke, Rose hearing her name mentioned.

Tiye squatted beside her, placing a hand on her shoulder. "Can you walk or do you need someone to carry you? I need to check you for injuries. A tent has been erected nearby that we can use."

"Yes, I think I can walk." With Tiye's aid, Rose got to her feet, Hedjet on her other side to lend help if needed.

The three walked over to a tent where a short, middle-aged ebony-skinned woman met them. They entered the tent, the woman leaving the flap partway open to provide light.

"Rose, this is Sitre, she is a healer." Tiye and the healer conversed for a minute. Tiye said to Rose, "Remove your garments so we can check you for injuries."

"It's just my right hip that's a little sore."

"This is no time for modesty. Remove your outer

robe but leave on your tunic." Tiye's tone was firm.

Rose removed her gloves and handed them to Hedjet along with the sash and outer robe.

"Show us where it hurts," Tiye said.

"Along my right hip."

"Lift up your tunic."

Tiye's tone let Rose know who was in charge, and she did as told. Before she could protest, Tiye untied the drawstrings of her sirwal and yanked it down to expose the right hip. Rose's long tunic hung enough in the center to cover her private parts. Tiye peered over Sitre's shoulder as the healer bent and pressed fingers along Rose's thigh.

"It's a little sore," Rose said.

The tent flap opened wider, Meryt standing in the entrance.

Rose smiled with relief to see that Meryt was unharmed. At the same time, her fear for Meryt's safety and the danger that she and Hedjet had been in, along with her pain, had the effect of making her a little cross. "Do you mind? Close that. I don't want the whole caravan to witness this."

The flap dropped as Meryt stepped close, her expression concerned. "Are you hurt?"

"Just bruised, I think. Hedjet saved my life."

Meryt turned to Hedjet and opened her arms. Hedjet stepped into the embrace and received a gentle kiss on her forehead. They exchanged words in Kemen, Meryt taking a dagger from her sash to hand to Hedjet. They exchanged more words, Meryt again kissing her, this time on the mouth.

Meryt turned to Rose. "Hedjet's dagger hit its target. I found it in the sand with blood on the blade. The man was able to ride away, but I think he will carry a scar as a reminder of this day."

The healer finished the exam and spoke to Tiye.

"Sitre says you will have bruising and not to ride or walk much for the next two days. She has herbs, and I will prepare a wet compress so we can put it on your injury tonight."

"Thank you," Rose said to Sitre. She pulled up her sirwal and retied the drawstrings.

Tiye translated Rose's thanks. Sitre grinned and nodded. The healer turned to Meryt and bowed her head. Meryt spoke to her in a kind tone, and then opened the tent flap for her to depart.

Meryt gathered Rose in a hug. Rose rested her head on Meryt's shoulder for a moment, feeling the soft stroke of a hand on her back. She lifted her head and offered Meryt a weak smile.

Rose's thoughts went to her mare. "Meryt. Izza?" She held her breath, almost afraid to hear the answer.

"Izza is safe. She came trotting after us as we headed back to the caravan. I have left her in the care of one of the grooms."

Rose let out a relieved sigh.

Meryt continued. "When we reach Iunyt Oasis, I will thank the Divine Isis and host a feast in her honor for protecting you and Hedjet. Hedjet will be honored for her actions."

"She deserves it," Rose said.

Hedjet beamed at the praise. "I think Re and Horus were with us, too."

"That they were," Tiye said. She regarded Meryt. "It's been a while since Imohags have raided our territories, or roamed this far east."

"They were probably on the way south for slaves to take to the Libyan coast and over to Morocco.

Unfortunately, I don't have enough guards to shadow them. I think they won't raid the caravan now that they have seen our strength and know their ancient muskets are no match for our more modern firepower."

"Who are these ruffians?" Rose asked.

"Imohags," Meryt said. "That is the name they call themselves, and means *freemen*. You might know them by the name Tuaregs."

"Oh, my God." Rose had heard of the fierce nomads many called the *blue men of the desert* because of the indigo dye they used for their turbans that stained their faces. The men were the ones who veiled their faces, not the women. They had a reputation for raids on caravans, villages, and oases, murdering and taking slaves.

Meryt drew Rose close and rubbed her back. "You are safe now. In three days, we reach Iunyt Oasis. There we will rest for a few days, then on to the Valley of Wind and Dreams."

A short while later Meryt walked a slightly limping Rose over to a white camel carrying a howdah that belonged to Hedjet. Rose would be able to stretch out a little in the roomy howdah and remove weight from her sore hip.

Meryt placed her hands on Rose's waist, then embraced her. "If they had captured you, I wouldn't have rested until I had you back." Meryt's tone was raw, her breath hot in Rose's ear. Meryt stepped back and pressed a fervent kiss on her lips.

In breathless abandon, Rose parted her mouth, and the kiss deepened as Meryt slid the tip of her tongue in to gently stroke hers. A rush of heat coursed through Rose and struck low in her belly releasing a groan from deep within her chest.

All too soon, the kiss ended. Neither woman said a word, but stared deep into each other's eyes. Those gold eyes drew Rose in. They were familiar to Rose in a way she couldn't explain. It was as if she had always known them, and in their molten depths, Rose saw they held recognition of her.

Meryt helped her into the howdah. Rose watched as she walked away. She touched her lips, confused by her enthusiastic response to Meryt's kiss, the warm taste of it still on her tongue. Maybe it was due to the trauma of thinking she could have died and the kiss was an affirmation that she lived, and felt. But, she wanted Meryt to come back and kiss her again.

≈≈≈≈≈

Meryt parted the tent flap and entered the glowing interior, smiling to see Hedjet there to greet her.

"Henut, I missed you." Hedjet kissed Meryt's cheek.

Meryt kissed Hedjet's cheek then scanned the area for the other two members of her household. "Where are Rose and Tiye?" She smelled a slight acrid odor.

"Rose is in bed and Tiye is applying a medicinal compress to her hip."

"So, that's what I smell." She removed her cloak, scimitar and baldric, and handed them to Hedjet.

"Yes, the odor is most foul." Hedjet scrunched up her nose.

Meryt headed to her room, Hedjet right behind. "How is Rose?" Meryt had checked Rose when the caravan stopped for a quick rest and meal, Rose assuring her she was fine.

"Sore. She went to bed right after our dinner. I can warm up something for you to eat."

"I shared supper with my guards after our patrol."

Hedjet helped Meryt undress. She dipped a cloth in a bowl of water, soaped it and wiped it over Meryt's body. "Were any Imohags about?"

"No signs of any. I assigned extra guards to patrol tonight."

Hedjet finished bathing Meryt, patted her dry with a towel, took a shift from the top of a chest and handed it to her.

After Meryt slipped on the shift, she drew Hedjet into her arms and bestowed a warm kiss on her lips. "I am proud of you my brave warrior."

Hedjet brightened at the praise. "My sole thought was to remove Rose from danger." Her expression became serious. "If he had taken Rose—" She flung her arms around Meryt's neck and pressed against her. "I knew you would come."

Meryt stroked Hedjet's back. The man would never inflict his malevolence on another. She didn't regret sending him to Maat for judgment. "I would have hunted the sons of Set down if they had captured either one of you and gotten you back." If Rose or Hedjet had been harmed, Meryt would relish killing the culprits with her own hands and slowly. They would beg to die.

Hedjet looked into Meryt's face. "Henut, if they had captured Rose, I'd have gone with you and made them curse their mothers for bringing their miserable lives into the world." Hedjet's lips tightened, her green eyes looking as bright and hard as emeralds.

"My brave little warrior, how fierce you are." Meryt kissed her again, this time with passion. Hedjet's zeal had stirred her blood.

"Ah, I see you're back without injury," Tiye said as she parted the curtain and entered. "Meryt, you should let your guards do their jobs and not go chasing after danger."

"A nisut's job is to be Ramses the Great when danger threatens."

"Yes, when there is an army of thousands at Nisut's side."

"Yes, yes, yes, O Wise Priestess."

"I take it all is well?" Tiye walked up to Meryt and kissed her cheek, receiving one in return.

"No sign of danger. How is Rose?"

"There are bruises. I applied the compress and gave her a draught for pain. She should fall asleep soon." She paused. "She stayed quiet tonight when we had our meal, and tense. Some is from pain I'm sure, but I think what happened today is now stalking her thoughts. I hope her dreams are not bad ones.

"I'll give you my bed so she doesn't have to sleep alone."

"Henut, why don't you sleep with her?" Hedjet asked.

"I think Rose would prefer you and Tiye protecting her, like you did on the night of the scorpions." It would please Meryt for Rose to seek comfort and refuge in her arms. However, she knew this would make Rose uneasy, even though Meryt would have no intent other than to protect.

"It was a trying day for you, too." Meryt lovingly touched Hedjet's cheek. She glanced at Tiye. "Put her to bed and take care of her. I'll join you two later. I want to see Rose. If she wishes not to sleep alone, I'll bring her here and sleep in your bed."

Meryt hugged both women before she parted the curtain that led into her Companions' section of the tent. The area was semi-dark, the only light emanating from over the top of the curtain of her room and a gap in the one of Rose's tent space.

She cautiously made her way past the two mattresses pushed together to make one and stopped beside the curtain to Rose's room. "Rose," she called softly.

After a long moment, Rose answered in a subdued voice, "Yes."

Meryt pushed open the curtain and entered. The muted glow from the oil lamp by the bed reflected in the tears on Rose's lashes, her eyes shimmering. Meryt knelt by the mattress and touched Rose's arm. "Are you in pain?"

"Only a little ache." Rose's bottom lip trembled as she attempted to choke back a sob.

Meryt slipped into the narrow space on the mattress beside Rose, slid her right arm under her and pulled her close to rest her head on Meryt's shoulder. "I have you. I won't let anything, or anybody hurt you." As she stroked Rose's silky hair, she touched her lips lovingly to her forehead.

Trembles wracked Rose's body. She pressed close to Meryt, her forehead against Meryt's neck. This action infused Meryt with tenderness. Something from deep in her heart caused a tight ache in her throat. She wanted to cry from the intensity of the emotion.

Only one time before had Meryt held and comforted one who cried and needed the arms of another to succor them. This happened many years ago when Tiye's beloved niece died from a fever. She cried with Tiye and with all her heart begged the Great One to unravel time to keep the child from death. Was she not the Setepenneit? Would not Neit grant her this favor? The Great One heeded not her plea. Time spiraled forward to forever circle outward, never to repeat the same path.

The ache and tightness in Meryt's throat subsided so she could speak. "The sons of Set are far away from here and won't return. There is nothing for you to fear." She rubbed Rose's back in a small circle, feeling the trembles lessen, then stop. "Soon, we will reach Iunyt Oasis, where I plan to stay for a few days. I will have a great feast dedicated to Isis, and to honor Hedjet, and you will have a place at my side. Shall I tell you what I have planned for the menu?" Rose remained silent, Meryt continuing to tell her of all the foods the cook would prepare. The sensation of warm and even breath on her neck let Meryt know Rose slept. Meryt nestled her face against the silky hair and soon fell into slumber.

✿✿✿✿

The rumbling resonance of a voice drew Rose from slumber. She woke to see the mellow glow of a lamp fill this section of the tent. The conversation between Tiye and Meryt was low. She stirred but Meryt's arm tightened around her back keeping her pressed to the warm body and her head resting on the comfortable shoulder. The shift Meryt wore felt soft against her cheek, the scent of it pleasant. Rose had her right arm draped across Meryt's waist.

A few more words passed between the two

women then Tiye departed, leaving behind the lit lamp she placed on the stool by the head of the bed. Rose felt Meryt's tender lips on her forehead as her hand soothingly stroked Rose's hair and back. A rumble of contentment sounded in Rose's throat, and she nuzzled into the warmth of Meryt, soaking her in.

Last night anxiety from what had happened had stormed into her thoughts, bringing with it loneliness and uncertainty as to the future. Then Meryt was there holding her, and it was what she required at that moment. Her need pushed truth aside, the truth that Meryt's arrogance and sense of entitlement put Rose in this situation.

"The first rays from the solar barque have greeted a new day, and Nisut with all her might from its course cannot sway."

"A nisut and a poet?" Rose smiled in amusement.

"I am Nisut, always. A poet only when inspired."

"Not always Nisut. Sometimes you're Benret."

Silence stretched for a moment, Rose holding her breath, afraid she offended, or stepped across a barrier Meryt didn't want her to. Or wasn't ready for her to...yet.

"Perhaps, sometimes I am." Slowly, Meryt pulled her right arm from underneath Rose, propped on her elbow, and stared down at her. "How is your hip?"

Carefully, Rose stretched her right leg and rolled onto her back to look up at Meryt. "Some stiffness that I'm sure is the result of sleeping in one position. When I'm up and about, I'll be fine."

"If you need help with your morning toilette, I can send Tiye or Hedjet."

"I think I can manage. Thank you."

Their eyes met. Rose felt shy and uncertain. Her

emotions were all jumbled and hard to sort out. Meryt had been so tender last night and the tenderness remained this morning. Rose knew Benret was with her now, and last evening, not Nisut. "Thank you for last night."

"I will always be here when you need me." A quick, but warm kiss caressed Rose's forehead. "I must go. I want to have the caravan depart before Re leaves the horizon. Go back to sleep for a little while longer. Tiye will wake you."

Meryt was soon on her feet and out of the room, leaving Rose alone.

Rose's thoughts swirled, pulled and pushed. There was no doubt left that she was attracted to Meryt, and dangerously so. Meryt had raged into her life like a storm that buffeted and lashed, leaving behind Rose's scattered emotions.

She thought back to the day in the museum when she first gazed into those gold eyes. As strange as it seemed, they had spoken of a connection, something waiting for discovery. Or rediscovery? The storm named Meryt had blown past and left the gentle rain. Benret was the gentle rain bringing life to a seed that was beginning to sprout in Rose's heart.

No. Preposterous. You are not falling in love with her. You will not entertain that notion.

Chapter Twenty-one

N isut Wer, noble one, Setepenneit, I beseech you, forgive your devoted servant for siring such a worthless child who is hated by the Gods. I will not stay the strength of my arm when I punish her."

Letting silence reign for what she was certain would seem an eternity to the guilty, Meryt studied the prone man, Bakenre, groveling in the dust in front of her. He was the headman of Iunyt Oasis and the father of the she-jackal, Satiah.

They had arrived at the oasis yesterday. Meryt had ordered the guards not to let Bakenre approach her as a sign of Nisut's displeasure for sending such an abomination as his daughter to the Temple of the Great Neit. Bakenre and his three deputies had knelt in the road as Meryt rode past without even a glance in their direction.

The bulk of the caravan was divided into three parts with each part sent to one of three separate areas that afforded adequate shade, ample water, and plenty of forage for the camels and horses. For the next few days, her household, attendants and guards, along with the camels carrying their provisions, would camp at the current location, a park area with three clear pools and a grove of date palms and olive trees.

Meryt occupied the throne under the grand tent's canopy. She wore gold robes and held the was-scepter. Rose sat to her right, the place of honor, which made it clear she stood high in Nisut's favor. The gold udjat around Rose's neck was the one that had belonged to Meryt and marked Rose as one granted the protection of Nisut. Both Companions had similar ones Meryt had given them, though smaller.

Behind Rose Tiye translated, and behind Meryt's left shoulder stood Hedjet.

"Beseech not my forgiveness, Bakenre, but the forgiveness of Nebet Rose, for she is the one your worthless spawn wronged."

Still on his knees, Bakenre directed his attention to Rose and bowed low to touch his forehead against the ground. He lifted his head to address her. "I beg your forgiveness, honored Nebet. Your compensation for this injustice I will render."

Meryt heard Tiye whisper the translation to Rose and instruct her in the expected response.

"When compensation is made, Maat will be served," Rose said the phrase in Kemen, her accent almost making the words hard to understand.

"Nebet Rose has accepted compensation from you for this injustice done to her by your benighted daughter, Satiah. May the Gods forever curse her. Rise and my guards will show you to the accursed one. What you do with her is your decision. Keep such filth out of my sight while I am here."

The man rose and backed away with his head bowed. When he was out of sight, Meryt summoned one of the guards. "Have the compensation brought before me."

Meryt turned to Rose. "Your compensation will be brought for you to examine. This morning, I instructed Hedjet to select twelve of the best fillies and mares from Bakenre's herd of thirty. Three of these are the she-jackal's horses. I think the selection will satisfy you."

"I'm sure they will."

The sound of whinnies reached Meryt's ear before four of the horse guards appeared, each leading a string of three horses to stop in front of the throne. The majority of the horses were gray, with two bays, a red roan, and a black filly around a year old.

"Come, Rose, let us examine your new found riches." Rose took Meryt's offered hand. Hedjet accompanied them, her manner and movements showing excitement. "Nebet Hedjet, it would please me if you would point out the finer qualities of the compensation to Nebet Rose," Meryt said formally in Kemen and with her voice raised so that the nearest spectators would hear. She added in English in a lower voice to Hedjet, but loud enough for Rose to catch, "Do this in Kemen and loudly. I want the people present to know Rose was fairly compensated." To have the compensation lauded would add weight to her decision in sparing Satiah's life. After all, for the aggrieved party to receive riches was far better compensation than having an enemy executed and naught but empty hands to show for it.

Hedjet nodded and turned to Rose. "Tomorrow, I will go over the quality of each of the mares with you."

"That will be fine," Rose said.

Meryt listened to Hedjet extol on the qualities of each animal. Even though Rose couldn't understand what Hedjet was saying, it was obvious by her manner that she was pleased with the horses. Rose and Hedjet would have a pastime in common and this would help to foster a strong bond between the members of

Meryt's household. She was aware Tiye held a fondness for Rose. She was as a lioness with a cub and someone Rose could go to with any questions or concerns.

A happy household meant a happy nisut.

☙☙☙☙

"And you are from this day forward to carry the title of Nisut's Foremost Warrior." Tiye smiled with pride as Meryt handed her scimitar with its ivory handle and silver studded baldric and sheath over to an elated Hedjet. Tiye translated the speech for Rose who stood by her side.

A multitude of whoops and ululations followed from the crowd outside the front of the open tent as they witnessed the presentation.

Meryt hugged Hedjet, her smile crooked, letting Tiye know she was up to something.

The crowd parted as a groom led a glossy black filly, part of Rose's compensation, into the tent. Meryt stepped back, turned to Rose, and motioned her over.

Rose strode up to Hedjet and gathered her in a quick hug. "I'm grateful to you for saving me. You would honor me if you accept this gift of appreciation." She gestured to the filly.

Hedjet's eyes grew big. She squealed in delight, handed the scimitar and baldric to Tiye, and drew Rose into a tight hug. The two hurried over to the filly.

Catching Tiye's attention, Meryt grinned. "You don't want to go over and admire the gift?"

"My eyes can admire it from here."

Meryt chuckled then fixed her sight on the two women, saying in a loud voice and in English, "Nisut is ready to announce the feast."

Tiye stifled a laugh when the two failed to heed Meryt's words, their focus on the filly.

"Nebet Hedjet, Nebet Rose, I require your presence," Meryt said forcefully, this time getting the two women's attention. They walked over to stand by Tiye.

Meryt ordered the groom to take the filly from the tent. She went to the opening and raised her hands into the air before the spectators. "I dedicate this feast to Nebet Hedjet, Nisut's Foremost Warrior, for her bravery, and to honor the one who protected her and Nebet Rose, I also dedicate the feast to the Divine Mother Isis. Celebrate this night in honor of them all."

The crowd cheered and began the festivities. Meryt had the guards close off the front of the tent so the household could dine in private. Later, they planned to partake in the celebration, Tiye hoping to get Rose to join her and Hedjet in a dance.

Meryt took a seat on a cushion, Hedjet to her right and Rose to her left. Tiye sat next to Hedjet.

Five servants brought out the food, placing it on the dining mat. Tiye smiled when Meryt placed tasty morsels in Rose's mouth to sample. Yes, Hathor looked favorably upon those two.

Then, much to Tiye's disgust, the conversation turned to horses.

"She's a beauty, like Black Beauty," Hedjet said. "Too bad I cannot name her Black Beauty."

"Why not?" Rose asked.

"Black Beauty is a boy."

"Black Beauty is a name that can apply to a filly or a mare."

Hedjet regarded Meryt. "Henut, would Black Beauty be a suitable name for a filly?"

"Yes, a very suitable name for a black filly." Meryt looked at Tiye with a crafty smile. "Is this not so, Tiye?"

Can they talk of nothing else but the smelly, accursed beasts? "Name her Ammut." Tiye thought the devourer of the heart of the wicked, with its head of a crocodile and torso of a lion and hippopotamus an appropriate name.

Frowning, Hedjet poked Tiye's arm sharply with her elbow and said in Kemen, "Ammut yourself, you ugly rump of a she-baboon in heat."

"Cease! I will not tolerate talk of that nature when dining," Meryt warned.

"Black Beauty is the name I give her," Hedjet said in English.

The conversation on horses continued. Tiye noticed the wine cups of the three were refilled two times. She directed a silent prayer to Isis to spare her from having to act as nurse to three over indulgent individuals.

The sound of music and celebration started. Dinner ended and Meryt directed the guards to open the front of the tent, and then commanded them to carry out her throne. She departed to don festive attire. Both Tiye and Hedjet offered to help her dress, but she told them to go enjoy the festivities.

After dance instructions from Tiye, Rose joined her and Hedjet in a dance around the bonfire with many of the men and women from the caravan as well as fourteen invited guests from Iunyt Oasis. As soon as the dance finished, a cup of wine was thrust into each woman's hand. Tiye became concerned for Rose when she watched her quaff the wine down. A second dance started, and the three joined in. After this dance, another cup of wine ended up in their hands.

"Rose, this wine is very strong. I don't think you should drink anymore," Tiye warned.

"I'm fine. A little more won't hurt."

Soon, another dance started up, and the three once more joined in. Tiye tightened her hold on Rose's hand to keep her from stumbling as they danced. Hedjet danced on the other side of Rose, her steps sure and steady despite the large quantity of wine she'd quaffed. Tiye and Hedjet were accustomed to the drink, and it would require a great amount to knock them off their feet. Rose was not, and it was Tiye's duty to keep a watchful eye on her.

The music of flutes, stringed instruments, rattles and drums swirled about them in a fast tempo. Tiye kept Rose from stumbling as Rose glanced over her shoulder to an attentive Meryt seated on the throne. Meryt wore her turquoise outfit and gold hair net, the fire light and torch light making her appear more like a goddess than a nisut. Meryt sent a broad smile in Rose's direction. It made Tiye's heart happy for Meryt, and for her friend, that these two by all appearances were progressing toward a joyful union.

The circle moved forward, pulling them along with it. Tiye dropped Rose's hand to perform the series of rhythmic claps and swirls, noticing Rose had missed the cue, forgot to clap and flailed more than spun. Tiye quickly caught Rose's arm to hold her up.

"Come, let us rest for a while." Tiye led an unsteady Rose out of the circle.

"I think the dance made me a wee bit dizzy." Rose gawked about then up into the night sky. "Everything is spinning. The stars are spinning."

Hedjet joined the two and placed an arm around

Rose's waist. "I know a little heifer of Hathor who needs to be put to bed."

"I don't want to go to bed. I want to dance." Rose pushed her lower lip out in a pout.

"Later," Tiye said. They stopped in front of Meryt, who now stood, concern for Rose evident in her face.

"Too much drink and celebration," Tiye said.

"Henut, you're one fine figure of a woman." Rose leered, her gaze wandering over Meryt's body in a lascivious way. "Why don't you dance?" She frowned. "Or don't pharaohs dance?" Her manner became flirtatious. "You'll dance with me, won't you?"

Tiye watched Meryt's expression change from delight at the praise, to amusement, to concern.

"Truth often falls from wine kissed lips," Hedjet said under her breath.

"Get her inside. I think it time we all retire for the night." Meryt ordered the two guards to close the tent.

"Hello! Ma baby. Hello! Ma honey. Hello! Ma ragtime gal!" Rose sang off key.

"Is that an invocation to her Gods?" Hedjet asked Tiye.

"Send me a kiss by wire! Baby, ma heart's on fire!"

"Perhaps a feast song." Tiye cringed, not understanding some of the words.

Hedjet grabbed a lit lamp hanging from a stand and led the way down the corridor to Rose's room. Once in the room, Tiye removed Rose's jewelry and then had Hedjet help her take off Rose's galabeya, leaving the shift on.

Meryt checked the bed for any uninvited

creatures before they put Rose in.

"Tiye, you take my bed tonight," Meryt said. "I'll take yours. If Rose needs help, I'll be able to hear."

Rose looked up at the three and started to giggle. "Libertines. I've fallen in with libertines." Rose's eyes closed, head lolling to one side, mouth open, and a loud snoring ensued.

Tiye had to think about the word 'libertine' for a moment. The word was familiar, yet she didn't know in what context.

"Does she mean Liberians?" Hedjet's expression was one of befuddlement. "Why would she think we're from Liberia?"

Meryt snorted out a laugh. "Libertines."

"Is that a place here in Africa?"

Then it came to Tiye. "Why yes, it is. You can find it right within Nesneit and in the palace of Merytneit the thirty-fourth." She remembered Nebet Eliza once remarked that libertines would embrace the Welcoming Feast of Hathor with its raucous behavior she described as *abandoned*. Nebet Eliza explained the libertine philosophy, and even commented that libertines would approve the practice of a nisut having many Companions.

"I still don't understand," Hedjet said.

Tiye gave Hedjet a seductive smile and clasped her arm. "Come with me, my little heifer of Hathor, and I'll *show* you what it means."

A large smile blossomed on Hedjet's face as she got the gist of Tiye's words.

Meryt's laugh followed the two as they headed toward her section of the tent.

Chapter Twenty-two

The Valley of Wind and Dreams lay a day's ride away. The sun had already passed the zenith when the caravan reached the depression. Rose noticed the gradual change in landscape, the desert floor now surrounded by low cliffs. They soon passed small settlements, groves of date palms, olive trees, and fruit orchards.

Meryt told Rose the depression was called Re's Pathway and descended one hundred and fifty feet below sea level. At its broadest point, it stretched approximately five miles wide and eighteen miles long, containing a number of small villages built around wells and spring-fed lakes. In some areas, aqueducts carried water to fields and groves. At the end of the depression, at its deepest point, the natural wall was one hundred and fifty feet high with a narrow cleft some sixty feet wide that ran close to ninety feet through the wall to exit on the other side.

This cleft, called the Gateway of Horus, led into the Valley of Wind and Dreams. The Valley was four miles wide and eleven miles long and surrounded by cliffs two hundred and fifty feet high. The Temple of Neit lay some three miles from the Valley entrance, and around it spread the city of Nesneit. Beyond the city stretched farmland and orchards, and a few small villages.

Rose rode beside Meryt at the head of the caravan,

four guards riding in front of them and four behind them. Meryt had donned her red cloak and keffiye this morning for their ride through the depression so her people could *gaze upon Nisut's magnificence,* as she declared in a dry tone.

"Henut, how many people reside in Nesneit?" Rose asked. She had to look up at Meryt, as Bakhu stood a hand taller than Izza.

Meryt regarded her with a lift of her eyebrows. Before she could answer, jubilant shouts greeted them from the yard of a mud-brick house. As Meryt raised her right hand in acknowledgement, Rose observed the group of men, women, and children kneel and bow their heads.

"Do they ever throw stones at you?" Rose asked.

Meryt's expression was surprised. "All my people adore me. You would throw a stone at me?"

"I beg your pardon. I would never do such a thing."

"Then I would have no need to discipline you."

"I would throw a rotten cabbage at you instead."

Meryt laughed, giving Rose a crooked smile. "For that offense, your discipline would be to clean out the stable for a week." She paused for a moment. "I believe you asked me a question concerning the Valley?"

"I believe I did. How many people reside in Nesneit? There must be many since its founding fifteen hundred years ago."

"The last census two years ago showed the population of the Valley and Re's Pathway at close to sixty thousand. When you count in the vassal oases, the population under the control of Nesneit is near seventy-eight thousand."

"That doesn't seem like many. Unless the original settlers numbered ten and everybody married their cousins."

"The original followers of the Great One who left Sais to come here were close to two thousand. The last time the population approached the current number was in the reign of Merytneit the twenty-first. However, a caravan to the Black Land in the Christian year 1347 A.D. brought back the Black Death, killing over three-quarters of the population. There have been other instances of plague and pestilence." She shook her head. "As long as we have caravans that go to the Black Land and to Libya, we risk that happening."

"I'm surprised you haven't been discovered by the outside world. I know you send out caravans, and some of your people leave the Valley to live in the outside world. Your brother, for one. Aren't you afraid they will talk?"

"For any who reveal the way to the Valley, a curse is put upon them by the Gods, and their heart consumed by Ammut when they die. I am not naive enough to think no one has talked, or will talk." She shrugged. "Who would believe them? It's only another fable told by storytellers. If it remains her wish, the Great One will keep us hidden."

Rose had yet to see Nesneit, and not too long ago she'd dismissed it as exaggeration. She no longer thought the descriptions imparted to her by Meryt, Tiye, and Hedjet as bold embellishments of the truth. She hoped, for the sake of these three women, the outside world would never intrude into Nesneit with its wars, cultural and religious intolerances, quest for power, and greed for riches.

Hedjet trotted Sah up to join them, the lower

portion of her face covered by the keffiye, her black robe dingy from dust. She lowered her keffiye to speak. "The dust is thick. I have swallowed half the desert."

"Ride next to me, there's less dust up here," Meryt said.

"How much further is it to Parherry?" Hedjet asked.

Rose was informed Parherry was the name of a house located next to a spring and built over two centuries ago for a nisut to rest after her journeys. The name translated into House of Flowers.

"At most, an hour away."

"I am favored by the Gods. I think I will sleep in the bathing pool tonight."

"I sent word ahead for the house staff to fill the pool with clean, hot water. By the time we arrive, it should be ready."

Hedjet glanced over at Rose with a sly expression. "Henut, perhaps Rose will scrub your back."

"Only if she scrubs mine." Rose smothered her laugh when she saw both Meryt and Hedjet's surprised expressions.

❧❧❧❧❧

Releasing a contented sigh, Rose relaxed against the wall of the round bathing pool, the warm water easing the tenseness in her muscles. She felt bold deciding not to wear a shift while in the pool. Although Meryt and the Companions would think nothing of it, and besides, Meryt had seen her naked before. She squirmed from embarrassment and a little arousal thinking about the time she went to Meryt. The bathing room's walls served to heighten her arousal as she surveyed the realistic and provocative murals depicting frolicking nude and nubile women, some engaged in intimate embraces.

They had arrived at the oasis a couple of hours earlier and were greeted by the house staff of nine. The house was situated amidst a garden area of ponds surrounded by shady trees and beds of flowers. The inside looked Roman to Rose with its atrium and rooms on each side. The walls in the main part of the house depicted realistic nature scenes representative of the Nile with water lilies, crocodiles, hippopotami, and areas of reeds through which a striped brown cat slunk stalking birds. Rose learned from Tiye that the name 'House of Flowers' was given to the estate because one of the past nisuts' concubines were called the Nisut's Flowers, and they had spent a portion of their time here.

Her eyes focused on a scene of a fair-haired beauty reclining against a cushion with legs parted as a pretty brunette lay between them about to place her mouth on the fair-haired woman's sex. Such a bold representation of physical love both shocked and fascinated her. She wondered what it would feel like to have that done to her. A rush of raw desire struck her hard as a vision of Meryt between her legs—

"The kiss of Hathor," Hedjet said as she slipped naked into the pool beside Rose.

"What?" Rose started, feeling the heat of a blush, embarrassed that it was obvious where her gaze had been focused.

"Ahh, this is delightful." Hedjet let out a blissful groan. She submerged to wet her hair then leaned on the wall next to Rose. Hedjet turned, imparting a smile Rose had difficulty deciphering. Was it amused or seductive? With Hedjet, it could be both. "We call it the kiss of Hathor. A most delightful way of pleasuring a woman. And of being pleasured by a woman." This time Hedjet's smile was definitely seductive as she dropped her gaze to Rose's breasts.

"I...ah..." Rose felt another blush, slumping so that the water covered her bosom. She fixed her attention back on the wall and tried not focusing on *that* particular spot.

"The golden haired one is my ancestor. She's the one who passed on the green eyes to the women in my family. Her name was Katia. She came from Russia."

"She was a concubine?" Rose took another quick glance at the scene.

"Yes, of Merytneit the twenty-eighth. She was the last nisut to follow the tradition of keeping concubines. Before her reign, to be a concubine of a nisut was a sought after position although, not as prestigious as being a Companion. Rather than select citizens, that nisut traveled to Alexandria every four years and purchased pretty slave girls. Katia was purchased there."

"I thought slavery wasn't practiced in Nesneit." This information alarmed Rose. Didn't Meryt tell her that there was no slavery in her kingdom?

"It was practiced in the past. Though it was rare since selling slaves by citizens was forbidden, and few people travelled to places where they were sold. Merytneit the twenty-ninth abolished slavery. She didn't keep concubines and chose to grant all her predecessor's concubines a stipend. Katia took a palace guard as her husband. She shared him with her true love, Alea, the one bestowing *the kiss*. They had many children and were a happy family."

Just then, Meryt slipped into the water beside Rose. "Ahh, the water is perfect." She submerged up to her shoulders.

Rose surreptitiously took a glance at Meryt, disappointed that the water didn't reveal much for her to see.

Tiye slid into the pool next to Hedjet. "Nice." She let out a contented sigh, then asked Hedjet, "Who had many children and a happy family?"

"I was telling Rose about Katia, the favorite concubine of Merytneit the twenty-eighth and my ancestor, the one in the kiss of Hathor painting."

"So you say every time we come here." Tiye focused on the scene. "How do you know that one is Katia when none of the women are named?"

"Family history says she had golden hair and green eyes. That one has golden hair."

"So do six other women. Besides, that one has blue eyes, not green." Tiye pointed to one playing a small harp. "Look. Green eyes." She indicated another woman with golden hair and her arm around the waist of a black-skinned woman. "Green eyes. Besides, no records exist of that nisut having a favorite."

Spluttering out angry words in Kemen, Hedjet stood and moved quickly to the other side of the pool. She sat stiffly and shot Tiye a peeved look. Tiye returned a few angry sounding Kemen words.

"Cease your bickering. I demand peace," Meryt said. "I can imagine why Merytneit the twenty-ninth didn't want concubines. Word probably reached her they bickered and fought...like you two do. A palace full of hissing and clawing she-cats, I am sure, is why Merytneit the twenty-eighth died while in her sixth decade of life. Her ba couldn't wait to flee to the West."

Rose had to laugh along with Hedjet and Tiye, although all this talk of concubines made her uneasy. She couldn't help but wonder if Meryt planned to start up the custom again, with Rose as her first.

"The story is that an over-indulgence in *pleasuring* killed her," Tiye said.

Hedjet moved back between Rose and Tiye. "What a delightful way to die. Henut, have you ever thought about restarting the old tradition of keeping concubines?"

"O Divine Mother Isis, have pity on us," Tiye said in exasperation. "Hedjet will recruit every woman in Nesneit who is a lover of women."

Rose couldn't help but laugh, also hearing a chuckle from Meryt.

"That is one tradition that holds no appeal to me." Meryt reached over the pool's edge to a copper bowl and an assortment of oil. "Come, Rose, sit in front of me and I'll wash your hair." There was a smile in Meryt's voice when she added, "And scrub your back."

Rose hesitated for a moment before sliding over between Meryt's legs, her back to her. The feel of the soft yet firm legs against the side of her thighs, the light brush of nipples on her back, and the warm hands massaging her scalp, made Rose imagine she was Meryt's favorite concubine. *Good Lord, what am I thinking?* She felt torn by the thought, both titillated and dismayed.

She wondered just what she was to Meryt. *She said I was a member of her household. I'm not a Companion. She doesn't want a concubine, and I'm certainly not a slave.*

What was she?

Chapter Twenty-three

Zerzura. This is Zerzura," Rose said in awe as they rode toward the cleft in the one hundred fifty foot basin wall that led to the Valley of Wind and Dreams.

Meryt threw back her red cloak as a gust of morning wind blew a corner of it across her front. She glanced at Rose dressed in white Bedouin robes, astride Izza. Around her neck was the gold udjat she had given her.

She could understand how Rose would connect the Oasis of Little Birds to the access into the Valley. On each side of the cleft entrance, a fifty-foot falcon of Horus was incised into the stone, their wings spread and heads crowned with sun discs. The morning rays of Re fully illuminated the vivid colors of their plumage, re-painted every two years in green, red, white, yellow and blue.

"Home," Hedjet said as she rode beside Meryt. That one word, home, contained all the love Meryt felt for the Valley. It had taken them a total of fifty-five days to cross the desert from al-Qahirah to the Valley of Wind and Dreams. That was thirteen days more than scheduled due to longer stays at the oasis of al-Bahariya, Ipu, and Iunyt, and an extra two nights at Parherry. The hot months had started, and desert travel would be dangerous in the extreme heat of summer. Those who had to cross the desert during the hot months often traveled at night. The Gods were with them as the weather had been mild while they journeyed from Ipu to Iunyt.

The broad road leading up to the cleft was lined with three hundred soldiers, the Gate Guard, standing at attention in their red linen tunics, round bronze shields held in their left hands and iron tipped spears in their right. Two days ago Meryt had sent one of her guards to Nesneit to inform the High Priestess of Neit and the city officials of their arrival date and the approximate time. In the message to the High Priestess was an account of Satiah's treachery.

Ahead of Meryt rode six of her black-robed guards. One of the front guards carried her standard: the gold falcon of Horus crowned with the deshret and positioned on a blue background. Behind her rode the other four guards, one who led Tiye's white camel, with Tiye gazing out of the howdah. The bulk of the caravan followed behind and would arrive in the Valley later, and the packs of goods would be unloaded and distributed among Nisut's merchants to trade in the main souk. The horses that Rose owned would join Meryt's equine breeding stock in one of the many pastures located in the Valley.

Into the cool and shadowed cleft they rode. Meryt watched Rose out of the corner of her eye as she examined the cleft walls, painted with scenes of the first Merytneit leading the Great One's followers out of the Black Land and to the Valley of Wind and Dreams.

The clatter of hooves reverberated off the walls. Ahead, she saw the light of day, and soon they emerged onto the broad terrace that overlooked the Causeway of the Netjeru, the main artery into Nesneit. Her view included green carpets of gardens, groves of palms and olive trees, estates of the richer citizens, artificial lakes and ponds constructed over the centuries and fed by springs, and the pastures dotted with camels and horses. In the distance lay the city of the Great One, made bright as a jewel in the first rays of Re that broke over the wall of rock behind them.

Meryt brought the party to a halt and addressed Rose. "Behold, the Valley of Wind and Dreams and its jewel, Nesneit, the eternal city of the Great One." She smiled as she watched Rose's mouth open and eyes widen in wonder. "What say you now, Rose?"

"I...I couldn't imagine..." Rose fell silent.

"Come, Nesneit awaits us." Meryt spurred Bakhu forward to enter the gradual downward slope of the road to the tan stone paved causeway; beside her rode Hedjet and Rose.

The front horse guards had slowed so they could catch up, the rest of the guards behind Meryt. The group descended onto the great paved way, greeted by people lining the road, their shouts joyous, many of them waving palm fronds in salutation. They rode on toward Nesneit, and were now joined by an escort of twenty cavalry troopers from Nesneit's military decked out in their red tunics and bronze helmets.

Meryt inhaled deep to savor the distinctive scent of home. She smiled when recognizing the smell of flora and fertile fields of grain. Her sight took in the aqueducts and irrigation canals that fed the life giving water to the Valley's groves and fields.

Majestic date palms lined the causeway as sentinels, the breeze moving the fronds as if they too celebrated the return of their nisut.

Devotees to the God Bes stood in front of his

brightly painted shrine and waved in greeting as Meryt passed. They would pass many more shrines and small temples of the Gods and Goddesses, several honoring the deities from ancient Greece and Rome.

On they rode, now in the outlying district of the city with its residential area laid in geometrical precision. One did not find the urban sprawl as in the cities of the Black Land. A quick glance at Rose showed her expression was one of wonderment as she absorbed the scenery.

They entered the official city limits, the temples now grander lining each side of the causeway. Many of the temples copied the old style of the Two Lands with columned porticos and flat roofs. A few mirrored the ancient Greek and Roman style. All displayed painted facades depicting the divinities, and had statues on each side of the doorways.

The roar of the welcoming crowd greeted them as they approached the manmade hillock upon which stood the thirty-foot whitewashed pylon of the Temple of the Great One. Its walls were vibrant with painted likenesses of the Netjeru. Here in Neit's great city, various aspects of the Divine still found representation in different forms.

The city's cavalry veered off, leaving Meryt's contingent to ride up the temple's incline and through the great portal of the pylon, the outstretched wings of Horus portrayed on the crossbeam. They entered the courtyard, which contained fountains and a garden. At the steps of the great-pillared temple, three of the guards rode to the right and the other three to the left. The guards in the rear of Meryt went to join the others, to form a line facing the courtyard, the temple behind them.

Meryt halted Bakhu, dismounted, and helped Rose dismount Izza. She gave Rose an encouraging smile as she took her hand and led her up the steps and past the painted columns of the portico. In front of the temple's tall door stood the High Priestess and four white-robed attendants. Meryt removed her gloves and tucked them into her sash before she clasped the outstretched hands of the High Priestess, and touched the knuckles to her forehead for a brief moment before releasing them.

"Merytneit, welcome home." The High Priestess' wrinkled, ebony face bore a welcoming smile, and her dark eyes were bright.

"It is good to be home, Nebet Wadjet. How goes the kingdom?" Meryt would not enter the temple until tomorrow, when she was properly rested and clothed. Then she and her Companions would pay homage to the Great One.

"All is well." Wadjet paused, her eyes crinkled at the corners in humor. "No gold-eyed girl child has been born in your absence."

Meryt laughed, then turned to Rose and motioned her forward. "Nebet Wadjet, this is Nebet Rose." She said to Rose in English, "Rose, this is Nebet Wadjet, the High Priestess of the Great One."

Rose held out her right hand, the High Priestess taking it in both of her hands. She looked into Rose's eyes, turned to Meryt and said, "She wears your udjat, as is destined by the Great One."

"Nebet Wadjet?" Meryt asked, puzzled by the statement.

"Answers will come from the most unlikely places." She focused on Rose and smiled warmly. "Welcome to Nesneit, Nebet Rose."

Meryt translated for Rose. "Thank you, Nebet Wadjet," Rose answered in Kemen.

Nebet Wadjet then started a conversation with Tiye and Hedjet. Meryt turned her attention to Rose and took her hand. She led Rose over to one of the yellow and blue painted pillars.

Rose regarded her with a smile, the blue eyes ensnaring Meryt. The sweet smell of incense wafted from the temple's interior and the echo of a sistrum caressed Meryt's senses into a sudden awareness. Deeper into the blue she fell until past, present, and future collided in a brilliant flash of light. She saw joy and love. *I love her. I have always loved her.*

Then the blue turned an ominous green and black. The rumble of thunder rolled through Meryt's senses like a contemptuous laugh.

"Henut? Are you all right?"

The voice pulled Meryt into the present. For a moment, she was confused, trying to catch the fragments of the vision before it faded like a mirage. The vision disappeared before she could grasp it.

"Henut. Meryt?" Rose's voice held concern. She grasped Meryt's shoulder and gently shook it.

Meryt blinked to clear her head and bring her eyesight back into focus. The only sounds were that of the three women in conversation nearby. Her nose inhaled floral scents from the temple garden.

The touch on her shoulder tightened and drew her attention to Rose. Meryt searched her face for a moment. "You asked me a question?"

"Are you all right? You seemed far away."

"Weary from the journey."

"I think rest is the tonic all of us could use for a few days."

Meryt looked into the blue eyes once again.

I love her.

Those three words filled her heart with exhilaration. Yet behind this joy, loomed fear.

Chapter Twenty-four

The warmth of the late morning sun bathed Rose's face as she rode with Meryt's party north along the cobblestone road heading away from the Temple of Neit. The smaller temples, mostly shrines to the lesser Gods and Goddesses were now in evidence. A sense of mild unease caught her at the sight of a shabby shrine with peeled paint. Two oversized painted statues, around seven feet high, of the God Set stood on either side of the entrance, their red eyes seeming to follow her. A vague sense of something connected to this god brushed her thoughts, but she couldn't recall what.

The crowd of citizens thinned out the farther north they rode. They entered what to Rose looked like an affluent residential area. A series of high, whitewashed walls lined the road, some with tall, double doorways and others with gates that were open. She caught a glimpse of courtyards in which sat flat roofed houses constructed from whitewashed brick. Geometric and floral friezes painted in bright colors decorated many of the houses.

Ahead, their destination lay on the rocky hillock upon which sprawled the palace of the nisut. She saw the high, tan stone walls that surrounded the estate and glimpsed the whitewashed rectangular structure on top of the palace's flat roof.

She had heard the history of the palace from

Tiye and Hedjet. The original palace was built soon after the Valley was settled. Selected as the palace's site was the Valley's highest point, which lay due north of the city's center. Construction took twenty years to complete, as removal of most of the hilltop was done to provide a pasture area for the guards' horses, a nisut's personal mounts and other livestock. Also on the grounds were barracks for the guards and apartments for the servants.

Over the centuries, the palace had been rebuilt and expanded, and now included a set of apartments on the broad, flat roof that contained the nisut's main bedchamber, one for the queen, and three other generously sized bedchambers, two of these occupied by Tiye and Hedjet. Tiye informed Rose that Meryt wished her to have the queen's chamber. Rose felt at a loss as to what to think of this and decided not to read anything into it.

The perpendicular surface of the hill now towered above them, blocking the view of the palace walls. They entered a road that climbed and exited onto the flat grounds of the palace area, then rode through the high wooden double gates and into the expansive courtyard. On the left side of the courtyard, a paved path led through a grove of stately sycamore trees to a small shrine, and on the right stood twenty-four blue tunic clad foot guards in four rows. The horse guards veered right and behind the foot guards before they came to a stop.

Meryt rode past the guards and brought the party to a halt in front of the seven broad steps leading up to the portico. Several grooms were there to take charge of the horses and Tiye's camel.

Rose stood by Hedjet and Meryt, waiting for

Tiye to join them. Once they were all together, Meryt took Rose's hand and led her up the steps and onto the columned and roofed portico. A distinguished looking elderly man, his white tunic immaculate with its starched pleats, greeted them. His smile was broad as he bowed at the waist. Meryt and the gentleman conversed for a short while in Kemen. The conversation concluded and Meryt introduced Rose to the gentleman. "Rose, this is my steward, Nefer. He also served as steward under the last nisut."

"I am pleased to meet you," Rose said.

"Welcome, Nebet." He bowed. "I and the house staff are at your service."

His use of English surprised Rose. Meryt must have seen her surprise. "Nefer and Nebet Eliza were great friends. Nebet Eliza taught him English."

Nefer placed his right hand over his heart, his expression somber, and sadly shook his head. "Nebet Eliza was a dear friend of mine. She was greatly loved by all who knew her." Then he smiled and said to Meryt, "Henut, all is ready. I am sure you want to rest and have refreshments."

He led them toward the main entrance to the palace and through a line of palace staff. Some dozen men of different ages were on the left of them, and a little over a dozen women on the right, standing straight and dressed in clean, blue tunics. They bowed their heads as Meryt strolled past, a slight nod her only acknowledgement of their presence.

They entered the palace and into a reception hall. After a few dozen steps, they went through an entryway on the right that led into a spacious room with several platforms situated along the long walls, cushions scattered about on them. At the far end of the room was a raised dais with a throne on it. Rose guessed this room was where Meryt entertained visitors and conducted meetings with important guests.

The walls depicted a pastoral scene of groves of trees, gardens and fountains painted in pastel colors. Various colored rugs and carpets covered areas of the blue-tiled floor.

Hedjet dove into a pile of cushions on the closest platform and leaned against an overstuffed one. "How I missed home. Although, I do like our trips to al-Qahirah where I can buy pretty galabeyas and silver jewelry."

"Yes, my purse can attest to that," Meryt said as she sat by Hedjet and motioned Rose to take the place on her other side.

Tiye settled into the large cushion beside Hedjet. "A good thing I kept control of the purse, or Hedjet would have had us out on the streets begging for food."

"I bought garments and jewelry to please you and Henutsen when I wear them." She looked over at Rose. "Henutsen should open up her purse and commission Ashayt to fashion beautiful outfits for Rose."

"I will leave that up to you and Tiye to arrange." Meryt regarded Rose. "Ashayt is the tailor I commission to provide my household with garments."

Three women carrying trays with goblets and platters of food entered, followed by Nefer. The three placed the trays on the platform near Meryt. She removed a goblet from one of the trays and handed it to Rose.

Rose tentatively took a sip of the beverage, the flavor a blend of fruit juice.

Nefer started to converse with Meryt in Kemen.

The conversation concluded, and Nefer departed.

"That is too bad," Tiye said in English. "Hedjet and I will conduct the interviews. I know of one servant here I think will do. Rose can have the use of my two handmaids until we find two for her."

"Mayti and Tenre will attend to Rose until ones are found for her." Meryt addressed Rose. "The two handmaids that were Nebet Eliza's both spoke English. When Nebet Eliza's ba passed to the West, both wished to leave the palace. Aisha married and is expecting her first child. Sadeh now takes care of her elderly parents. My two handmaids will attend you."

"I think I can manage without handmaids," Rose said.

"You *will* indulge me in this." Meryt's tone and voice were very much that of Nisut. "You will need them to prepare your baths and help manage your wardrobe."

"I thank you." Who was she to argue with the commands of Nisut? *When in Rome.*

≈≈≈≈≈

Rose stood at the rail on the southern end of the roof terrace and watched as the three litters departed through the front gate of the courtyard. Each litter rested on the broad shoulders of their eight bearers, the group accompanied by twelve guards on foot and twelve horse guards. The litters were Meryt's and her two Companions' mode of transportation this morning to the Temple of Neit. Once at the temple, most of the day would be spent in homage to the Goddess and performing rituals, which Rose learned were privileged to only those who were priestesses.

She hadn't awakened until she heard the sounds of voices in the hallway, just as the first rosy hued rays of the sun shone through the entrance to the terrace. At first, she didn't recognize the surrounds and had lain in the comfortable bed for a bit longer to collect her scattered thoughts. She had slipped out of bed and donned a downy robe then walked onto the terrace to watch Meryt and her Companions depart.

Turning away from the rail, she walked around to the west side of the terrace. She glanced through the entrance to Tiye's room and saw a young woman making up the bed. A few steps more down the terrace and she stood at the entrance to Hedjet's room. A quick glance showed her bed neatly made. That could mean it was tidied this morning, or Hedjet didn't sleep in it and had shared Tiye's bed—or Meryt's. If Meryt's bed, then they were quiet as she heard not a sound from Meryt's room, which was next to her room.

She continued on to the north side of the terrace, where she gazed down into the bathing area that was open to the sky and surrounded by a peristyle. Various potted plants and small trees in containers were placed near the two bathing pools. Last night, she'd bathed in a three-foot long, oval-shaped, copper tub in the tiled bathing room across the hall from her bedchamber. The tub sat off the floor on brown-glazed bricks. Four young men had carried pots of hot water heated in the kitchen up the back stairs and emptied them into the tub.

Meryt's two handmaids wanted to assist in her bath. Rose had called Tiye, whose bedchamber adjoined the bathing room, to tell the two that she didn't require their aid. After the bath, she pulled the wooden plug from the tub's drain and watched as the water whirled out and presumably into a pipe or hole in the floor under the tub.

Beyond the enclosed bathing pools, lay the garden with its stately trees, flowerbeds, grape arbors, and garden pool. A rugged knoll lay beyond the garden, a winding path going up to a ledge where a lone tree grew. She had yet to explore the garden and grounds. This afternoon, when Hedjet returned, she would take Rose on a tour of the stable, something Rose looked forward to doing.

She strolled around the terrace to the east side, stopping in front of Meryt's chamber, and peered into it. The room was similar to hers, though the bed was much bigger. She chuckled, thinking if Meryt had twenty concubines like that past nisut, she would require a bigger bed. The mural on the wall was of the Valley as seen from the Gateway of Horus, with the fields and lakes spread out in quilted patterns, and Nesneit shining in the distance.

She walked on and entered her bedroom, now able to inspect it in the full light of the morning sun. The walls were painted with the scene of a desert oasis where graceful gazelles grazed by pools surrounded by palm trees. The blue-tiled floor held a carpet woven in a blue and green floral design. One wall had a full-length mirror with a gilt frame of antique French design.

A door next to the mirror led into a room with racks for items of clothing and shoes. Last night, Meryt had her handmaids carry over armloads of clothes and footwear from her room. Rose had protested, only to have Meryt tell her she had so many outfits she could wear a different one each day of the year and still have not worn them all. The door to Meryt's room was on the other wall. Against the wall by the main door leading into the hall, sat a dressing table of European design. Beside it was an ornate desk with a pen and inkwell on top.

Seeing the pen and inkwell made her think about Father. Meryt said the caravan to Alexandria would leave in October and Rose could send a letter to her father. It had been almost two months since she'd seen him. She missed him and knew he worried about her. But a part of her now relished this adventure, the new friends she'd made, and the possibilities she was discovering outside her own world...and inside herself.

Where would these possibilities and discoveries lead? She wasn't sure, but one person was playing an important part in them.

Meryt.

Chapter Twenty-five

Meryt went back over the reports she had received that morning from the three western oases concerning the recent incursions into the area by Imohag raiders. She wondered if it were the same ones her caravan ran into in the eastern part of the desert. So far, no attacks had occurred, but the continued presence of the Imohags would make it dangerous to travel back and forth between the oases and the Valley. She had arranged for a conference that evening with the senior officers of Nesneit's military to discuss sending troops to bolster the oases' defenses.

Since her arrival home five days ago she had spent the days and most of the nights going over reports of events and matters that had occurred in her absence. Just when she thought she was caught up and could spend time with Rose and her Companions, this new crisis arose.

A soft knock on the doorframe to the library room diverted Meryt's attention away from the reports. She placed the reports on the table in front of her chair and motioned for Tiye to enter. "Has the selection of Rose's new garments finished yet?"

Tiye took a seat on a stool by Meryt's chair. "It has not. Ashayt and her two assistants are buzzing around Rose as bees around a nectar-filled blossom. Hedjet's ba has entered the blissful realm of the Gods at the choice of materials and designs."

"O Great One, no! I had better go and give my approval to the designs selected or Hedjet will have *all* the garments fit only to wear for the Welcoming Feast of Hathor," she frowned, *or for a concubine*. Not that Meryt knew what concubines wore since she had only the murals in the House of Flowers to go by, and they provided very little information as most of the women wore nothing. However, she did know Hedjet's tastes, and this is what worried her.

"I have already approved many of the designs. I think they will meet with your approval."

Tiye had an eye for fashion and advised Meryt regarding her wardrobe. She was sure the garments Tiye approved would compliment Rose's coloring and figure. "I want to see the designs. The reports can wait a little longer." She started to stand. Tiye placed her right hand on her knee to stop her.

"There is something I wish to know," Tiye said.

"What is it?"

"Since we arrived home five days ago you have seemed distracted. I know part of that is due to your days and nights spent catching up on reports. However, I think part of this distraction has to do with Rose. When you are in her company, you sometimes watch her as if something is worrisome to you. Hedjet has also noticed. She told me last night that when she and Rose went riding to the north wall of the Valley yesterday, you had two guards ride along as escort. Why is this, Meryt?"

Meryt closed her eyes, letting out a weary sigh before she regarded Tiye. "It is hard to explain. When I stood beside Rose near the doorway into the temple, I sensed danger for her."

"Danger? From what and whom?"

"I don't know."

"Do you wish to send Rose back to her father in al-Qahirah where Ahmose can watch over her and she will be safe from this danger you think she is in?"

"No! I love her! She is mine."

"That you love her has been obvious to see." She studied Meryt for a moment. "Did you receive a premonition of danger when you returned to the temple the next day to pay homage?"

"I did not."

"I am not saying that your premonition has no basis. Yet sometimes our worries spring from other sources. Love is a powerful emotion and can bring so much happiness. These joyous emotions illuminate, yet light casts shadows and sometimes we allow the shadows in. We fear we will lose that love, or the loved one. This fear can diminish the happiness. Do not let fear control you, Meryt, or your love for Rose will never bloom to its fullest."

Meryt ran a hand through her hair. Perhaps that's all this fear was. The Great One wanted her happy or she would not have given her Rose. "You are right, I know." She laughed. "I should set up a school of philosophy and make you the grand philosopher."

"I learned that bit of philosophy from my teacher in the Temple of Hathor."

"I thought what you learned in the Temple of Hathor was how to please a woman."

"You would be surprised what bits of wisdom one can pick up while in bed."

Meryt's laugh was full and hearty as she stood and brought Tiye up from her seat and into her arms, hugging her tight. "O Wise Priestess, who am I to doubt your wisdom?" Meryt placed a tender kiss upon

Tiye's lips.

Tiye stepped slightly out of the embrace. "If it will make you feel easier, continue to have guards accompany Hedjet and Rose when they leave the palace grounds to ride. If you wish, I will explain to Hedjet why. Rose will think it routine and need not know the reasons."

"Do that. I would feel better if the guards accompanied them for a little while longer."

"As the Wise Priestess, I have more advice to give you. Tell Rose you love her."

"No."

"Why not?"

"I think it might frighten her. She's not ready. "

"She is more ready than you think. Rose is in love with you."

"No, Tiye, she has a liking for me. Perhaps not a liking for Nisut."

"Nisut is Nisut. For Rose, it is the woman she loves. Tell her you love her."

"I'm not prepared to do that, just yet."

"You're afraid to tell her."

"I'm not afraid."

Tiye stayed silent, Meryt seeing disbelief in her expression. Meryt frowned and glanced away. "Perhaps, I am...a little." She looked back at Tiye. "I want her to come to know me better before I declare my love."

"Then you should continue to woo her. Now that we are home, you will have the privacy you need without the presence of others interfering." Tiye snickered. "Although Hedjet would be an enthusiastic and rapt audience should you require one."

"And you would not?"

"Only to see your happiness and the happiness of my friend, Rose. Don't wait long to reveal your heart to her."

"I won't."

"You might be Ramses the Great when it comes to chasing away Imohags, but you have become a timid gazelle when it comes to Rose."

"That I have. Come." Meryt took Tiye's hand. "Let us see what garments Hedjet has managed to order for Rose in your absence." Meryt then smiled slyly. "Although, I think I might like a few of Hedjet's choices."

Tiye laughed. "I do have to admit, I like a few of Hedjet's choices on Hedjet."

They left the library, Meryt feeling a bit foolish that she had let fear control her. Did not Neit give her Rose? The Great One's blessing would protect them both.

After all, she was Nisut and the Setepenneit.

Chapter Twenty-six

The market behind the Great Temple of Neit bustled with business. Rose and Meryt had arrived earlier by a litter that had rested on the shoulders of eight litter bearers, and with eight guards to accompany them.

Rose took in the surrounds, finding it similar in many ways to the market scenes in Cairo with its vendors extolling their goods to customers. Many of the whitewashed, two-story narrow houses belonged to the merchants. The bottom part of the houses opened to the street where the wares were displayed, and the upper part were the living quarters. The differences in the market places here as compared to Cairo were the presence of many women merchants and the way the people were dressed.

Robes, turbans, and head coverings were sparse, although a few women did wear headscarves. The prevalent dress seemed to be short tunics for men and dresses for women. Some women wore short mantels over the dresses, or shawls. Children, for the most part, were dressed like the adults. Though the younger ones of both sexes ran about naked, most adorned with necklaces and girdles of beads and amulets.

Last night Meryt had invited her to go on a tour of the market. Rose accepted the invitation, eager to see the city. She was also glad the tenseness Meryt seemed to display around her soon after their arrival in Nesneit was no longer in evidence. Meryt's behavior had confused and made her feel hurt. Now it pleased Rose to see Meryt meet her gaze once again and see her gold eyes flood with warmth.

Rose was aware of the many curious stares, thinking most of the gawkers were probably more interested in their nisut, rather than the pale-skinned, redheaded stranger. Everyone seemed respectful and did not approach them, though a handful of people, mostly children, trailed at a short distance. Rose thought Meryt's eight guards had a lot to do with keeping Nisut's admirers and the curious at a distance.

Their attire was modest, Meryt dressed in a knee length red tunic, and Rose wore a sea-green tunic. Around her neck hung the udjat Meryt had requested she wear to show that she had the 'protection' of Nisut. Her sandals were of the Roman type with the straps laced up the shins. They were a tad large, having been Meryt's, but comfortable. Two nights ago a shoemaker had come to the palace right after the visit from the dressmaker and had measured her feet, promising he would have ten pairs of footwear delivered in five days.

They were now on the street where the farmers from the Valley and the oases sold their fruits and vegetables, most of the items spread out on woven mats. The vendors sat behind the mats on rugs, surrounded by baskets of produce, and under makeshift canopies made from linen cloth or striped blankets.

Meryt held Rose's hand as they walked down the colorful and fragrant rows of fruit, vegetables, and wooden cages holding chickens, ducks, and pigeons. They stopped by a mat upon which was displayed different kinds of melons. The elderly vendor moved to his knees and bowed at the waist several times.

Meryt spoke to him, and he glanced up, Rose noticing he didn't look directly into Meryt's face. Meryt pointed to a creamy-skinned melon and said a few words to the vendor who nodded enthusiastically, his grin revealing his absent front teeth. The man picked up the melon and handed it to her.

Meryt sniffed the top. "This one smells ripe." She held the melon under Rose's nose.

Rose smelled a slight musky scent. "That's not the way you tell if it's ripe." She snapped her right forefinger on the melon. "That's how you tell if a melon is ripe."

"By attacking it?"

"Listen carefully." Meryt brought the melon close to her ear and Rose again thumped it. "Hear the deep sound, not too hollow and not a dull thud?" She thumped it again. "This one's ripe."

"My nose and your attacks are in accord. We shall see if they prove right." Meryt handed the melon to the vendor and said a few words. He took a two-edged knife and cut the melon in several slices, exposing the milky green interior studded with numerous seeds.

The man handed a slice to Meryt. She brushed off the seeds and took a bite, nodded, and held out a silver coin taken from her belt pouch. The coins were minted in Nesneit, one side bearing the image of the falcon of Horus, and the other the image of the Temple of Neit. Rose learned from Tiye that silver and gold coins from Egypt and Libya were also acceptable currency.

The man vigorously shook his head and put out his hand in a gesture indicating he didn't want the money. Meryt put the coin back in her pouch and then bent to retrieve a piece of the melon, handing it to Rose.

"Is it a custom for Nisut not to pay when she comes to the market?" Rose took a nibble of the melon, finding the taste very good.

"Yes, even though he could use the money. You did notice I left over half of the melon? He will sell the slices for a good profit when I leave." Meryt grinned. "It will bring good fortune to whoever purchases them, for my hands held it."

"Not only a nisut, but a saint?"

Meryt's short laugh was one of amusement. "I am the Setepenneit, after all. Even so, don't expect miracles of turning lead into gold or making the desert into a paradise." Meryt bit into the melon. "Good. My nose proved right."

"It was my thumps."

"My nose."

"My thumps."

"Let's call a truce and agree it was both."

"Agreed."

When they finished eating the melon, Meryt handed the rinds to a nearby guard who then stepped over to a wooden cage holding five chickens, and stuffed them between the slats.

Rose watched the fowl peck at the rinds. "Will the chickens get lucky and avoid the stew pot?"

"Of course."

Before they strode away, the old man walked up to Rose and bowed, holding out a round melon. He spoke a single word, Rose thinking it sounded like, 'himnisut'. Two of the guards stepped toward the old man. Meryt said a few words to them, and they backed away.

"Go ahead and take the melon," Meryt said to

Rose.

Rose took the melon and thanked him in Kemen. The man bowed again before leaving.

Meryt removed the melon from her and handed it to one of the guards. She then grasped Rose's hand, lacing their fingers together.

"What is that word he said to me, himnisut?"

Meryt whispered close to her ear, "Hemenisut."

"Is it one of your titles?"

"No."

"What does it mean?"

A long moment of silence followed. Meryt glanced away, her voice small. "Wife of the King."

"Oh." Rose was at a loss for words for a second. "Why would he think that?" She fingered the udjat. "It's because I'm wearing this. That's why, isn't it?"

"He's a foolish old man. I could have been with any woman...Tiye or Hedjet...or both of them, and he would've said the same thing."

Their eyes met. Rose noticed Meryt's eyes widen slightly as if she discovered something, but Meryt broke the gaze, her expression uneasy.

"Forget his foolish talk." Meryt smiled. It looked a little strained to Rose. "Let's walk over to the leatherworkers' section," Meryt tugged Rose's hand, "I want to look at the saddles."

Rose walked beside her, wondering what Meryt had seen in her eyes.

Chapter Twenty-seven

Sounds from the terrace drew Rose's attention. She slipped her sandals on and walked over to peer out the entrance. Two servants were setting up a table and two chairs in preparation for supper. During the last two weeks, she and Meryt had supped on the terrace alone six times, usually after a day spent in each other's company during which Meryt escorted Rose around the city to visit the various temples and give her a history of Nesneit. Yesterday she and Meryt had visited one of the parks in the Valley to ride their horses and have a picnic. The guards accompanying them stayed at a discreet distance, giving them their privacy.

Rose smiled when recalling the laughter they shared over humorous incidents and stories of their childhoods. Meryt's eyes reflected not only her happiness when in Rose's company, but her desire. She knew Meryt held her desire in check, letting Rose set the pace. She also knew her own desire for Meryt was apparent in her own eyes.

That pace would remain slow. Rose wasn't prepared to act on her desire. Acting on it would involve another emotion, one she was trying hard not to acknowledge given the complications surrounding it. She had yet to cut through the Gordian Knot of her feelings. Such emotions she didn't want to think about tonight. She went over to the mirror and fastened around her neck a gold necklace with teardrop dangles. Yesterday, Meryt had presented the necklace to her, along with six gold bracelets that now adorned her wrists.

She took a critical look in the mirror to make sure she was presentable and smiled at her reflection. She had her hair pinned up, leaving a tendril free at the temples. Earlier, her two handmaids, employed last week, had applied cosmetics to her face and helped her dress. She had dismissed them with the Kemen words for 'leave me now' that she had learned, glad not to have the two girls underfoot.

She smoothed her hands down the turquoise gown, its linen material so fine it felt like silk against her skin. The dress was one of the loveliest ones Rose had ever owned, making her look like she stepped out of a Greek or Roman frieze. The color flattered her blue eyes and red hair.

Tiye had recommended the dress design and material, along with other designs for outfits. Rose found them acceptable and tasteful, unlike the more bold and revealing ones Hedjet wanted her to get, for, as she put it, 'those nights blessed by the Goddess Hathor.' The coquettish look Hedjet sported left Rose no doubt as to what Hathor *blessed* on those nights. Rose was thankful Tiye had stepped in and stipulated her wardrobe was to consist mainly of outfits she could wear in public and around the palace.

Hedjet's crestfallen expression caused Rose to concede to the Companion's selection of a white dress, shot with silver thread, as sheer as the blue one she had worn on the night in the desert when she dined alone with *Nisut*, the night she wanted to forget. She wondered why she'd followed Hedjet's suggestion on that particular dress, as well as if she'd ever get a chance to wear it. It was hardly one she would pick under normal circumstances. *These aren't your normal circumstances, are they, Rose McLeod? Nor have they been for almost three months.*

A sharp rap resonated on the door between Meryt and Rose's bedroom. She smiled wryly. *Deny it all you want, but the reason why you got that dress is knocking on the door.*

"Come in."

The door opened and Meryt entered, Rose watching as her eyes and smile widened when she stopped to look her up and down.

"Isisnofret. How beautiful you are."

Rose held her arms out to her sides and did a slow turn so Meryt could get a good view of the dress. "I take it you approve?"

"I do, very much so." Meryt stepped forward, placing her arms around Rose and gave her a peck on the cheek. A smile graced her face and shone in her eyes when she stepped back. "I am but a plain wildflower next to the bloom of a red rose."

"My, but you have a silver tongue."

Meryt stuck out her tongue and attempted to look at it, causing Rose to laugh.

"Is a silver tongue a sign of an illness?"

"It means you're clever in your use of words." She looked Meryt over, admiring how the long, peach colored tunic with its thin, white belt circling her waist accentuated the feminine curves. "You're very lovely tonight. That color looks very good on you."

"I shall have all my future garments made in this color."

Rose shook her head. "A nisut should dress in

all the colors of a rainbow."

"A rare sight in the desert. I've seen one twice in my life."

"A rainbow or a nisut?"

A laugh burst from Meryt. "A rainbow. Nisuts are common. My eyes see one every day. They like to stare at you from a mirror."

Rose's smile froze, Meryt's words calling to mind the night in front of the mirror with Nisut's eyes gazing upon her reflection. The night when the first stirrings of passion had awakened in her. In her dreams she returned to that night, and Meryt did not stop. Rose did not want her to.

"Let's see what's on the menu tonight?" Rose hooked her arm through Meryt's and they headed to the terrace.

⊰⊰⊱⊱

Meryt went over in her mind what litigations were on the roster for her to hear today in the Great Hall of Maat, as her two handmaids, Mayti and Tenre, dressed her. First on her court schedule was the trial of two individuals for the theft of a keg of beer from a tavern. The tavern owner and her two sons caught the two culprits as they rolled the keg down the road before the first light of Re. The second was a disagreement between relatives over the division of an estate of a man who had left no will and had no spouse or offspring. A shared responsibility with the three appointed district judges in the city, it was important for her to preside over some of the trials so people would see that their nisut was aware of what transpired in the kingdom.

This was the first day of resuming her judicial responsibilities since arriving home a little over two months ago. She was resuming many of her duties, and they would take her away from the palace for long hours on many days. She would miss spending time with Rose and seeing the wonders of the Valley through her eyes. However, for today, Rose would accompany her to the Great Hall of Maat and observe Nisut performing part of her responsibilities.

Sharing these past weeks together had made her fall more deeply in love with Rose. She smiled when recalling the warmth in Rose's smiles and eyes when they were in each other's company. She believed this warmth echoed her own feelings and desire. She let go a chuckle. Rose was unknowingly teaching her patience, a quality that she hadn't possessed in abundance before.

It had been hard not to declare her love, and hard not to take Rose into her arms and show her passion. From all indications in Rose's manner toward her, she felt it was time to reveal her heart. Based on her birth chart, her astrologer said five days from now was an auspicious time to bring into the light secrets and wishes. She would declare her love then.

Mayti finished pinning up her hair and stepped back so Tenre could place the deshret upon Meryt's head with its gold uraeus, the spitting cobra with ruby eyes. Tenre finished the task, and Meryt gave the image reflected back in the mirror a keen eye. Red ochre stained her lips, black kohl outlined her eyes and green paint shaded the lids, making the gold of the irises seem more brilliant.

Her official dress for this duty consisted of an ankle-length, deep red sheath that reached up to cover the breasts and was held up by two straps. It was made of the finest silk from China, the silk purchased on one of her trips to al-Qahirah several years ago. Small gold discs decorated the bodice, and the hem was banded with gold zigzags. The design was an ancient one often seen worn by Neit on the statues and artwork that depicted her. A collar of gold embossed with the falcon of Horus, his wings outstretched, circled her neck.

Satisfied with the results, she left the bedchamber and went down to the palace entry, her steward and a house guard opening the double doors. She exited onto the portico where Rose and her Companions waited. Two of the guards, dressed in their ceremonial blue tunics with black-plumed bronze helmets, bowed before her.

Her inspection of Tiye and Hedjet showed the two had dressed the part as advisers. Their simple dark red sheaths, cut similarly to hers, were unembellished. Around each woman's neck hung a gold udjat. They wore black wigs with many tight braids weighted with gold beads at the ends. A white ostrich feather representing the Goddess Maat was stuck in the back of each woman's red headband.

Hedjet carried Meryt's ornate flail with its gold handle and three beaded strands, and Tiye the blue and gold-banded crook, both ancient symbols of a nisut. Meryt controlled the urge to laugh when Hedjet smiled seductively, giving a slight flick of the wrist that made the strands of the flail shake. She knew Hedjet was reminding her of their little pastime they had indulged in last night.

Her gaze lingered on Rose, taking in the simple, long blue gown she wore with its gold sash. Her hair was coiled in a long braid on top of her head. Meryt's eyes moved to Rose's face, noticing the blue kohl-lined eyes and red ochre-stained lips.

"You are very becoming," Meryt said.

"You are very much a pharaoh." The admiration in Rose's voice and eyes pleased Meryt.

Meryt held out her arm for Rose. "I want you to ride with me to the Great Hall of Maat."

"Ride with you? I thought we were going in litters. I don't know how we will manage on horseback, unless we ride sidesaddle."

"Tiye and Hedjet are traveling by litters." She escorted Rose through the portico and to the steps leading down into the courtyard. "Behold, my Nebet, your chariot awaits you." Meryt smiled with pleasure when seeing Rose's amazed expression as the gold chariot, pulled by two sun-colored horses, stopped in front of the steps. The horses' white manes and tails were braided with blue ribbons, their heads plumed with white ostrich feathers, and the blue and gold striped blankets on their backs dripped fringe.

Ahead of the chariot were ten of the horse guards dressed in their ceremonial tunics of blue. Behind the chariot were the litters of Tiye and Hedjet, the litter bearers also dressed in ceremonial blue tunics.

"Impressive, truly impressive," Rose said as Meryt led her down the steps and up to the chariot.

The driver stepped down from the chariot. Grasping the handrail, Meryt stepped into it, then assisted Rose to stand beside her. "Hold on to the rail," Meryt said.

"Promise me we won't reenact Rome's Circus Maximus."

Meryt assumed a pompous air, her voice

officious. "By decree of Nisut, no racing is allowed in the city limits." She smiled and added, "Besides, I own the only chariot." With a quick motion of her left hand she signaled for the guards to proceed. Then with a flick of the reins she started the chariot forward.

The procession exited the palace gates and went down the hill, taking the road that led toward the heart of the city. Already the crowd gathered.

Meryt recalled the day she and Rose had gone to the market and the old man who sold melons. The words of Nebet Wadjet echoed in her mind. *Answers will come from the most unlikely places.* Looking into Rose's eyes that day, she had seen the truth in the word he had called Rose. Meryt's smile was proud as she glanced at Rose. She wanted her people to see the beautiful woman beside her. She wanted her people to see their future queen.

The Hemenisut.

Chapter Twenty-eight

H ere with a loaf of bread beneath the bough, a flask of wine, a book of verse, and thou beside me singing in the wilderness." Meryt beamed as she placed a piece of honey cake in Rose's mouth, her fingers lingering a moment on her lips.

Rose enjoyed both the treat, and the touch.

They sat on a rug under a lone olive tree perched on a ledge that overlooked the palace gardens, having just finished a late morning meal of goat cheese, ripe olives, and half a loaf of yeast bread. The basket still contained a variety of sweet treats of a honey cake, dates, figs, and a flask of fresh milk.

"And wilderness is paradise enow." Rose completed the verse from the *Rubaiyat of Omar Khayyam* she'd learned in college. She had seen Edward FitzGerald's first edition translation in Meryt's library.

With a quick move, Meryt turned her back to Rose, leaned back and placed her head in Rose's lap, stretching out her legs. She used her left foot to push off the right sandal and the right foot to remove the left sandal.

Rose admired the slender feet and the curve of Meryt's calves and the rest of the shapely brown legs visible below the hem of the sleeveless, knee length butter-yellow tunic she wore. She wore a tunic of the same pattern but in pale blue, an embroidered band of a pink and black wave design around the hem.

"With you, the desert would be a paradise." Meryt gazed up into Rose's eyes. "Your beauty could make it bloom." Meryt clasped Rose's left hand and held it between her breasts.

"My, my, but you can flatter."

"I never flatter. I have no need to."

Rose knew what Meryt meant. She could get what she wanted because she was nisut. It was others who flattered Meryt.

"What are you thinking that has made your pretty blue eyes sad?" Meryt squeezed Rose's hand.

Rose hesitated as she weighed the prudence of saying what she thought. "That sometimes it must be hard to know there are those who want to be your friend because you're Nisut and not because you're Meryt."

Meryt sat up and faced Rose. "I know that's not true with you. I don't think you like Nisut very much."

Rose delivered a small laugh. "Let's not tell Nisut that, shall we?"

"I would never tell." Meryt scooted close to put an arm around Rose's shoulders. She slipped her hand under Rose's chin, searching her eyes. "It is not Nisut I wish you to know. Or love."

It was the woman, and that woman had awakened in Rose an emotion she was afraid to name. Hearing Meryt say *that word* called it forth from where she kept it hidden, exposing it to the truth. She could no longer deny it to herself. Yet she must keep it hidden from Meryt.

Meryt's eyelids dropped and her lips parted, as she pressed an achingly tender kiss onto Rose's lips. Meryt drew away, brushing back a strand of hair from

Rose's forehead. "I love you." Meryt's voice held a slight tremor, her eyes shimmering gold.

"Do you? Do you truly love me?" Rose's bottom lip trembled, and her eyes started to tear. Was Meryt sincere? She almost hoped not, for if Meryt were sincere, Rose's defenses would crumble.

Meryt cupped Rose's face in both hands and looked into her eyes. Rose saw the confusion and hurt.

"You doubt my love? You are the only one I have ever said the words *I love you* to."

"You say you love me, yet you love Tiye and Hedjet, too." Rose's words were more like an accusation.

"You ask me to choose...you...or them?" Meryt's tone was stricken, hurt showing in her expression.

"No, in all fairness, I have no right to do that, for I believe you do love them. I know that they love you."

"I do love them. Nisut loves them. I will not deny them my love, or forsake what we have shared between us for so long." She pressed Rose's right hand on her left breast, over her heart. "You are the one who holds the heart of Benret. The woman, Benret, loves you. You complete me in a way I don't understand."

Their eyes met, Rose read the truthfulness in Meryt's.

"And you, Rose? Do you have some loving regard for me?" Meryt sounded almost afraid, her eyes holding a vulnerable look.

Rose hesitated. *Oh dear God, I'll not lie to her.* "I love you."

Meryt's eyes and expression beamed. The kiss Meryt bestowed on Rose's lips was warm and gentle. They separated slowly.

Meryt sighed happily. She stood and reached out to Rose. "Come, my beloved, I want to share pleasure with you."

Rose started to cry. Her desire had become a part of her love. Once she went down that path, there would be no turning back. In her eyes, sharing pleasure with Meryt would be a symbol, a part of the vow of marriage.

Meryt knelt beside her. "Why do you cry?" Meryt wiped the tears away with her thumbs, then tried to draw Rose close.

Rose put her hands on Meryt's shoulders to stop her. "I don't know that I can share pleasure—" Rose's throat closed, choking the words.

The look on Meryt's face was one of devastation. "Would you deny yourself love? Deny yourself physically sharing the love that dwells in our hearts? Deny yourself this?"

With one hand behind Rose's head, and the other behind her back, Meryt drew her in for a kiss. Rose accepted the kiss, hungrily devouring the sweet caress of Meryt's tongue against her own.

No. She did not want to deny herself Meryt, did not want to deny the physical expression of love with her. Yet, she knew accepting Meryt in all the ways that love entailed also meant accepting that Meryt loved and was bound to two others in all ways. Could she accept that? Was she ready to accept that?

Rose slowly and reluctantly broke from the kiss. Tenderly, she caressed Meryt's cheeks with both hands while looking into her gold eyes. Meryt nuzzled into Rose's right hand and kissed her palm.

Rose swallowed against the tightness in her throat, not sure how to phrase what she wanted to say. "I do love you, my darling. Believe that. But I'm not ready to share pleasure with you. Tiye and Hedjet, what will they think?" Although she thought she knew what the answer would be, she wanted to make sure.

"They are aware of my love for you. Tiye is my confidant and she has given me support and encouragement. Hedjet has too, in her own way. They have accepted you as a part of my household and hold you in warm affection."

Tiye and Hedjet were Rose's friends and protectors, both women warm and generous. She acknowledged she did feel a little jealousy. In time, when she became more trusting of Meryt's love for her, she might come to understand how the human heart is capable of love for more than one. She doubted her love would ever be that encompassing, but she couldn't deny it for Meryt and her Companions.

Meryt held Rose's hands in hers. "Rose, I can wait until you are ready."

"Thank you." Rose's smile was encouraging. "You know, I've never been in love. Nor have I ever said *I love you* to anyone else."

"I am honored."

"Why is it you have never told Tiye and Hedjet you love them?"

Meryt startled. "I...I think it is because they chose to love Nisut, and it's Nisut who loves them."

"Do you believe that? That they love only Nisut and not the woman?" How could they not love the woman, as did Rose? "Do you believe only Nisut, and not the woman, loves them?"

Meryt's eyes closed, Rose knowing she searched her heart for the truth. She wouldn't have to search far for the answer. In truth, Rose felt Tiye and Hedjet knew Meryt in a way she would never know her. Their blood bound them together through traditions and beliefs from an ancient time, and source.

"Grant me a request, my darling?" Rose touched Meryt's cheek.

"If I have it within my power to do so."

"Tell those two beautiful and wonderful women that you love them."

Now it was Rose's turn to brush away the tears from Meryt's cheeks.

❦❦❦❦❦

A shower of red rose petals plopped onto her head and fell around her knees. Tiye stilled the pruning knife she held against the head of a rose blossom past its prime.

"Do you come to help, or hinder?" Tiye said crossly as she brushed the petals from her hair.

Hedjet knelt close, encircled her arms about Tiye's neck and kissed her cheek. "Why do you do this when we have gardeners?"

"I enjoy it." Tiye put the pruning knife down and fondled one of the red buds. "It brings back memories of Nebet Eliza." Red roses had been Nebet Eliza's favorite flower. Meryt had brought back ten bushes from al-Qahirah four years ago for Nebet Eliza to plant. Tiye picked up the knife and carefully shaved the thorns from the stem holding the bud before she cut it to place the flower against Hedjet's lips. Hedjet kissed the flower as she offered Tiye a sweet and seductive look. Tiye rotated the bud to where Hedjet's lips had been and kissed the velvety flower while holding Hedjet's gaze. She drew the bud gently across Hedjet's cheek, watching the green eyes close in pleasure and the lips part in a slight smile. Just as she leaned in to kiss those enticing lips, the sound of scrunching gravel caught her attention.

"Ah...," Meryt said as she looked from Tiye to Hedjet. "It can wait until later."

Tiye and Hedjet began to stand, but Meryt stopped them. "Stay where you are."

Tiye saw the nervousness and uncertainty in Meryt's demeanor, which was something foreign to Meryt who almost always displayed a confident manner.

Both women rose to their feet anyway, Tiye sure something was wrong. "Meryt? What is it?"

"I came to speak to you alone...and later, Hedjet."

Tiye looked at Hedjet, noticing confusion and concern in her expression.

"Henut, have we done something wrong?" Hedjet asked apprehensively.

"You have done nothing wrong. Don't even think it."

"Can you not tell both of us together what this is about, if it concerns all three of us?" Tiye asked.

Meryt sat and motioned for them to sit in front of her. Meryt reached out and stroked each woman's face with tender regard, her eyes soft and unguarded.

"I love you, Tiye." Meryt turned to Hedjet. "I love you, Hedjet." Meryt's voice held the strain of deep emotions. Tears welled in her eyes. She opened her arms, welcoming them into an embrace. Meryt kissed Tiye lovingly on the lips, then Hedjet.

"I have always known you loved me, and I love you." Tiye rubbed the tears from her cheeks.

"I love you, too, Henut," Hedjet said. "I always knew you loved me."

Tiye knew Rose had something to do with this declaration. "You have revealed the love you hold in your heart for Rose, have you not?"

"I have. And she has said the words *I love you* to me."

"This pleases me, Meryt. I hold a fondness for Rose."

"Me too, Henut. Rose is as a sister to me. She is a *very* beautiful Isis."

Tiye rolled her eyes. She was aware Hedjet held affection for Rose one shouldn't entertain for a sister. She said a silent prayer to Neit to still the tongue of Hedjet from seeking permission from Meryt to share pleasure with Rose. Tiye would choke her if she ever brought up that subject with Meryt. Meryt might choke her if she dare mention it. She might even choke her just for thinking it.

"It gladdens my heart to hear you two say it. It was she who told me to tell you that I love you both." Meryt looked from Hedjet to Tiye. "She understands what we share between us is strong and true. However, truthfully, it's strange to her for a heart to hold love for more than one the way we do."

"It is also the physical aspect that bothers her, is it not?" Tiye asked.

"Yes, in part. Her views of desire and love reflect that of her culture. For her, I think, the two emotions intertwine. She has not reconciled what she holds in her heart with her passion. That will occur, and I will wait."

"You will not have to wait long, Henut," Hedjet said with a large smile. "You are a beautiful

Isis and Hathor has favored you with passion. Lots of passionate passion. Why, that little pot—"

With a push to Hedjet's shoulder, Tiye hissed, "Shuss," and curled her lip in displeasure.

Meryt laughed. "Have your priestess friends at the Temple of Hathor beseech the Goddess' favors for me."

"Rose is a fortunate woman. You are also a fortunate woman to have her love. She is worthy of your love." Tiye meant it. Meryt and Rose were of one heart, separated but now rejoined. She did not doubt that this had occurred to them many times in the past and would occur again in the futures to come. It was her hope that she and Hedjet would accompany these two on their journey.

Tiye dared to be brave. "She will be your queen...our queen." Tiye knew with certainty that Rose would fill this role, but didn't know if Meryt had acknowledged it.

"I haven't asked her yet, but yes, she will be our queen...if she accepts."

"Why would she not, Henut?" Hedjet asked.

"Our ways are strange to her. She needs time to adjust and become comfortable with what is a new way of life for her before I ask her to be our queen."

"Hedjet and I will be here for you and Rose."

"Yes, Henut, we will." Hedjet nodded in agreement.

Meryt placed a hand on each Companion's cheek, her words sincere. "How fortunate I am the Great One sent you both to me."

Tiye reached for Hedjet and Meryt's hands. "We are fortunate she chose you as nisut."

Chapter-Twenty-nine

"Where are Nebet Tiye and Nebet Hedjet?" Rose said in Kemen, pronouncing each word slowly and carefully to the two young women she found in the main hall dusting the chairs. They shared a questioning look with each other before one acknowledged Rose with a smile and a nod, and motioned for her to follow.

Just yesterday she and Meryt had declared their love to each other, and she hadn't had a chance to see Tiye and Hedjet since then. Late yesterday afternoon, Meryt found Rose in the library, informing her of her talk with Tiye and Hedjet about her feelings. Meryt informed Rose that she planned to spend the evening and night with her two Companions. Rose thought it proper for the three to share after opening their hearts to one another.

After taking supper alone in her room last night, Rose had retired to read one of her favorite books, *Pride and Prejudice,* borrowed from Meryt's library. Her reading was interrupted by the faint sounds of pleasure coming from Meryt's room, sounds she had heard on many other nights. She hadn't allowed jealousy to invade her heart, although it was hard for her to concentrate on reading and not imagine what the three were doing.

She had awakened early that morning thinking of Meryt and their love. She wanted Meryt in all the ways of love. She thought it right to tell Tiye and Hedjet she loved Meryt, and that she respected the relationship between all three of them.

Meryt's business this day with her military officers to discuss defenses against any future Imohag problem would afford her the privacy she needed to talk with the two Companions. Not that Meryt would demand she be included, but she might inquire why Rose wanted to see the two in private and she just didn't feel up to an explanation.

The woman led her through a door at the side of the main hall and into a gallery. At the end of the gallery, they entered into a hallway and walked to a room where the woman stopped and gave Rose a bow of her head then departed.

Rose looked into the room lit by a long row of windows near the ceiling. Shelves and cubbyholes, containing rolled papyruses and manuscripts, lined the walls. She spied Hedjet and Tiye sitting on a mat with a low, oblong table in front of them, its top filled with books. Hedjet held a piece of paper from which she read aloud in Kemen. Tiye wrote in a book using a reed pen.

A bout of nerves assailed Rose and she drew a long breath. "Excuse me."

Both women looked up in surprise.

"Rose, come in," Tiye said.

They stood as she entered. Her gaze darted between them. "I hope I'm not interrupting anything important."

Tiye made a dismissive motion with her hand. "Keeping tally of the household expenditures is a chore we can do later." She grasped Rose by the elbow. "Come, let us sit over here where we will be more comfortable." She led Rose to a space in the corner of the room filled with cushions. Rose took a seat on one of the cushions with Tiye and Hedjet sitting beside each other and facing her.

A strained silence followed, Rose staring down at her hands, uncertain how to begin the conversation.

"Would you like tea?" Tiye asked. "I can have a pot brought to us."

"No, thank you. I'm fine." Rose sucked in a deep breath and blurted, "I love Meryt."

A gentle laugh came from both women as they hugged her.

"And Meryt loves you," Tiye said with a pleased smile.

Hedjet kissed Rose on the cheek. "Tiye and I knew Hathor had struck Henutsen's heart with love for you the day when she first saw you in the museum at Giza. Why Henutsen could think of nothing—"

"Shuss!" Tiye said and gave Hedjet a stern look. She gently touched Rose's cheek. "This pleases us both and makes us happy."

"Yes, it does," Hedjet said, giving Rose's arm an affectionate squeeze.

Rose saw the sincerity in Tiye's eyes and heard it in both women's words. She choked back tears. "Thank you. I know Meryt loves you both very much, and I know you love her. I wanted you to know that I respect that."

"Thank you, Rose," Tiye said.

"There is something else." Rose felt nervous about what she wanted to say next, but thought it necessary. She felt the heat of an intense blush as she blurted out, "I would like both of you to grant me permission to share pleasure with Meryt."

Shock reflected in the two faces, Tiye's eyes huge and Hedjet's mouth open.

Then Tiye laughed, not unkindly, and held Rose's hand, giving it a gentle squeeze. "Sweet, sweet friend, permission is not ours to give. Were it so, I would not give permission for you to share pleasure with Meryt, but order it."

"Yes, I'd order it done tonight if Henutsen didn't have to attend that dinner her military officers are hosting." Hedjet's expression became artful and her voice a little seductive. "In two nights the moon is full. It will be an auspicious time to discover the mysteries of Hathor."

"O Divine Mother Isis." Tiye looked up as if beseeching the Goddess. "Do you think of nothing else?"

"I seem to remember you singing the praises of Hathor last night...and loudly." Hedjet focused on Rose. "For that night, Tiye and I will make you into a goddess for Henutsen. Not that you aren't already an Isisnofret. I do remember that dress I helped you choose. Henutsen will find you irresistible in it. Don't delay."

It was inevitable and something Rose wanted. Why delay? "Tell me how you two can transform a mere mortal into a goddess for Henutsen."

Chapter Thirty

The moon god, Aah, in all his majestic splendor, ascended golden and huge, following in the wake of the last bright ray of Re's solar barque. Tonight, he would rule supreme over stars, desert and valley.

Meryt stood on the terrace, in front of her room, watching him embark on his journey. She thought of the evening meal earlier. Rose and her Companions often glanced at one another, their small smiles betraying intrigue. She wondered what the three schemed. That it involved her was certain.

The balmy evening breeze parted her robe and she hugged it more tightly around her.

"Lovely, isn't it?"

The voice sent delight through her and she turned to behold the beauty of the woman who joined her at the rail. Her breath caught at the enchanting sight. Rose's hair fell in waves about her shoulders, a silver headband holding it in place. Her white and silver gown fastened at the right shoulder with a silver fibula, leaving the left shoulder bare. The sheer material revealed the outline of her figure, her alabaster skin glowing beneath, the coral tips of her breasts visible.

Meryt could not resist. She pulled Rose into her arms, pressing their bodies together. "Isisnofret, Aah is rising to see your beauty." A pleasant scent, delicate and floral, wafted from Rose's warm skin.

Rose's soft arms closed about Meryt and held tight before she slid her right hand behind Meryt's head to draw her mouth to her warm lips, her tongue gently seeking entrance. With a ragged inhale of breath, Meryt opened to Rose, hungrily drawing her in to return the gentle exploration stroke for stroke.

Passion coursed through Meryt's veins to the very core of her womanhood, causing the tight ache that craved a deeper touch.

A throaty groan sounded from Rose as she withdrew from the kiss, her breathing shallow. Without a word, Rose grasped Meryt's hand and led her through the portal to Rose's room, bathed in moonlight and the glow of two lamps burning with jasmine scented oil. Rose led her to the mirror and gazed at their reflections.

"Don't move until I give you permission." Rose's voice was soft yet firm. She stepped behind Meryt and pressed their bodies together. "I dream of that night in front of your mirror." Rose's voice held a quiver as she stroked Meryt's shoulders and down her arms.

Meryt closed her eyes, not wanting to see the censure in Rose's face. Images tumbled into her mind, not only of that night in front of the mirror, but the night she humiliated Rose. "Forgive me, please." Meryt did something she had never done before—ask forgiveness.

"No, my darling, open your eyes for me." Rose tenderly stroked Meryt's arms. "The dreams are ones I desire. Open your eyes and see the truth."

Meryt opened her eyes.

"Shall I tell you that your touch was the first to awaken passion in me, and your kiss became the lightning strike that sparked the ember?" Rose pressed her face to Meryt's hair. "Had you not stopped, I would have been yours that night." Rose nuzzled aside Meryt's hair to bestow a gentle kiss on her cheek. "I'll not lie and say I wouldn't have regretted it." Rose locked her gaze to Meryt's. "Why did you stop?"

"I saw the fear in your eyes. I didn't want to destroy your spirit and make you hate me."

"Not fear, surprise and confusion. I was bewildered...not knowing what to do with this new awareness your touch awakened in me." Rose's arms encircled Meryt's waist. "I'm grateful you did stop. I think if you had continued, I would have hated you, for you would have always been Nisut to me, and not the woman. It's the woman I love and desire."

"Then it is the woman you shall have."

"Yes, it's the woman I'll have tonight and always." Rose pulled the robe slowly from Meryt's shoulders, sliding it off to fall at her bare feet. The revealed beauty of the Meryt in the mirror received the caress of Rose's eyes. "Oh, so lovely you are. You are the Isisnofret. My Isisnofret." Rose cupped Meryt's breasts. "So soft and beautiful." Her palms lightly caressed the stiffened nipples, bringing forth a soft moan from Meryt. Rose then smoothed her hands down Meryt's sides and encircled her arms around her waist and pulled her close, Meryt feeling the silkiness of Rose's gown made warm by the body it covered.

Then a nuzzling aside of Meryt's hair to place a tender kiss on her neck and whisper into her ear, "Lightning has sparked the ember. Fan the ember to flame. Love me, Meryt. Show me how to pleasure you."

Meryt turned to take Rose into her arms. "Beloved one, I wish to pleasure you." Placing her hands in the red hair, she pressed against Rose's body, and bestowed a kiss on ready lips. Tongues caressed as sounds of pleasure passed from one to the other until, for the moment, the need to kiss was satiated. Their kiss broke slowly, leaving Meryt breathless. Meryt removed the headband from Rose's hair, flinging it aside, then unpinned the dress, sliding it down and over the swell of hips, to pool at Rose's feet. Meryt knelt before her and ran her hands down Rose's thighs and legs to her feet to remove soft slippers. Hugging Rose about the hips, she leaned her head against her abdomen, feeling the brush of the rough, red hair against her breasts.

She inhaled the scent of this beautiful woman, as sweet as any flower and as potent as any wine. With tenderness, she pressed a kiss onto Rose's abdomen, feeling Rose's hand in her hair, and hearing her gasp of pleasure. She stood slowly, her sight feasting on the alabaster skin that shimmered in electrum from the mating of the silver moonlight and the gold glow of the lamps. "You are Isis come to walk among us."

She held Rose's hand and guided her to the bed where she slid upon the cool sheets, bringing Rose to rest atop her. "Lie against me and let my skin drink you in."

Rose relaxed against her. Meryt spread her legs allowing Rose's right to nestle between them. The silken tresses of Rose's hair spread across her bosom, a loose strand across her face. With worshipful gentleness, her hands caressed Rose's back, gliding smoothly to firm buttocks, there to linger and lightly clasp. She hugged Rose close and slowly rolled over, Rose now beneath her. Meryt gazed down into her eyes. As lovers had since Neit created humankind, they smiled into each other's eyes, pouring out the joy kindled by the mere presence of the other.

"I love you, Isisnofret."

"And I love you, my darling." Rose reached up and entwined her arms lightly around Meryt's neck, drawing her in for a deep kiss.

A stab of desire hit Meryt hard in her core, bringing a gasp and a surge of her hips against Rose's thigh. Tonight was for Rose's pleasure. She lifted from Rose and moved to lie on her side. Tucking back a lock of Rose's hair, she said, "My Isisnofret, I wish to pleasure you. This night is for you. Will you accept the gift of this night from me?"

Rose rested a gentle hand on Meryt's cheek. "Yes, I will."

Drawing Rose against her, Meryt began the tender worship of Rose with her mouth and touch. She was the priestess guide, leading the initiate through the mysteries of life and love, pleasure and passion.

Then again, perhaps her beautiful Isis would guide her this night, and Benret would be born anew.

❧❧❧❧❧

Meryt's warm body pressed to her own, the caress of her loving hands, and the sound of her voice became Rose's whole existence in this place and time. She arched into the sensations flooding her senses from Meryt's ardent mouth that suckled her right nipple, her tongue softly caressing. Rose's sounds of pleasure flowed in soft sighs, an ardent request for fulfillment. Coolness on her nipple as Meryt's mouth departed, and then a sweet kiss left on each breast as a promise to return.

The heat of Meryt's mouth pressed on her own and with excitement, she opened to allow a deeper kiss that raged through her, causing a cry to escape as she surged against the solid warmth of thigh pressed hard between her legs.

"My Rose, how I love you." Meryt rained small kisses on Rose's face and the corners of her mouth. Meryt lifted from her to nestle against her side. Her fingers journeyed over Rose's stomach and through the patch of hair to massage with exquisite care over that point requiring salvation from the ache of desire.

Rose moved her hips in a small circle as warm fingers traced around her opening to catch the wetness that seeped from within, stroking it over that tender place at the apex of her thighs. Her breath caught and she released it in a cry of need, clutching the covers, her eyes shut tight. "Please, please."

"Tell me you want this, my beloved."

She opened her eyes to peer into those of Meryt that were now darkened to bronze by the fusion of moonlight and firelight. "More than anything."

Meryt's eyes held hers as her finger pushed carefully through the wetness and entered the portal and paused. "You must tell me to stop if I cause you pain."

"Ahh." Rose surged upward, the need outweighing the dread of pain. She felt slight resistance, then a gentle finger caress within her. She pushed her hips upward as muscles pulled the touch deeper. The rhythm of passion, the thrust and retreat, thrust and retreat, thrust and retreat, drove her higher.

"Isisnofret, so very beautiful you are." Meryt's mouth descended on Rose's to catch the cries. The thrust of her fervent tongue matched the rhythm of passion repeatedly stroking the sensitive place as it entered her.

Rose tore from the kiss, her breathing ragged and hot. With a cry and final arch to keep the touch deep within her, she splintered and then plummeted.

"For me, Isisnofret, for me."

Meryt's soft lips were on her eyelids and moved to the corners of her eyes to catch the tears. Rose felt the gentle retreat of a finger from inside her, Meryt's hand remaining as a mantle to protect her secret place.

Meryt rolled onto her back and brought Rose to rest partially on her, Rose laying her head on Meryt's shoulder. Meryt's right arm slid farther under her, drawing her closer, warm and protective.

"Rest now and let me hold you." Meryt nuzzled her face into Rose's hair.

The pleasure left Rose drowsy and she drifted into a warm place lulled by the sound of soft breathing and the steady heartbeat beneath her ear.

Later, the feel of Meryt's caress on her hair opened her eyes to a semi-darkened room. She removed her head from her darling's soft breast and rose up, gazing down at Meryt's tender smile and gold eyes deepened to bronze by the moonlight and fire from the one lamp that remained lit.

Meryt brought Rose back down to rest her head on her shoulder. "So beautiful you were when your passion peaked." Meryt pressed a tender kiss on Rose's forehead. "How are you feeling?"

"Hmmm, wonderful."

"Yes, it was that." Rose heard a smile in Meryt's tone. "Any pain?"

Rose moved her legs, feeling a trivial amount of soreness. Meryt's touch vanquished all the worries about the pain she had heard there would be when the maidenhead was breached. "You were very gentle."

"I never want to hurt you."

"You won't." Rose lifted her head from Meryt's shoulder and kissed her. "Now, darling, I believe it's my turn to pleasure you. You will have to guide me—show me what you like."

Meryt rolled them over, Rose now beneath her. "Tonight is for you. Your pleasure is my pleasure."

The warm slide of Meryt's silky skin and hair descended, followed by open kisses and the quick traces of tongue over Rose's stomach as Meryt settled between her legs. Soft kisses grazed her inner thighs.

The realization of what was happening froze Rose. The kiss of Hathor would bring, for Rose, the abandonment of all control, the surrender of herself to another in a profound way.

"Open to me, my beloved."

With love and trust, Rose opened.

৯৫৯৫৯৫৯৫

The delicious feel of fingers stroking that pleasure place between her legs drew Meryt from sleep. A tender ache filled her chest, spreading to tighten her throat and bring tears to her eyes. "Isisnofret. Come here. Kiss me."

Rose slid up along Meryt's side, her fingers now still on that place needing a deeper touch. Warm kisses rained on Meryt's face and mouth. The kisses stopped as Rose pushed herself up, Meryt seeing her eyes glisten in the light that heralded the rebirth of Re.

No words were spoken as Rose once again stroked that place which became the point of Meryt's sharpest need.

Drawing Rose against her, she placed her hand over the fingers that stoked her hunger to press them more firmly on the need. Their hands moved in tandem until Rose caught the rhythm of Meryt's hips and led the steps of the dance.

With a fierce cry, Meryt peaked, the torrid touch of fingers stilled for a moment before again seeking the cadence.

"Inside." Meryt guided Rose's finger into her, the rhythm and steps of Hathor's dance quickly found by Rose's hand and Meryt's hips. The dance quickened, the drum of heartbeats thundered in her ears, the breath gathered in a great inward rush to leave in the gust of a desert wind.

She opened her eyes to see Rose made flame and alabaster in Re's emerging light.

In her Isisnofret's arms, Benret was reborn.

Linda North

Chapter Thirty-one

The bare breasted, nubile, honey-skinned dancer arched backward, her dark chestnut hair sweeping the floor. Her arms and hands weaved sensuously and reminded Tiye of two cobras in a mating dance slithering in rhythm to the beat of the drums and tambourines. The throaty sounds of the one reed instrument added to the sensuality of the music. A lute and two flutes played the melody.

The dancer's small, black cat tattoo on the upper right thigh marked her as a devotee of Bast and peeked from the dangling strands of beads girdled about her waist.

Tiye glanced around at Meryt's twenty-five dinner guests, seeing their looks of enjoyment.

"Grrrl," Hedjet leaned over from the cushion by Tiye's side to growl in her ear, the warm breath sending a delicious shiver down her back. Hedjet scooted closer to place an arm around Tiye's waist. "We should pay homage at the Temple of Bast and pet the temple cats."

"Mmm. As long as they don't scratch." Tiye had to agree with Hedjet's appreciation of the young dancer as she watched her slowly rise to stand straight, her body now rapidly shimmying to make the beaded girdle shake and rattle, and the small breasts jiggle.

"Grrrl. I wouldn't mind that Bast cat scratching my itch." Hedjet nibbled Tiye's neck. "Or giving me a little bite or two."

"I've kept my teeth sharp for you." Tiye lightly nipped the rim of Hedjet's ear.

Meryt had Tiye and Hedjet hire the best entertainers, and purchase the finest food for tonight's private feast to mark the first night of the annual celebration of the Welcoming Feast of Hathor. This holiday honored the completion of the Temple of Hathor in Nesneit fourteen centuries ago. For the next three days, celebrants would throng the city's streets, most of them inebriated and out to honor Hathor's aspect as the goddess of physical love. Nine months from now Nesneit would see a boom in Hathor babies. Many believed these children blessed, and it mattered not that some mothers were not betrothed or married, or that some of the children born didn't have features similar to the mother's husband.

A wry smile formed on Tiye's lips when she recalled how Nebet Eliza would always go into a discourse on how the celebrants of this holiday were in step with the debaucheries of ancient Rome. Her smile stretched into one of warm amusement when she recalled the time years back she had returned from the Temple of Hathor to hear sounds from the library. She went to investigate and discovered Nebet Eliza and Nefer celebrating Hathor in the corner among the cushions. Tiye had slipped out of the library unobserved and never revealed what she'd glimpsed.

She focused her attention on Meryt and Rose sitting beside her. Rose leaned back in the embrace of Meryt's arms that encircled her waist, their heads close together. They seemed to be enjoying the dancer's sensual performance, and it pleased her to see that the only red on Rose's cheeks came from cosmetics and not from blushes.

Rose had discovered her passionate nature. Tiye felt that a part of this awareness was why Rose appeared more comfortable when seeing sensuality, such as this dance, expressed in her presence. Although, the sense of what was Remenneit propriety remained something, she was sure, far removed from what was customary in Rose's society.

Not much of Remenneit propriety would be in evidence in the streets of Nesneit for the next three nights. Tiye thought it good Meryt never liked to take part in the public revelry, which could, and probably would, in many instances become lewd. Meryt always hosted a feast for friends on the first night. To take Rose out in the streets would make her run across the desert back to al-Qahirah.

The dancer concluded her performance. The appreciative audience tossed coins in her direction, which she deftly scooped up. A group of acrobats tumbled onto the floor, Tiye not interested in their antics. She wanted to see more dancers or for the singers to perform.

When she, Meryt, and Hedjet would leave to pay homage to Hathor tomorrow night, the guards would clear the way to the temple. On that night, only those who carried the title of priestess were allowed into the Temple of Hathor. This privilege included priestesses from the temples of other goddesses. Meryt, as the Setepenneit, was an honorary priestess of Hathor on that night, and she was obligated to pay homage.

It was custom for the three to honor Hathor in pleasuring when they returned from the temple. However, this year Meryt wanted to honor Hathor with Rose. Not that she minded. For now, Meryt's desire was only for Rose.

Hedjet had complained that Meryt hadn't shared pleasure with her in four weeks. Tiye had laughed and reminded Hedjet of when she first joined the household. Tiye had not seen either Hedjet or Meryt in her bed for almost a month.

To Hedjet's credit, she hadn't brought up the subject to Meryt of sharing pleasure with Rose. Tiye had warned her not to do it, saying it was up to Rose to approach Meryt with that request. She didn't think that would ever happen.

She slipped her arm around Hedjet and nuzzled her neck, catching the sweet scent of the perfume she wore. Glancing down, she admired the yellow, almost diaphanous gown Hedjet wore for the occasion and how her dark nipples were noticeable and deliciously enticing. She did love to suckle and kiss Hedjet's breasts.

Yes, she'd celebrate the blessings of Hathor later tonight in the arms of the one who lodged in that special place in her heart.

❧ ❧ ❧ ❧

The sound of distant revelry in the city streets of Nesneit drifted in and out of that drowsy place between wakefulness and sleep. Rose reached out her hand and touched the space on the bed beside her, finding it empty.

A rustle of fabric and the muffled tread of feet let her know that Meryt was returning from paying homage to Hathor.

She smiled in welcome and rolled onto her back, eyes still shut. "Hmm, darling, come here. I've kept the bed warm for you."

She barely had time to draw in a breath when a hand was roughly pressed over her mouth, and a sharp point jabbed her neck, causing her eyes to shoot open. She instinctively recognized the tip of a knife pricking her skin, and she stilled, trying to suck air through her nose.

Rough words from a male voice were muttered, Rose not understanding, except for one, "Shuss," a warning to keep silent.

Her eyesight adjusted to the subdued light of a lamp, allowing her to see the dark, frowning visage of a male wearing Bedouin robes and a keffiye. The hand at her mouth moved off and grabbed the front of her shift to pull her up into a sitting position, the point of the knife still at her throat.

"Shuss!"

She sucked in a harsh breath and gasped. She wanted to cry out but the knife pressed to her neck kept her silent.

The man tugged at her shift in an indication that she was to stand. She complied, her wobbly legs weak and breathing shallow. Her sight took in two other figures, dressed in desert garb, one a young but brawny male who held a lit lamp. He placed the lamp on a nearby table and stepped behind her. The other person lurked in the shadows where the lamp's light weakly pierced, his back to her. His stature appeared short, a black and white striped keffiye obscuring the sides of his face. He peeked into the dimly lit hallway through the thin crack between the door and doorframe.

There was movement by the man behind her and his hand grabbed her hair roughly at the base of the neck, forcing her head back. The round opening of a small, water skin was pressed against her lips. A bitter liquid flooded into her mouth, and she swallowed rather than choke. Then there was the slide of a thin cloth against her mouth and a yank, forcing it between her teeth. A tug on her hands brought them behind her back where they were tied together at the wrists.

The man facing her dropped the knife from her throat and stared hard into her eyes in an ominous warning as if to convey that if she caused trouble, she'd pay. He grasped her by the arm and forcibly walked her to the door.

The man at the door shot his hand up to stop all movement and stepped back from the door. Rose saw the faint glint of the lamplight reflect from the blade of a knife the man removed from his belt. The door swung open, and like a cobra, the man sprang out, his hand with the knife quickly thrust forward. He swiftly stepped back, the knife slipping from his hand to clatter onto the floor.

In horror, Rose watched as Meryt stood in the doorway, the dim light from a hallway sconce showing her stunned expression, a dark blossom of blood from the left side of her chest staining the white dress.

A scream issued from Rose's throat, muffled by the gag, as she saw Meryt stagger back and hit the far side of the hallway wall. Meryt slid down the wall and sank to her knees, clutching her chest. Her gaze locked with Rose's, holding love, an apology, and sorrow.

Rose struggled to go to Meryt, her cries smothered by the gag. She sagged, blackness and light fading in and out as her eyesight dimmed. She felt the sensation of being lifted and thrown over a shoulder, then jostled from the stride of the abductor.

It became hard for Rose to draw breath through her nose, and she thought she'd suffocate. She weakly struggled, wanting to go to Meryt. The jostling from her abductor's hurried stride continued and the muffled clomps of feet sounded as if they descended a stairway. A female voice issued a question, then a panicked cry as the thuds of feet retreated and a voice yelled in alarm.

Then coolness surrounded Rose and she realized they were outside in the night air.

Her head spun, and consciousness faded as black descended.

Chapter Thirty-two

The barque swayed gently back and forth on the Nile. The full moon's reflection glinted on the river's surface in broken ribbons of silver caused by the flow of water as it coursed around submerged obstacles not evident to the sight. There were no luminescent eyes of crocodiles or hippopotami visible, giving her some relief that this frail barque wouldn't be rammed, and she wouldn't tumble into the water to be devoured.

"So, you're back," a voice boomed from behind her.

She twisted around, seeing Set at the stern. He did not frighten her. She had travelled with him one time before, though the memory of that time was as murky as the Nile floodwaters.

"I still await your directions," he said.

"Directions?" Set's words tickled a memory. Home. She had the vision of gold eyes holding her reflection.

"Take me to her...to the Valley of Wind and Dreams."

"Ugh. Never could abide that place. I only go there at Maat's bidding." He snickered. "I did enjoy my last bidding. Even dropped in to see my shrine. Such as it is." He slowly shook his head. "Pitiful. The paint peeling off, no coins in the donation box, dried up old priests. I get no respect any more. Not even from that

wife of mine, Nephthys. Evil. That's what they say about me." He stared at her, his eyes glowing red. "You know, I'm not an evil God—just misunderstood. Light casts shadows. I have my Maat side, just as you have your Set side."

She knew of the stories told about him. He started out as a God with some respect and power. The politics of men had corrupted him into the murderer of his good brother when the kings who worshipped him were defeated, and the gods of the conquerors ruled in his place. He was still the protector of foreigners, like her, and the guardian of the desert.

Now a vision filled her memories of Meryt falling, blood on her chest, the gold eyes meeting hers in a final goodbye, full of love and sorrow. She cried aloud, the tears streaming hotly down her cheeks. The one she loved was taken away, and she had no home.

"Ugh," he rumbled. "I never could abide the tears of a woman ever since Isis cried for Osiris. Seeing her tears made me regret killing my brother. I should say almost made me regret doing it." He sighed. "All right, dry your tears. Not that I have a choice...but I'll help. Even we Gods must serve Maat."

"There is no help. She's dead." She wiped the tears from her eyes, only to close them against the pain.

"Dead?" He snickered. "Dead is all a matter of interpretation. Death is neither here nor there, up or down, back or forth, in or out. You'll see."

The sweet fragrance of incense filled her nostrils, the sound of chants, drums and sistrums filled her ears. She stood behind her beloved Nofret in the Temple of the Great One. She beheld the Venerated One with her hand resting over the left breast of Nofret, chanting the ancient invocations to call the Great One. Time

seemed to unravel in a spiraling hoop, when suddenly
the Venerated One and Nofret jerked as if tugged by a
rope. Ancasta caught Nofret against her, and with the
help of two friends of Nofret, lowered her to the floor.

Nofret opened her eyes, their irises the gold color
of those of the falcon of Horus.

Those eyes ensnared Ancasta and she soared with
the falcon through the ages to come.

Kasia had left Constantinople to travel with her
father to Alexandria on one of his trade ships. She had
always heard stories of pharaohs and of Cleopatra and
wanted to see for herself this ancient land. After much
cajoling, her father had agreed she could come with
him, but she was to go no place unaccompanied. After
all, she was a virtuous Christian girl, and Egypt was
under the control of the followers of Muhammad. These
pagans wouldn't be above kidnapping her to sell as a
slave or concubine.

She watched from the deck the bustle of brown
men and broad-shouldered Nubians with skin the color
of ebony carrying cargos from, or to, the holds of nearby
trade ships.

Her eyes caught sight of a white Arabian horse
prancing proudly through the crowd. The rider was
richly dressed in robes of silk, his turban of yellow
silk, and the lower part of his face covered. From his
slimness and small stature, he appeared to be a boy,
yet, sitting astride his mount straight and proud he had
the manner of a person of importance. Accompanying
him were two brawny guards dressed in black robes and
mounted on black horses.

He rode nearer, now a few yards away from the
ship. She noticed his small and delicate hands adroitly
holding the reins. He looked up, his eyes locked with

hers. The golden gaze sent her spirit flying.

Maria knelt in the tent on the soft carpet and shivered, wondering what her new master would be like. She knew why he had bought her, for what purpose he would use her. She cringed from the memory of standing naked on the platform in the market place. She had closed her eyes, not wanting to see the lustful beasts' leers feasting on her body. That she remained a virgin was a miracle. However, she learned that her virginity and blue eyes would bring in much gold in the slave market in Tripoli.

She shivered again, a prayer on her lips. How futile to pray. Where were Jesus and his mother when her drunken father sold her to the Moorish slaver in Granada to pay his debts?

The rustle of robes made her cringe and drop her gaze to the rug. A man knelt in front of her. She could see part of the brocaded, blue robe he wore.

A soft, delicate hand slid under her chin and lifted her head. She gazed into the face of a beautiful woman, her skin as black as that of any Moor's. Their eyes met. The gold eyes of an angel captured Maria, and she ascended.

Naomi poured the water from the pitcher into two cups and placed them on a tray. Her father, Moses Israel, was the principal scholar and seller for ancient Egyptian manuscripts. He had a prospective buyer for some ancient papyruses from the Ptolemaic period. Customarily, she and her younger sister were kept out of sight of any prospective buyers. However, this customer was different. This one was a woman.

Her younger sister, Miriam, hurried into the kitchen. "I saw the lady. Her gown is beautiful and her hat has a blue jewel."

"Have you been spying?"

"I did peek through the curtain. I know she is beautiful beneath her veil. Her carriage is very pretty with gold decorating it and has red curtains. I think it came from Paris and belonged to a sultan."

"There are no sultans in France. They have kings. King Henry the fourth." Naomi picked up the tray and headed to the library. She went through the curtain and over to the library table where the lady stood as she studied the papyruses. Embroidered flowers and vines decorated her dark blue robe, the round hat that perched on her head held a large sapphire in front. An almost sheer veil hid the lower portion of her face.

She lifted her head, the gold eyes meeting Naomi's. The tray clattered to the floor, the cups breaking. Those eyes took Naomi beyond the earthly realm.

Although startled, Rose found herself looking into the most beautiful and mesmeric eyes she had ever seen. The irises were golden yellow, the shape catlike, and the lashes black and long. These eyes captivated her. She 'recognized' those eyes.

The vision scattered as she felt a rough shake to her shoulder. She opened her eyes to see not her darling, but the snarling face of Satiah.

࿊࿊࿊࿊

All was dark around her, a void without form, no sound, not even that of her breath. Then her ears caught a faint thumpa, thumpa, thumpa. Was it a heartbeat she heard? Was it her heart?

A dim light appeared in front of her and grew brighter until she saw the glowing form of a golden scale suspended before her in the void. The left pan of *the scale held a heart, her heart, still beating.*

She knew this was judgment and Maat would weigh her heart.

A menacing growl somewhere to the left drew her attention. Red glowing eyes fixed on her heart. Now a sickly red light revealed Ammut, demon eater of the soul. Her head was that of a crocodile with the grin forever fixed in mocking disdain, the front of her body that of a lion and the rear a hippopotamus. Ammut stood ready to devour her heart and send her ba to oblivion if her heart failed the test of Maat. If her heart passed the test, she would go to the West, ascend into the starry night, and dwell with the gods.

How she came to be here she couldn't remember. Did she have a name or a past? Her heart held all of what she was, what she had been, and if she had followed Maat.

Silver light appeared above her head, and she observed the slow, spiraling flutter back and forth fall of a white feather. Maat's ostrich feather plucked from her headband, the weigher of souls.

She watched as the feather floated toward the right pan of the scale, now a finger's breadth away. She held her breath and waited to see if the heart sank or rose.

Time stopped, the feather hovering above the pan.

A brilliant flash of light blinded her, the heat a blast from a smelting furnace. The seat beneath her felt solid, yet she had the sensation of movement. She forced open her eyes, shading them with her hands as she squinted against the light. "Where am I?" *she cried out in alarm.*

"Daughter of Kemet, do not fear. The solar

barque of Re carries you back to the beginning." The voice was gentle and that of a young woman.

"Who are you?"

"My names are many, for I am many, yet one. Your need for me has called out, and I come to you as Isis."

She held her hands above her eyes in an effort to see the Divine Mother. All she saw was the blinding light. "O Nebet, Divine Mother, she who conquered destiny, I have lost who I am. You, who have succored the lost, have loved us mere mortals. Tell me who I am, why I am here?"

There was coolness and the smell of incense and herbs. She stood naked, her bare feet planted on the cold stone floor. With eyes closed, the clanks of sistrums, chants, and beats of drums vibrated through her consciousness, pulling her out of time and place.

"Daughter of the Two Lands, you are the Setepenneit."

The words moved through her, not touching her ears. She opened her eyes to see the beautiful face of the Great One. Her smile was serene, her gold eyes holding the secrets of the beginning of time and the hidden age to come.

"Many will bear the name, Merytneit, yet you are the one I love."

"I am blessed, Great One."

"The time will come when I will send Maat back to rule. Through you, I will do this. That time, to you, is far in the future, and you are still a child with much to learn. Many times will I return you to the worldly realm to grow and learn."

"As you decree it, Great One."

"Your heart has chosen Ancasta as mate. She will

travel with you on your journeys. Love and respect her, Merytneit, for she holds half of your heart. Heed to the lessons she has to teach you. Some will be harsh, yet each is a step toward purpose."

Neit placed her right hand over Merytneit's left breast. The touch raced through her as a lightning bolt, restoring her heart and with it, her ba. She forever would belong to the Great One, would forever serve her. She lost herself in the gold eyes. Then blackness fell.

Merytneit, Setepenneit, and first nisut for Neit's people took her first breath of life. She opened her eyes. "Ancasta," she whispered, reaching up her right hand to touch the gold curls and trail fingers down the soft cheek.

"Nofret." Ancasta looked into her eyes, Merytneit falling into the blue depths, spinning and spinning into a wide spiral, the rattle of sistrums and the scent of incense blending into light and images. She closed her eyes against the intensity of a flash of light brighter than the rays of Re.

A woman's happy laughter. Meryt also laughed at the brown tabby kitten's playful antics as it grabbed for the wiggling fingers of her beloved Kasia. Kasia picked the kitten up, hugged it against her cheek, the kitten burrowing its face into her dark hair. Kasia laughed again, her blue eyes meeting those of Meryt who fell into them.

"Mi amada," was said in a heated moan as the woman arched in Meryt's arms, her rich brown hair spread across the pillow, her breath suspended for a moment, then released in shuddering cries as she peaked.

The blue eyes opened as Meryt groaned out, "Maria," and fell into the blue depths of the vortex.

"*Isisnofret,*" Meryt breathed out in a soft sigh as Naomi waded out of the pool's water toward her, the moonbeams kissing her hair and skin. Naomi's blue eyes were silver in the night, Meryt pulled into their depths.

"*Rose,*" Meryt cried out in a heated rush of breath as her passion crested in the arms of her love.

"*Rose,*" she cried again, this time in fear as her beloved was taken from her embrace by the rough hands of a black-robed figure, the end of the keffiye pulled across the lower portion of his face.

"*No! You cannot have her. She is mine!*"

The figure clutched Rose to his chest. His fiery red eyes mocked, and his voice boomed, "*Yours?*" He laughed. "*Your arrogance has deluded you.*"

"*Neit gave her to me.*"

Rose lifted her head, meeting Meryt's gaze, blue eyes filled with sorrow.

"*Rose!*" She reached for her beloved. A searing burn in her chest knocked her to the floor. She watched helplessly as her love was taken away.

"Be still, Meryt," Tiye said, pressing Meryt's arms to the bed. "Try not to move, you'll start to bleed."

"Rose?" The vision scattered and fled. Meryt stared into Tiye's face and watched as her dark eyes became as desolate as the heart of the desert.

"Rose!"

Chapter Thirty-three

Our lives are forfeit." Satiah's cousin, Penre, paced with a slight limp from one end of the tent to the other. He stopped and contemptuously glowered at Satiah. "We will be hunted down like jackals and killed."

"Shuss, you worry too much." Satiah wished Penre would just shut his mouth.

"You accursed fool. A servant recognized you and now Nisut's guards will find us."

"All is chaos in Nesneit. No one will follow us."

Penre grabbed his hair in both hands and pulled it, shaking his head, and then started to pace once again. "It will be simple, you said. We will go into the palace of Nisut and take her on the second feast night of Hathor, you said. Nisut and her Companions will be in the Temple of Hathor paying homage all night, you said. The palace servants and guards will be celebrating and we can easily get away with the woman, you said."

He stopped in front of Satiah, his face twisted into an angry grimace. "Except Nisut stayed not in the Temple of Hathor all night, did she? You have murdered Nisut, the Setepenneit. The Goddess will curse you...and me." He raised his voice to a shout. "Our own people will curse us!"

A laugh of amusement was Satiah's response. Neit had forsaken Nisut for turning her heart against

Maat by unjustly punishing Satiah when she tried
to free Nisut from Serpent Woman's poison. Maat
had guided the knife in Satiah's hand into Nisut's
corrupted heart.

As for her people, they already cursed and spit
on the ground at the mention of her name. Women
who had claimed to love her, whom she'd lain with,
now looked at her with disgust as if she were droppings
from a dog.

Her father turned his face away, refusing to let
her take meals with him. Then there were her two
mares and filly paid as compensation to the Mercan.
But the worst insult was when her father had taken her
to the village souk, tied her to the whipping post, and
stripped her to the waist. He then beat her back with
his horsewhip until she bled. Almost the entire village
witnessed the humiliation. The welts had faded, but a
couple of lashes had cut deep, leaving scars that were
still puckered and red. These two scars would forever
remain. Compensation was due her for this injustice.
Maat demanded it.

Penre shook his head. "I shouldn't have paid
heed to this foolish plan of yours."

Satiah snorted. "You want to remain in Iunyt all
of your life, an object of pity? There goes Penre, the
poor cripple who takes care of his family's goats."

His scowl and darkened cheeks let Satiah know
her words struck his heart. Penre had often spoken
to her of his dream of going back to al-Qahirah, ever
since he first visited that city almost two and a half
years ago when Nisut took her camels to sell. He had
signed on as a camel drover. But a little over a year
ago a fall from an olive tree had broken his leg and
left him with a permanent limp that would prevent

him from walking the miles a caravan would travel in a day. There was no inheritance for Penre, or for his younger brother, Khian. Their older sister would inherit their parents' small land holding. It had been easy for her to sway them to her plan with the promise of the gold they could get for ransoming the Mercan back to her father. Her only concession was giving in to Penre's demand that when the Mercan was theirs, he would make the major decisions.

"With the gold we get from the Mercan's father, we will live well in the Black Land."

"Al-Qahirah is far away. We are still in the shadow of Nesneit. Nisut's guards have swift horses and camels." He looked at her with a sardonic lift of his eyebrows. "Who is it you have found to lead us across the desert? That old drunk, Titus."

"He knows well the caravan route and a way that will take us around Ipu where I would be known." She had gone into the desert to a well and by it, a mud-brick shelter built long ago, its roof gone, and found the grizzled old man. He was once a caravan guide until a drunken brawl led to the death of another guide and his banishment from Nesneit. He had agreed to act as guide and interpreter for a share of the gold.

Her plan for revenge and riches was a good one. She and her two cousins had ridden their camels into the Valley on the first feast day of Hathor along with a throng of other celebrants. The guards at the Gateway of Horus hadn't recognized her. Titus had stayed in a camp area outside the Gateway to tend to the two pack camels.

Once at the hill on which the palace sat, they surveyed the area and found a secure place in which to tie their camels along with the one carrying the howdah for the Mercan. The second night of the celebration, they watched from a discreet distance as Nisut and her Companions left the palace to pay homage to Hathor. She guided her cousins up a back path of the hill and through a large crack in the garden wall. Once in the garden, they went into the tunnel that led to the underground storage below the kitchen. From there, they entered the kitchen and went up the back stairs to the rooftop. Serpent Woman was in one of the bedrooms just like Satiah thought she'd be. The Mercan wasn't a priestess of any of the Goddesses and couldn't offer homage in the Temple of Hathor.

How was Satiah to know Nisut would not give homage all night to Hathor? Satiah had joined Nisut's household two months before the Feast of Lamps in honor of the Great Neit, and Nisut along with the Companions had spent all night in homage, not leaving until the first light of Re touched the temple. She inwardly groaned. *Fool, of course Nisut would pay homage all night in the Temple of Neit. She was the Setepenneit.*

"You worry like an old woman," Satiah said. "We are already long on the way before there is anyone with enough wits about them to send pursuers after us."

They had ridden through the night and most of the morning, putting in many miles. It was the hot season so they'd rest today and resume the journey tonight when the temperature cooled. Their camels that she had stolen from her father were bred for swiftness and endurance. The supply packs were light so their camels could travel almost twice the distance in a day than that of a fully loaded caravan. Al-Qahirah could be reached in eighteen or twenty days if they limited the number of days of rest along the way.

A groan came from where the Mercan lay on a carpet. The sleep potion forced down her throat was starting to wear off. Satiah went over to the Mercan, bent and grabbed the red hair, lifted Mercan's head and slapped her hard across the face, satisfied to hear a moan of pain.

She raised her hand again, only to have it grabbed by Penre.

"Stop! Do you want to return her to the father marked?"

"She will heal by the time we get to al-Qahirah." Satiah snatched her hand from Penre's grasp.

"We will return her unharmed to the father."

"Spread her legs and take her if you wish. The father will still pay for her return." She glanced at his crotch and laughed. "Ah, yes cousin, if she had a beard and a hairy chest she'd appeal to you. If you don't want her, perhaps Khian will, or Titus."

"Your brain is full of maggots, cousin, that gnaw at it, driving you mad. When my ba goes into the West, I will not have Maat weigh my heart and give it to Ammut to devour."

"Your heart is already in the gut of Ammut for what you have done."

He looked at Satiah with contempt. "I have never killed. I did not take the life of one chosen by Neit. I will not have Hathor's curse upon me for violating a woman, or allowing a woman to be violated who is within my care, and neither will my brother."

Satiah's sneer mocked. Penre's heart always held pity for sick animals and the weak.

He looked at the steaming pot of stew over the cook fire. "Tend to the food while I help Khian with the camels." He focused on the Mercan. "Untie her. There is no place she can run." He fixed a hard stare on Satiah. "If I find a mark on her, I will mark you." He pivoted and strode with a limp out of the tent.

She made a face at him, cursing him under her breath. Her attention went to the Mercan. She lay on her side with eyes closed. The track of dried tears streaked the dust on her face. The red hair tangled about her shoulders, and the blue outer robe Satiah had managed to pull over her was askew. Satiah walked over to the Mercan and pushed her roughly around, smiling when she flinched. It took only a few seconds to undo the rope from the wrists.

Penre returned with Khian, the two going to the stewpot. Satiah joined them, her stomach roiling from the hollowness of hunger. Khian filled two bowls with the stew, leaving the tent to share a meal with Titus who kept watch.

Penre handed a bowl of stew to Satiah. "Take this to the woman."

She scowled at him. "Take it yourself."

He glared back, their eyes locked in a war of dominance. With a growl of defeat, she snatched the bowl from him and walked over to the Mercan who now sat up with slumped shoulders and head down, the tangled hair shrouding her face.

Satiah knelt beside her and thrust out the bowl of stew. "Here, take." Before she could react, the Mercan was upon her, screaming in rage as she attempted to scratch Satiah's eyes out. Satiah managed to grab the woman's left wrist, but not the right, feeling the searing agony of sharp nails as they raked down her left cheek.

Then the weight of the angry she-cat vanished,

leaving Satiah free to jump to her feet and confront the Mercan now held by Penre. She brought her fist back to deliver punishment only to have Penre quickly thrust the Mercan to the side and grab her arm.

A scream of rage tore from Satiah as she fought to get free. Penre delivered a slap to the side of her head that stunned.

"Touch her, cousin, and I'll make you pay," he growled into her face.

She ended her attempts to get free, glaring at Penre.

"Go to the other side of the tent and stay there." Penre released her with a push.

She did as told and watched with satisfaction as Penre bound the woman.

Rage still burned in her and something else. Lust. Despite her disheveled appearance, the Mercan was still attractive, the anger imbuing her with a spirit of strength Satiah wanted to crush.

The sting of the scratches started to throb and she brought her left hand up to her cheek, feeling the sticky ooze of blood. The salve she packed to treat camels would work on her scratches.

She sneered at the Mercan. Too bad she didn't have a phallus, for she wanted to ride the woman until she screamed.

Chapter Thirty-four

"A l-Qahirah. Ab." This was the second time the grizzled old man repeated the words as he knelt on the rug by Rose and looked her in the face. Rose tried not to recoil from the foul odor of his breath.

She knew al-Qahirah was Arabic for Cairo. *What is ab? I've heard it before. Ab...father...Arabic for father.* Her breath hitched. Dare she believe it? "Al-Qahirah—Cairo! You're taking me to my father, to ab?"

"Cairo, aywa, aywa. Ab, aywa." He nodded vigorously, his smile now a toothless grin.

Aywa...yes. Rose brought her right hand to her mouth to help stifle the cry of shock. Her eyes closed as her head spun, more from the lack of food and the after effects of the drug given her on the night of her abduction two days ago than from the hope she was going back to Father.

But why would they take her back to her father? What was in it for them? She was sure Satiah would like nothing better than to kill her. *Ransom.* That's what it had to be. They would return her to Father for money. Or were they taking her to a slave market somewhere? With a sigh, she resigned herself to the fact that these four individuals were in charge. She said a silent prayer to whatever gods would listen that Cairo and her father were indeed their destination.

The old man, she thought he was named Titus, stood and moved away from her, Penre now taking his place. His hands held a bowl of stew and a piece of flatbread that he thrust toward her.

His smile was friendly and his manner kind. He nodded and said, "Rose, wenum."

Rose recognized the Kemen word for *eat*.

She took the offered food even though her appetite was gone. She'd try to eat, not wanting to have the food forced down her throat as Penre and Satiah had forced her to drink water. Besides, she wanted to live if their destination were Cairo and her father.

Maybe she could have Satiah arrested when they reached Cairo. She knew it was Satiah who killed her darling. Rose hadn't seen her face that night, but Satiah still wore the same black and white striped keffiye and robes. But the most damning evidence was the empty knife sheath attached to the belt she wore. Rose couldn't have Satiah arrested for murder because she would never reveal the whereabouts of the Valley of Wind and Dreams, not even to her father. Not that anyone would believe her, and Nesneit lay far outside of Egyptian law. It would have to be for kidnapping. For the death of her darling, Rose was prepared to perjure herself and swear Satiah was behind her disappearance, having kidnapped her within the city bounds of Cairo.

She looked up to see Satiah staring at her with a malevolent sneer. Satisfied to see the long, raw scratch marks down Satiah's left cheek, Rose smiled with slow deliberation. She wished it were Satiah who had brought the food to her, for she'd relish the opportunity to scratch her eyeballs out and rake nails down the unmarked right cheek.

Rose thought it probable Satiah planned to hurt her in some way. But she had a good idea from Penre's actions that he would prevent it. As for the old man and Khian, they avoided Rose, not deigning to pay her much attention, for which she was relieved. But, she was still wary of them.

She continued to stare at Satiah with a disdainful smile and saw her derisive expression turn into a puzzled one. For now, Rose would not grieve, would not give Satiah the satisfaction of seeing her tears. For Satiah to witness her grieve for her darling would somehow be a sharing, and to Rose, that would be a desecration.

Rose's smile turned into a triumphant grin.

Justice would be served.

Chapter Thirty-five

Tiye jumped to the side as Meryt's handmaid, Mayti, came through the door of the bedchamber carrying a pot of used bathwater, closely followed by the other handmaid, Tenre, who clutched an armful of soiled bed linens.

It had been ten days since Meryt was stabbed, and her prognosis was good. Fortunately, the dagger blade had hit a rib that deflected it away from the heart and lungs. However, Meryt lost much blood, and the blade had cracked the rib, which posed the danger of further breaking and perhaps puncturing a lung if Meryt moved too much. Meryt's physicians had ordered complete bed rest for two weeks followed by a period of little physical activity.

Nothing could be done for the pain in Meryt's heart over Rose. Bad dreams invaded her nights and made her scream out. Tiye and Hedjet took turns sleeping on a mat by her bedside so they could keep her from thrashing about and injuring herself when she was in the throes of one of the dreams.

On the night Meryt was stabbed, a kitchen maid had identified Satiah as one of the culprits who absconded with Rose. She had summoned the two guards at the front entrance. The guards immediately searched the palace, finding Meryt, and sent for the physicians. They had also called in the perimeter guards and launched a search of the grounds for Rose and the felons.

Tiye and Hedjet were returning to the palace late after catching up on news from some of their priestess friends when a guard met them and imparted the bad news. Tiye immediately contacted Nesneit's military heads and Nebet Wadjet, informing them of what had occurred. The military and men from Meryt's guards mounted a search for Rose and Satiah in the Valley and sent out search parties to the oases and caravan routes. Meryt had also identified Satiah as her attacker and had offered a reward to anyone with information that would lead them to her or Rose.

Now Tiye smiled to see Meryt in bed propped up on a couple of cushions and Hedjet kneeling on the bed by her as she combed Meryt's hair.

"You have news?" Meryt gave her an expectant and hopeful look. Tiye was heartened that Meryt's voice sounded stronger today, and that her skin didn't appear as sallow, though the dark circles under her eyes from the nights of interrupted sleep were evident.

"No more than I reported two days ago." Tiye stepped up to the side of the bed, leaned over and kissed Meryt's cheek, smelling her freshly bathed scent.

It was two days ago that they had received word from one of their agents at Iunyt Oasis, that Satiah's two cousins and an old caravan guide were accomplices. A bedmate of the youngest cousin imparted this information for the reward. Khian had boasted to the girl how he, his brother, Satiah, and Titus were going to the Black Land to become rich. He didn't discuss details or mention Rose.

Based on the information that a caravan guide was involved, the military had expanded its search further along the desert routes leading to the Black Land and Libya. Messengers were dispatched to Nisut's agents in the Black Land to conduct a search for Rose and the culprits. Meryt feared the culprits would sell Rose as a slave. Tiye voiced the hopeful opinion that Satiah would ransom Rose back to her father and that al-Qahirah was their destination. She and Hedjet prayed to the Great One and Isis that the latter was Satiah's intent.

"The Great One and the Divine Mother Isis has heard our prayers and are protecting Rose," Hedjet said.

"I want a donation given to the priests of Set and have them beseech him to protect Rose," Meryt said.

"Set?" Hedjet stopped combing Meryt's hair, her eyes big and her expression one of distaste.

This request even surprised Tiye. The Temple of Set, more like a shrine, had only three priests who attended it. Set's followers were scarce in the Valley, although he did have more living in the oases as he protected those places. Some caravan attendants did make offerings at his shrine before they embarked on a journey. This had nothing to do with love for the God, but was more to bribe him not to send sandstorms or the rare desert deluges that flooded the wadis and depressions.

"He is the protector of foreigners, is he not?"

"He is that," Tiye said. "I'll do it today."

"Make it a generous donation."

"It shall be done, Nisut Wer." Tiye held no enthusiasm for this task. The one and only time she had gone to the Temple of Set was to discuss a request from the priests for funds to repair the roof of the structure. The inside of the temple had made her jumpy in the same way as did being in a dark room of an abandoned house, where one was apt to see scorpions and spiders scurrying about. The three wizened, ugly old priests had given her lascivious looks that made her feel unclean. As soon as she had returned to the palace, she had taken a long, hot bath.

Meryt shook her head. "Not Nisut. Meryt is doing this. Do it discreetly. I don't want my people to think their nisut is paying Set to work mischief against enemies. Nisut will carry out justice through Maat."

"I will see to it." Yes, Nisut would see that Maat was served. As for Meryt, Tiye knew she'd appeal to any god, even those in the shadows, to get her beloved Rose back.

Tiye would make an offering to the Great One and beseech her not just to protect Rose, but also to bring Maat back into Meryt's heart.

❧❧❧❧❧

The night was awash in the half moon's light, Meryt's room bleak in ashen luminosity and deep shadows. A grunt of pain escaped as she pushed out of bed. She swayed for a moment and carefully straightened her posture. The scar on the side of her left breast, close to the sternum, pulled and throbbed and her rib ached. With care, she reached out and picked up the robe from the foot of the bed, slipping it on.

Her tread was light and slow. She passed the open door to the queen's chamber, hearing no sounds from her Companions asleep within. They had moved to the room a few days ago after her bad dreams ceased, instead of sleeping by her bedside.

She exited the room and onto the terrace, walking with care to the north side. She listened to the night, hearing the nocturnal insects in the garden. No breeze carried the scent of the garden or the desert beyond the Valley. She viewed the deep cobalt hued cloak of night dusted with brilliant diamonds and the half-moon. It gave her little solace to know the same night sky blanketed the desert that hid Rose from her.

How could she have prevented Rose from being taken from her? Did not she have a premonition? Yet, who would have thought there was someone brazen enough to enter the palace of Nisut without permission? Nothing like this had ever happened in Nesneit's history. Why had Neit allowed this to happen? Why had the Great One abandoned her? No. Neit had never abandoned her. She had abandoned Neit. She had failed to follow Maat.

In her arrogance she thought herself due everything she wished. Was she not Merytneit the beloved of Neit? Who would deny her? Her arrogance had blinded her to the truth of Rose's true purpose. Neit had not given Rose to her as a possession. Rose completed her, had always completed her from the time when Meryt took her first breath as Setepenneit and gazed into those blue eyes and into eternity. For in truth, Rose, too, had always been Merytneit the beloved of Neit. Whatever guise Rose wore, or name she carried, in the ages to come, she would always hold half of Meryt's heart.

Yes, Rose would come to her again in the future, but pain existed in the now. And what of Rose's pain? Did she deserve to pay the price of Meryt's folly?

"Forgive me." She asked this not only of the Great One, but of Rose, too.

She searched the heavens. All was tranquil in the night sky, the stars and moon sailing their ageless course. Did she really expect some sign that Neit heard?

"It will be as you decree, Great One."

Turning to go back to her room, she paused as the sound of a faint breeze stirred through the garden. The breeze caressed her face. With her right hand pressed over the pain in her chest, she brought in a slow and steady breath, catching the night scents of the garden. The sweet fragrance of roses filled her nostrils, flooding her heart with hope.

She smiled as she cried.

Chapter Thirty-six

Cairo
September 16, 1901

J ames, you don't know how I've prayed for this
day...that my Rose would be returned to me."
Arthur McLeod sat on the edge of the seat in front of
the desk in the library of Colonel James Walters, the
latter behind the desk scrutinizing the lock of red hair.
He wrapped the lock in the parchment and handed it
back to Arthur.

Life for Arthur had been agony ever since he
had wakened from a drugged sleep at mid-morning
six months ago to find his Rose gone.

"Arthur, we must exercise caution here. This
could be a ruse to get monies from you. Rose could be
leagues from here. She might not be in Egypt—"

"No!" He almost came out of the chair when
he hit the desktop with his fist. He knew the belief
of James, and others, that she could be in a harem
somewhere out of the country. "That lock of hair
belongs to her. I'd know that color anywhere."

Arthur hadn't given up hope that his daughter
would return to him, even though the authorities had
no leads and held out little hope of him ever seeing
her again. He had shown them the letter from Rose
found slipped under the front door four days after
she disappeared. He didn't bother to show them the

second letter he received a little over a month after her disappearance, only sharing its content with James.

Hassid bin Hassid could not be found for questioning. He had disappeared soon after Rose's abduction, leaving no clues as to his whereabouts. A native in the service of the British Agency, informed James that word was he left Cairo in fear after two men in his employ had their noses cut off for offending a powerful enemy.

"That's not in doubt. What's in doubt is how this man came about it. You can't take the word of this native that he has her in his care. Dishonest, the whole lot of them. These Bedouins are nothing but bandits and cutthroats."

"I'll have to trust this one. If he did not have some compassion, or honesty, he would have prevented Rose from writing me." He stood and stared across the desk at James. "What would you do if you were in my place and this was Emma?"

James leaned back in his chair and studied Arthur for a moment. "I would do everything in my power to get my daughter back."

"So will I, to get my Rose back."

"A man who won't give you his name is not to be trusted. Not that he would give you his real name, or be a man you could trust if he did give it to you."

"My servant, Jabbar, asked him for it twice, but he refused to give it." The bedraggled, elderly man had shown up at his house early that morning with the lock of Rose's hair. He claimed he had rescued her from slavers, and for this deed, he was due a reward. "I tried to have Jabbar ask him more questions, but the only thing he would say was one hundred gold ten qirsh coins as a reward for the return of my daughter.

His instructions were to bring the coins at sunrise tomorrow to the west side of the Pyramid of Khafre. He would have Rose there. I have to have faith…faith in Providence that my Rose will be returned to me alive." He hadn't included the word 'unharmed', not wanting to dwell on the indignities she might have suffered. His first priority was to have his daughter back.

"I'll accompany you. I can arrange to have some trusted natives from the Agency there before he arrives. I'll provide them a description of Rose and this Bedouin cutthroat—"

"No! I don't want you to do that. He might get wind that something is up and the deal would be ruined. I can't risk that he wouldn't harm Rose. I'll not have anyone involved."

"Man, be reasonable, we may have the chance to have Rose in our custody in case this fails. If he doesn't have her, we can have him followed and he may lead us to her. Or have him detained and questioned as to her whereabouts."

"It's too risky."

James' expression was one of disappointment, but he remained silent, Arthur knowing he debated on whether to continue the argument.

James nodded in agreement. "I'll have the banknotes you gave me converted to gold coins in another hour, two at most. I'll gladly lend you the rest."

"I knew I could count on you. I'll write my bankers in Baltimore right away for the funds to pay you back and have them send you the draft. I'm not sure how long it will take to get to you, but I'm good for it."

"I know you are. And I'm glad to be of help. Emma will be happy to hear of Rose's return. This will lift a great burden from her." He shook his head, his expression somber. "Emma was so distraught over Rose's disappearance, that I almost had a physician come and attend to her. The main reason she returned to England was her heartbreak over Rose. She and Rose are close." He smiled. "Rose is more than a friend to Emma. She is like a dear sister."

"I'd like to ask another favor of you."

"Anything, my friend."

"I want to leave this god forsaken country as soon as possible and take Rose back to America. Can you arrange transportation for us on the train to Alexandria to take place within the next week?"

"I can do that."

"Once in Alexandria, I'll set up passage on a ship to Italy and then one bound for America with the earliest departure date. I'll take nothing but our clothes. I'd like to arrange for you to have the artifacts shipped to America. I'll send you reimbursement for the fees as soon as I'm back home in Baltimore."

"I will be glad to help you in that. Make an inventory for me and what port in America you want me to ship them to."

"Thank you, James. Thank you for everything."

Chapter Thirty-seven

Giza
September 17, 1901

The three triangular sentinels to Egypt's past glory stood majestic and black against the backdrop of the emergence of dawn over the land of the pharaohs. They had made camp two days ago within sight of the three pyramids. To Rose, they represented beacons of hope, the hope that she'd soon find herself free and in the loving arms of her dear father.

For the past twenty days, hope was her lifeline to keep going, to keep alive. Yet, along with hope there had clamored a sense of emptiness borne from loss and sorrow, and only kept at bay by her determination not to let Satiah see it. When this hope was fulfilled, she knew sorrow would own her heart for a time. And rightly so, for sorrow also must have its day and homage paid before healing could begin.

The stubborn donkey that Rose sat astride was urged onward with a stick held by the donkey boy. She darted a quick glance up at Satiah, sitting on the back of her camel and dressed as a Bedouin man. Rose also wore the disguise of a Bedouin man, the robes given to her by Penre in the dark of predawn.

Rose knew Satiah was there to make sure she didn't go trotting off to Cairo. Not that Rose thought she could make it across the Nile while riding this cantankerous beast, but she could enlist the aid of American or English tourists lodging at the Mena House, a hotel near the Great Pyramid. It was a certainty there would be a few romantic individuals up early who wanted to see the sunrise from the east side of the Pyramids, or watch the new day's light illuminate the face of the past as it had done for thousands of years.

On they rode in a beeline to the middle pyramid, built by Khafre. His tomb lay empty, the treasure pillaged long ago by grave robbers. But his monument, for as long as it stood, would uphold the magnificence of his name.

She glanced up again at Satiah, not in hatred, but in pity. Over the past days of their journey across the desert, she'd come to pity her for she sensed Satiah would never find what she sought in this world. However, Rose couldn't find it in herself to forgive. Satiah would have to seek forgiveness somewhere else. Although Rose thought Satiah would never possess a sense of the evil she carried within her, and forgiveness from any person or god would never be granted.

As for Penre, Titus, and Khian, they had shown kindness, even protection. She had always been in the watchful eye of one of them. She knew it was to keep Satiah from harming her. Penre had always stood guard outside the lean-to the few times she bathed. She hoped the price Maat exacted from them would be harsh enough to teach them a lesson. She wasn't charitable enough to forgive them either.

The first rays of the sun illuminated the pyramid that cast its shadow over the land. Out of the looming shadow of the pyramid, a camel trotted toward them. Satiah called out a question, Titus answering. A triumphant laugh came from Satiah, and after quick orders to the donkey boy, and a coin tossed to him, she turned her camel in the direction from where they had come as Titus joined her. Satiah looked back at Rose with a mocking smirk before riding off.

The breath rushed from Rose in heaves, leaving her faint. *You will not have the vapors.*

She was free.

The boy now goaded the donkey to trot into the shadow of the pyramid as he ran beside it, onward toward the giant itself. She threw off the keffiye, letting the red banner of her hair identify her as Rose McLeod, not born in this land, though her heart remained in a distant valley.

"Rose! Rose!" The sweet sound of her father's voice brought a strangled cry of relief.

There he was astride a donkey with his long legs dangling. He urged the beast forward with a slap of his hat on its rump as the donkey boy ran behind and shouted in broken English for him to stop.

Her vision blurred as the world spun. She fought hard to keep away the enclosing darkness that circled the edge of her consciousness. Suddenly, a pair of strong arms pulled her from the saddle and enclosed her in an embrace.

"My darling baby girl, my darling baby girl." Her father's voice spoke of love and the anguish he had suffered.

She clung to him and cried. They both cried.

Rose's tears weren't only those of relief. A keen sob of pain and loss rushed out as she opened the gates to her heart and let sorrow enter.

Chapter Thirty-eight

Baltimore, Maryland
October 28, 1901

08, October 1901

Dearest Friend

I know it is quite possible this correspondence will reach your home in Baltimore before you do.

My heart rejoiced at the wonderful letter I received from Papa yesterday informing me you are safe and reunited with your loving parent.

It was with great relief and a thankful prayer to the Almighty that I learned you were in no way harmed. Papa did impart that your ordeal had exhausted you.

My concern over your wellbeing had been such that I returned to England, as I could no longer abide in such a wretched and savage country as Egypt. It is no place for civilized young women to visit, even with the protection of a father or other male relative.

Now I have some good news about myself. I have recently become reacquainted with a second cousin I have not seen since childhood. Her name is Caroline Melton and she is related to me through my mother's side of the family. I was reintroduced to her at a party hosted by my Aunt Margaret shortly after my return to England. I was quite taken by her, and we quickly became friends. My sentiments for her grew, and much to my delight, her sentiments for me grew also.

I have recently taken up residence in my home in Bath that I inherited from my mother. Carolyn has agreed to share my home with me, and this has brought immeasurable amounts of joy to my heart.

I wish you to meet Caroline. And, to that end, I am inviting you to visit us here in Bath. Caroline expresses that she, also, would like to meet you. My home has ample room to accommodate you for an extended stay. Please, do me this favor and say you will visit. I know it will not be right away as you have only recently returned to your home. Anytime you feel you are ready, my home will be open to you.

I look forward to receiving a letter from you. Please, write soon.

I will keep you in my prayers.

With Sincere Regard,
Emma Louise Walters

Rose smiled as she read the letter from Emma. The letter had reached her home in Baltimore today, almost two weeks after she arrived. On the ocean voyage back to America, she'd stayed in her cabin. She allowed all the grief she'd suppressed to flow forth. Father had summoned the ship's physician who had recommended a sedative, but Rose refused to take it. For her father, she did make an effort to eat.

What she told Father was that she had spent her time at a distant oasis, and that a dear friend had lost her life in a tragic accident. She assured him that no physical harm was done her, and that her hosts were respectful and kind. Rose knew he suspected more to the story, but he never pressed for details.

As soon as she reached the safety of home, she retired to her room, not wanting to see friends or relatives who called. Nor did she take telephone calls from her many friends. Father, or their housekeeper, Mrs. Keys, made excuses, declaring her ill from the trip.

The bedroom and the house she'd known since childhood seemed strange, not at all familiar as it once was. She longed to see the Valley of Wind and Dreams even though Meryt no longer lived. But Rose knew that Meryt would return someday to look anew through the gold eyes of a baby girl destined to be nisut. Destiny would bring Rose to Meryt again as it had many times in the past. For she believed that, she truly did. Had not her vision in the desert been a revelation?

She wondered what would become of the kingdom without their nisut. Was the kingdom plunged into sorrow and mourning, possibly chaos, with no nisut to lead them?

What of those two wonderful women, Tiye and Hedjet? Did they return to the Temple of Neit to serve their Goddess? Or was the responsibility of governing the kingdom alongside the High Priestess now theirs? Rose felt some solace that the two Companions had each other to lean upon in their time of grief.

Not knowing of her fate and if she lived or died, did they grieve for her too? It was her fervent prayer Ahmose would somehow learn of her fate and return word to them.

She read Emma's letter again, happy for her friend finding someone to share her home and love. For love was the greatest gift the gods could bestow on mortals. She smiled. The Gods? Who was she to deny their existence? Had not she met one? Even talked to him? A vision or a dream? Could they not flow from the same source and speak the same truth? One need only listen with the heart.

Opening the drawer to her desk, she removed a box of writing paper. She would write Emma and wish her happiness, but a visit to Emma wasn't in the foreseeable future. She also wanted to answer the many cards and letters mailed by friends wishing her a speedy recovery. Then after she wrote the letters, she'd dress and take them to the post office. She must make an effort to go on with her life. Over time the sharpness of this sorrow would fade to a dull ache. Yet, her love for Meryt never would fade.

Rose closed her eyes, remembering vivid gold eyes. The image of those eyes would accompany her through the rest of her life until she once again gazed into them in some future place and time.

"Until then, my darling. Until then."

Chapter Thirty-nine

"In these cool grottoes within the—"

"Henut, Henut!"

Tiye looked up from the volume of poems, *Songs of the Solitary Heart* by Satkamose, to see an excited Hedjet running up the gravel garden path toward where she and Meryt rested in the shade of an arched trellis of jasmine.

Meryt lifted her head from Tiye's lap as Hedjet approached, almost tripping when she came to an abrupt halt. She dropped to her knees beside them, breathless, and waved a letter in front of Meryt. "Ahmose."

Meryt quickly sat up, snatched the letter from Hedjet's hand, and ripped open the heavy envelope, almost tearing the parchment in her haste to remove it.

Tiye watched Meryt's hands tremble as she unfolded the letter and started to read. A sharp cry tore from Meryt as she covered her mouth with her left hand and started to cry.

"Meryt." Tiye felt her heart turn to stone, certain the letter contained bad news.

Meryt uncovered her mouth, smiling brightly as tears fell, unable to speak. She handed the letter to Tiye. A quick scan of the contents stated that Rose had been returned to her father for a ransom, the two departing al-Qahirah five days later to return to America. The messenger had arrived two days after Rose's departure from al-Qahirah, so Ahmose did not have the opportunity to meet with her and inform her that Nisut was well. He did hear from a trusted individual in the employ of the British Agency that no harm had come to her, although the ordeal had exhausted her. His men were presently searching for Satiah and her accomplices and when found, they would reap the punishment as decreed by Nisut.

"This is a joyous day," Tiye said, feeling her eyes start to tear from relief.

Hedjet grabbed the letter from her hand and read it.

Meryt wiped the tears from her eyes and gave a laugh of joy when Tiye hugged her, careful not to squeeze hard.

"Henut, I knew the Gods would grant Rose protection." Hedjet kissed Meryt on the cheek and hugged her neck.

Meryt pushed carefully to her feet, Tiye noticing the slight wince. While Meryt no longer suffered severe pain, she still felt tender when she breathed deeply or moved quickly.

"Come. We must make plans." Meryt held out her hands to Tiye and Hedjet.

"Plans?" Hedjet asked as she took Meryt's hand.

"We're going to America."

"Meryt, you're not healed enough to go." Tiye clasped Meryt's other hand.

"By the time our plans are made, I will be."

"Henut, we're going to find Rose in America and bring her back?" Hedjet asked.

Meryt's face was radiant. "We're going to America and I will *ask* our queen to come home to the Valley of Wind and Dreams."

Chapter Forty

Small village outside of Luxor, Egypt.
February 20, 1902

The taste of the coffee was sweet on Satiah's tongue from the extra sugar she put in the cup. She patted the sash at her waist, smiling when she felt the outline of the belt beneath containing the gold and silver coins tucked into the hidden pockets. There were plenty of coins and she could afford the extra sugar and the other little luxuries she craved such as sweet cakes and coffee.

She recalled how the vendor in the local souk who sold her the sugar thought she was a young man. It was so very easy to deceive the eyes with the proper disguise and garments. She had added to the illusion by applying a smudge of smut to her upper lip to darken the fine hairs growing there, some already naturally dark. The only other requirement was to appear confident and deepen her voice. She had learned a few words of the language now spoken in the Black Land and could purchase the items she wanted. If she were unsure of the word for the item, she pointed at it.

Yes, in the days to come, she would do fine for herself. She, her two cousins and Titus had made a good start since arriving in this small village a month ago. Penre sold the male camel Titus had ridden, for a high price. The buyer, the village headman, had been impressed with the beast's sleek look and quality. Of course, it was far superior to any of the local stock, coming from the same line as that of Nisut's white racing camels, though of a cream color. One of the three female camels was pregnant, the village headman already expressing an interest in the offspring. The three female camels and one young bull made a good start to the herd she planned.

With the profit from the sale of the camels, she planned to purchase Arabian horses for breeding stock and start a herd. She would break and train them herself and sell them for a good profit. She looked across the room of the mud-brick house at her two cousins and Titus already asleep in their pallets in the corner, Titus snoring.

Yes, the Gods smiled upon them. Penre found favor in the headman's eyes due to his knowledge of animals and their ailments. He had recommended a cure for one of the man's colicky horses and the animal had quickly recovered. In payment, the headman allowed them the use of this house with its two rooms and penned area behind the house for their camels. He would also recommend Penre to others in need of an animal healer. This would bring in even more coins and give Penre prestige, thus lending her prestige as well.

Khian had found steady work as a groom. Titus planned to leave them in a few days, his destination, Sudan. She was responsible for caring for their camels. Yes, in a short time, she and her two cousins would be somebody in this town. She envisioned her own land and house and a young woman to help care for the place and provide her with pleasure. After the woman tasted the pleasure Satiah could give, she'd keep silent as to the fact Satiah wasn't a man.

As for their old life and names, they were as footprints in the desert sand, quickly blown away by the wind. They had changed their names to those common in the Black Land. She was now Ali, Penre now Rashad, and Khian now Samir.

Nesneit was far away, its reach not extending to this place she was sure. Since the death of Nisut, Nesneit would have other problems to attend to besides searching for them. They were safe, no longer needing to run and hide.

Her thoughts turned to the Mercan and she grinned. Too bad she'd never had the chance to take Serpent Woman for a night of pleasure, Satiah's pleasure. But the pain she saw in the Mercan's eyes from the loss of her lover would always bring Satiah satisfaction. Yes, Maat had exacted vengeance and the scales now tipped in her favor with compensation.

She rose from the floor and took a terra-cotta lamp, bending over to light the wick from the embers of the cooking brazier and walked the few feet to her room and through the beaded curtain over the doorway. After placing the lamp on a low table by the bed, she removed all her garments except the long shirt she wore.

Kneeling by the bed, she threw back the blanket, her throat seizing up when she saw the horror of the five deathstalkers as they scurried about on the mattress, their poisonous stingers raised and ready to strike.

☙ ❧ ☙ ❧ ☙

The sound of a woman's scream ripped through the night, reaching the ears of the watcher in the shadows. He grinned.

Nisut's reach was long. No place in the Black Land, or the Red Land, existed where the accursed ones could hide from the gold eyes of the falcon of Horus, or from Maat.

Chapter Forty-one

Al-Qahirah
March 1, 1902

"Miss Preston, would you like more tea?" Meryt asked the American nebet sitting across from her. They were in one of the reception rooms of the nisut's residence in al-Qahirah. This room was small but elegant, with its furniture imported from France in the early 1700s. The tea service came from England and was made in the early 1800s. She knew the room's furnishings and tea service reflected wealth and a high social station.

"No, thank you, Your Highness."

Meryt studied the young woman for a moment. She looked to be close to Hedjet in age. Her features were pleasant, though the spectacles she wore lent her the appearance of an owl. She conducted herself with confidence, dressed appropriately, was properly groomed, and her manners were respectful. She was educated and planned to enter the teaching profession when an appropriate position somewhere near her home in Elmira, New York became available.

Meryt and her Companions had arrived three days ago and were now engaged in arranging their trip to America with the help of Ahmose who planned to accompany them. Ahmose's network of agents had learned that a young American nebet, Miss Violet

Preston, was in al-Qahirah visiting her uncle, Ralph Preston, an official on the staff of the United States Consulate.

Miss Preston was due to go back home soon. Ahmose had presented her uncle with official appearing documents that designated him as the representative of Sultana Malika, the daughter of Sultan Zafar bin Abdullah, ruler of the newly formed African Sultanate of Omar that lay between Algiers and Libya. He explained to the uncle that the Sultana wished to visit America, but needed a lady of good character to act as her agent, secretary and guide while there. He informed Mr. Preston that he had it on good authority, from a respected official in the Egyptian government, that Miss Preston was a well-bred young woman and would make an excellent choice to fill the position.

Ahmose relayed to Meryt that Ralph Preston seemed pleased his niece could render assistance to the Sultana and had assured Ahmose that she was educated and her manners impeccable. Mr. Preston was most eager to learn more about the Sultanate and its Sultan and hoped the United States could become the new nation's friend.

"May I inquire as to when your departure date for America is, Your Highness?"

"If arrangements go according to plan, within another two weeks. Should you accept the position, I will need your help in arranging passage for me and my party of three." Meryt indicated the clothes she was wearing by a sweep downward with her hands. "As you can see, my garments are those of a proper Egyptian lady. I can see by your comely apparel that a lady in America dresses much differently. Your advice will be welcome in selecting the best American fashions for the trip, not only for me, but for my two personal attendants."

"That may present a problem. I'm not sure what Cairo has to offer. I can ask a few female acquaintances from America. They may know of a shop or dressmaker here in Cairo that can provide what you need. If not, I'm a customer at a few shops in New York City that cater to ladies of quality, such as yourself, and can make arrangements to visit these places soon after we arrive in America."

"Very good." Meryt smiled, pleased that the young nebet talked as if she'd already accepted the position. "I have the contract drawn up in English for you to look over as to the fee we discussed and length of service. My secretary, Tiye, will give it to you before you leave. Show it to your uncle and see if he thinks it agreeable. If you find it acceptable, please sign and have it returned to me no later than tomorrow afternoon."

"Your Highness, from what we discussed, I don't anticipate any problems, and I look forward to assisting you."

"Good. Now, Miss Preston, tell me of America and New York City. Do you know Calamity Jane?"

Chapter Forty-two

Baltimore, Maryland
April 8, 1902

The sound of a door opening at the back of the study hall in Girls' Latin School caused Rose to pause for a moment during her speech on the Pyramids to the school's Latin, Greek, and history students. A glance showed her the new arrival, a fashionably dressed woman who proceeded up the side aisle to take a vacant seat close to the podium. Rose noticed that a diaphanous veil shrouded the woman's brimmed hat and also covered her face. The veil and hat's color matched her blue Eton suit and short cape.

With a peek down at her notes on the podium top, Rose said, "The Pyramids will forever remain the symbols of the land of the ancient Nile. When future generations gaze upon their magnificence, they, too, will wonder who the ancient Egyptians were and what beliefs they held that inspired them to build such monuments."

The sponsor of the school's history club, Mrs. Alice Monroe, stood and started the applause while giving Rose an appreciative smile. After a few moments, the applause subsided, and she addressed the students. "Miss McLeod has graciously agreed to answer any questions you may have on the Pyramids and ancient Egypt."

Several hands shot up.

"Yes, you there, Miss Andrews." Mrs. Monroe pointed to a bright-faced girl of around sixteen, her brown hair in two long braids.

The girl stood. "My name is Sally Andrews. Miss McLeod, did you visit the tomb of Cleopatra when you were in Egypt?"

Rose couldn't suppress a smile when hearing a few professors laugh and Mrs. Monroe mumble under her breath.

"If you mean Cleopatra the seventh, the great enemy of Rome? Then no. Plutarch writes that Cleopatra and Mark Antony were buried together, but we don't know the location of where their tomb might be. That it is in Alexandria seems the most likely place." She smiled and added, "It would be the discovery of a lifetime to find her final resting place."

Rose answered a few more questions.

"We have time for one more question." Mrs. Monroe looked at the seated attendees, pointing to the woman who came in late, now with her hand raised and standing. "Yes, you have a question for Miss McLeod?"

The woman walked down the aisle toward Rose, paused and asked, "Would you like to return to the Valley of Wind and Dreams?" She lifted her veil.

"Meryt."

The gold gaze snared her and she saw not the face of her darling, but that of a beautiful woman dressed in a sleeveless red gown, the bodice covered in gold discs, the deshret upon her head.

Rose felt the tranquil sway of the reed barque traveling on the flow of the river. She glanced up to see the brilliant blue sky, but no sun was visible. She turned her attention back to the bow where the woman stood, seeing the small smile from the serene, brown face, reflecting secrets and wisdom.

"Who are you?"

"I am The All." Her voice sounded as if a chorus of thousands spoke, all in harmony.

"Neit?"

"At times."

"Why am I here?"

"You have lost your way, my daughter."

"Can you help me find home?"

A melodious laugh, not one that mocked, but one of affectionate amusement. "See into the one that sees into you."

The sharp scent of smelling salts jerked her to consciousness. She whipped her head to one side in an attempt to escape the pungent odor.

"Rose. Wake up."

She twisted her head toward the voice, her heart stilling as she stared into the concerned face of her darling. "Meryt." She touched Meryt's face.

"It is I, beloved." Bringing Rose's hand to her lips, Meryt kissed her fingers. "Are you all right?"

"I think so." Rose gaped unbelievingly at her darling. If this were a dream, she hoped to never awaken.

"Miss McLeod, can you get up?" Mrs. Monroe said from the other side of Rose. "I can take you to the teacher's lounge where you can rest."

"I think I can." With help from Meryt and Mrs. Monroe, Rose sat up. She took a long drink from a glass of water handed to her by one of the teaching staff. After a few moments she stood. Her legs shaky and weak, she held tight to Meryt who slipped an arm around her waist.

Neither spoke as Mrs. Monroe led them to the teacher's lounge and over to a divan. Rose sat with Meryt beside her, holding her hand.

Meryt said to Mrs. Monroe, "Would you give us this time alone?"

Mrs. Monroe turned to Rose. "Miss McLeod, you experienced quite a shock when seeing this person, Mrs.—"

"Sultana Malika, the daughter of the Sultan of Omar. I have newly arrived from Egypt to visit your fair country, and while here, to visit my friend, Miss McLeod."

Mrs. Monroe's expression reflected skepticism, prompting Rose to say, "It's all right, Mrs. Monroe. I'd like some time alone with my friend, Sultana Malika." Meryt's new title amused her. It sounded much more convincing than Pharaoh Merytneit of the kingdom of Nesneit and the Valley of Wind and Dreams.

"Very well. I'll be in the study hall." Mrs. Monroe gave the two women a long and slightly puzzled look before departing.

As soon as the door closed, Rose was in Meryt's arms, hugging her close. All control slipped, and she started to cry, her words strangled. "I thought you dead."

"Not dead. No girl child with gold eyes has been born. Yet."

Rose laughed a little through her tears. "Why didn't you write to me and let me know you lived, and were coming here?"

"I wanted to stand in front of you and see in your eyes if your love for me still held true, or if time and distance had taken you from me."

Meryt searched Rose's face, apparently seeing the answer, her smile one of elation. Meryt slipped a hand behind Rose's head and drew her in for a kiss.

The warm lips pressed fervently on Rose's own left no doubt that this was a flesh and blood woman. Her darling was very much alive.

When both were breathless, they separated, Meryt taking a lace handkerchief from her jacket pocket to wipe the tears from Rose's face.

Rose shook her head. "It's a miracle. I was so sure..." She brought Meryt into another hug. "Oh, my darling." she started to cry again.

Meryt soothingly rubbed Rose's back. Her voice held a tremor. "You are *my* miracle."

After a few moments, Rose stopped crying and Meryt once again used the handkerchief to wipe away the tears. Rose smiled tenderly as she took the handkerchief and dabbed away the tears from Meryt's cheeks, then tucked it back in Meryt's jacket pocket.

"When did you get here to America? Are Tiye and Hedjet with you?"

"Yes, they are. Ahmose is with us, too. Also, accompanying us is a young American nebet, Violet Preston, whom I hired in al-Qahirah, as an agent to assist us while here. We arrived five days ago to your New York City."

"Where are you staying? How did you know where I lived—that I'd be here?"

"The Hotel Altamont. We arrived this morning." She stroked Rose's face, brushing back a strand of hair that had come loose from the bun. "Ahmose got your address from a friend in the British Agency. I could wait no longer to have my eyes gaze upon your beauty so Ahmose hired a carriage to take the two of us to your home. Your woman servant informed us you were here. The carriage driver knew the way. Ahmose waits in the carriage and is eager to meet you. Tiye and Hedjet are at the hotel awaiting your arrival."

"And I am eager to see them and meet Ahmose."

Meryt kissed each of Rose's palms, and then held Rose's right hand on her left breast, over her heart. "I have missed you, beautiful Isis. My heart is a desert too long without rain because you do not share it. Give me your love and make my heart bloom again."

Rose's heart also had been a desert.

"Come home with me as my hemenisut, my queen."

"Queen?"

"I know I might not be deserving of your love. In my arrogance, I failed to see that the Great One sent you to me, not as a possession, but as an equal. And for my arrogance, she took you from me. Our destinies entwine, have always entwined. You complete me, and I need you by my side." Meryt smiled a little sadly. "One of your duties will be to keep me from the folly of pride and arrogance." She brought Rose's right hand to her lips and kissed it. "I humbly ask for you to forgive me."

"My darling, I forgave you when I said the words *I love you*. As for Nisut, I do think a little humility should be cultivated."

"Nisut will endeavor to cultivate and harvest a crop."

Rose laughed and shook her head. She watched as Meryt's smile faded into a serious expression.

"Be my wife and my queen, Isisnofret."

"Tiye and Hedjet?"

"Tiye and Hedjet love you and want you as our

queen."

"And I love them. Not in the way you do," she smiled, thinking of the two women, their goodness and their beauty, "but even that may come in time." She lifted her eyebrows in part teasing jest and surprise. Surprise she could entertain that notion.

"Why Rose. You? A libertine?" Meryt grinned. "It must be the company you kept in the past. When that time comes, I will endeavor to rein in my jealousy."

Meryt's eyes were molten gold, lips soft and inviting. Rose closed her eyes and the distance, kissing those lips. She brought her hands around Meryt's head to hold her close, to drink from the sweet mouth love and life. The desert once again bloomed.

Rose gazed into the gold eyes that saw into her heart and soul, finding what she had longed for all her life. "Take me home, my darling. Home to the Valley of Wind and Dreams."

About the Author

Linda is a fifth generation Floridian who lives in North Florida with her partner and adopted furry friends. She is an unabashed romantic who believes in happy endings.

You can find out more about Linda North at:

www.sapphirebooks.com

or on facebook at:

www.facebook.com/linda.north

CPSIA information can be obtained at www.ICGtesting.com
Printed in the USA
BVOW08s1459280716

457006BV00001B/33/P